Waiting for him to make the first move

Nighttime has officially arrived, and the streets are abuzz. I feel as if I'm floating. Glancing, smiling, blushing. Both of us. My voice has abandoned me. Josh's left hand grasps his right elbow, an anchor to keep him in one place.

How does one proceed in a situation like this? If only the discovery of mutual admiration could lead promptly into making out. If only I could say, "Listen. I like you, and you like me, so let's go find a secluded park and touch each other."

We steer around a group of tourists pawing through bins of miniature Notre-Dames. Josh swallows. "Just so we're clear," he says, "I wasn't, like, trying to steal you away from Kurt when I asked if you wanted to go to the store with me. I was trying to, you know . . . be your friend. I don't want you to think I'm a creep."

I smile up at him. "I don't think you're a creep."

This entire evening has been surreal. We cross another bridge, the Pont d'Arcole, onto the Right Bank. The scent of metal and urine wafts up from the Seine, but even this barely registers. We're in a two-person bubble. The noises that I should be hearing—cars speeding, pedestrians rushing, construction clattering—are muffled. Instead, I hear my heart thumping against my rib cage. Josh's steady footsteps against the pavement. The occasional swish of his pant legs catching against each other.

Ask me out. I chant it like a mantra. *A̶s̶k̶ ̶m̶e̶ ̶o̶u̶t̶, ask me out.*

OTHER BOOKS YOU MAY ENJOY

ISLA

and the

 HAPPILY
EVER AFTER

STEPHANIE PERKINS

speak

SPEAK
An imprint of Penguin Random House LLC
375 Hudson Street
New York, New York 10014

First published in the United States of America by Dutton Books,
an imprint of Penguin Group (USA) LLC, 2014
Published by Speak, an imprint of Penguin Random House LLC, 2015

LIBRARY OF CONGRESS CATALOGING-IN-PUBLICATION DATA IS AVAILABLE.
ISBN: 978-0-525-42563-2 (hardcover)

Speak ISBN 978-0-14-242627-2

Printed in the United States of America

9 10

CW

For Jarrod, best friend & true love

chapter one

It's midnight, it's sweltering, and I might be high on Vicodin, but that guy—that guy *right over there*—that's him.

The him.

His posture is as familiar as a recurring dream. Shoulders rounded down, head cocked to the right, nose an inch from the tip of his pen. Absorbed. My heart swells with a painful sort of euphoria. He's close, only two tables over and facing my direction. The café is boiling. The atmosphere is clouded with bittersweet coffee. Three years of desire rip through my body and burst from my lips:

"Josh!"

His head jolts up. For a long time, a very long time, he just stares at me. And then . . . he blinks. "Isla?"

"You know my name. You can *pronounce* my name." Most people call me Iz-la, but I'm Eye-la. Island without the *nd*. I erupt into a smile that immediately vanishes. *Ouch.*

Josh glances around, as if searching for someone, and then cautiously sets down his pen. "Uh, yeah. We've sat beside each other in a ton of classes."

"Five classes beside each other, twelve classes together total." A pause.

"Right," he says slowly. Another pause. "Are you okay?"

A guy who looks like a young Abraham Lincoln with a piercing fetish tosses a single-page laminated menu onto my table.

I don't look at it. "Something soft, please."

Abe scratches his beard, weary.

"But no tomato soup, chocolate pudding, or raspberry applesauce. That's all I've had to eat today," I add.

"Ah." Abe's mood lightens. "You're sick."

"No."

His mood darkens again. "Whatever." He snatches up the menu. "Allergic to anything? You kosher? Vegetarian?"

"Huh?"

"I'll have a look in the kitchen." And he stalks away.

My gaze returns to Josh, who is still watching me. He looks down at his sketchbook, and then back up, and then back down. Like he can't decide if we're still having a conversation. I look down, too. I'm getting the increasingly alarming notion that if I keep talking, tomorrow I might have something to regret.

But . . . as if I can't help it—because I *can't,* not when I'm around him—I glance up. My veins throb as my eyes drink him in. His long, beautiful nose. His slender, assured arms. His pale skin is a few shades darker from the summer sun, and his black tattoo peeks out from underneath his T-shirt sleeve.

Joshua Wasserstein. My crush on him is near unbearable.

He looks up again, too, and I blush. Blushing. The curse of redheads everywhere. I'm grateful when he clears his throat to speak. "It's strange, you know? That we've never run into each other before."

I leap in. "Do you come here often?"

"Oh." He fidgets with his pen. "I meant in the city? I knew you lived on the Upper West, but I've never seen you around."

My chest tightens. I knew that about him, but I had no idea that *he* knew that about *me*. We attend a boarding school for Americans in Paris, but we spend our breaks in Manhattan. Everybody knows that Josh lives here, because his father has one of the New York seats in the United States Senate. But there's no reason for anyone to remember that I live here, too.

"I don't get out often," I blurt. "But I'm starving, and there's nothing to eat at home." And then, somehow, I'm dropping into the empty seat across from him. My compass necklace knocks against his tabletop. "My wisdom teeth were removed this morning, and I'm taking all of these medications, but my mouth is still sore so that's why I can only eat soft foods."

Josh breaks into his first smile.

Accomplishment puffs up inside of me. I return the smile as full as I can, even though it hurts. "What?"

"Painkillers. It makes sense now."

"Oh, shit." I tuck up a leg and smack my kneecap on the table. "Am I acting that loopy?"

He laughs with surprise. People always laugh, because they don't expect words like *shit* to come out of someone so petite, someone with a voice so quiet, so sweet. "I could just tell something was different," he says. "That's all."

"Side effects include the cruel combination of exhaustion and insomnia. Which is why I'm here now."

Josh laughs again. "I had mine extracted last summer. You'll feel better tomorrow."

"Promise?"

"Not really. But definitely in a few days."

Our smiles fade into a reflective silence. We've rarely spoken to each other at school and never outside of it. I'm too shy, and he's too reserved. Plus, he had the same girlfriend for, like, forever.

Had.

They broke up last month, right before her graduation. Josh and I still have our senior year to go. And I wish there were a logical reason for him to show a sudden interest in me, but . . . there's not. His ex was tenacious and outspoken. My opposite. Maybe that's why I'm startled when I find myself pointing at his sketchbook, eager to prolong this temporary state. This miracle of conversation.

"What are you working on?" I ask.

His arm shifts to block the exposed drawing, someone

resembling a young Abe Lincoln. "I was just . . . messing around."

"That's our server." I grin. *Ouch.*

He looks a bit sheepish as he pulls back his arm, but he only shrugs. "And the couple in the corner."

We're not alone?

I twist around to discover a middle-aged man and woman, all the way in the back, sharing a copy of the *Village Voice.* There isn't anyone else here, so at least I'm not too out of it. I don't think. I turn back to Josh, my courage rising.

"May I see that?"

I asked. I can't *believe* that I asked. I've always wanted to look inside of his sketchbooks, always wanted to *hold* one. Josh is the most talented artist at our school. He works in several mediums, but his real passion is the comic form. I once overheard him say that he's working on a graphic novel about his life.

An autobiography. A diary. What secrets would it contain?

I content myself with doodles viewed over his shoulder, paintings drying in the art studio, sketches tacked to the doors of his friends. His style is almost whimsical. It's melancholy and beautiful, completely his own. The lines are careful. They reveal that he pays attention. People don't think he does, because he daydreams and skips class and neglects his homework, but when I see his drawings, I know they're wrong.

I wish he would look at me the way that he looks at his subjects. Because then he'd see there's more to me than *shy*, just like I see there's more to him than *slacker*.

My cheeks burn again—as if he could hear my thoughts—but then I realize . . . he *is* studying me. Have I overstayed my welcome? His expression grows concerned, and I frown. Josh nods toward the table. His sketchbook is already before me.

I laugh. He does, too, though it's tinged with confusion.

His book is still open to the work in progress. A thrill runs through me. On one page, Abe's face stares with boredom at the sketchbook's spine. Even the rings in his septum, eyebrows, and ears seem dull and annoyed. On the opposite page, Josh has perfectly captured the middle-aged couple's studious, gentle frowns.

I touch a corner, one without ink, oh so lightly. To prove to myself that this moment is real. My voice turns reverent. "These are amazing. Is the whole thing filled with portraits like this?"

Josh closes the sketchbook and slides it back toward himself. Its pages are thick with use. On the cover is a blue sticker shaped like America. A single word has been handwritten across it: *WELCOME*. I don't know what that means, but I like it.

"Thanks." He gives me another smile. "It's for whatever, but yeah. Mainly portraits."

"And you're allowed to do that?"

His brow creases. "Do what?"

"Like, you don't need their permission?"

"To draw them?" he asks. I nod, and he continues. "Nah. I'm not using these for anything special. This isn't even my good sketchbook. See? I can't remove the pages."

"Do you do this a lot? Draw strangers?"

"Sure." He reaches for his coffee cup with an index finger. There's a splotch of black ink near his nail. "To be good at anything you have to practice."

"Do you wanna practice on me?" I ask.

Pink blossoms across Josh's cheeks as Abe slaps down two dishes. "Chicken broth and cheesecake," Abe says to me. "That's all we had."

"*Merci,*" I say.

"*De nada.*" Abe rolls his eyes and walks away.

"What's with that guy?" I ask, shoveling in the cheesecake. "Ohmygod, sogood." I mumble this through a full mouth. "Youwannabite?"

"Uh. No, thanks." Josh seems flustered. "You look hungry."

I begin happily devouring the rest.

"So you live close by?" he asks, after a few moments.

I swallow. "Two minutes away."

"Me too. Ten minutes."

I must look surprised, because he continues. "I know. Weird, right?"

"That's cool." I glug my broth. "Ohmygod. This is incredible."

He watches me quietly for another minute. "So . . . you were serious? You wouldn't mind if I sketched you?"

"Yeah, I'd love that." *I love youuuuuuuuu.* "What should I do?"

"Don't worry about it. Just keep doing what you're doing."

"Ha! You'll draw me eating like a horse. No. A pig. I meant pig. Do I mean a pig or a horse?"

Josh shakes his head in amusement. He opens the sketchbook

to a new page and looks up. His eyes lock on to mine. I'm dumbstruck.

Hazel.

The word adds itself to my internal list of Facts About Josh. Sometimes his eyes had seemed green, sometimes brown. Now I know why.

Hazel. Josh's eyes are *hazel.*

I float into a green-brown fog. The *scritch* of his pen mingles with the *scratch* of an old folk song coming from the speakers. Their combined tune is yearning and turmoil and anguish and love. Outside, storm clouds burst. Rain and wind join the score, and I hum along. My head clunks against a window.

I sit up, startled. My bowl and plate are empty. "How long have I been here?"

"A while." Josh smiles. "So. Those drugs you're on. Good stuff, huh?"

I moan. "Tell me I wasn't drooling."

"No drool. You look happy."

"I *am* happy," I say. Because . . . I am. My eyes dim.

"Isla," he whispers. *"It's time to go."*

I lift my head from the table. When did it get there?

"Kismet is closing."

"What's Kismet?"

"Fate," he says.

"What?"

"The name of this café."

"Oh. Okay." I follow him outside and into the night. It's still raining. The drops are fat and warm. I cover my head with my bare hands as Josh stuffs his sketchbook underneath his shirt. I catch a glimpse of his abdomen. *Yummy.* "Yummy tummy."

He startles. "What?"

"Hmm?"

A smile plays in the corners of his lips. I want to kiss them, one kiss in each corner.

"Okay, Loopy." He shakes his head. "Which way?"

"Which way to what?"

"To your place."

"You're coming over?" I'm delighted.

"I'm walking you home. It's late. And it's pouring."

"Oh, that's nice," I say. "You're nice."

The traffic lights glow yellow on the wet asphalt. I point the way, and we run across Amsterdam Avenue. The rain pours harder. "Up there!" I say, and we duck underneath a city block covered in scaffolding. Weighty raindrops clang against the aluminum like a pinball machine.

"Isla, wait!"

But it's too late.

Scaffolding is generally ideal for escaping bad weather, but occasionally the bars will cross together to create a funnel, which can collect water and soak a person completely. I am soaked. Completely. My hair clings to my face, my sundress clings to my figure, and water squishes between my sandals and the soles of my feet.

"Ha-ha." I'm not sure it's real laughter.

"Are you okay?" Josh stoops under the scaffolding, swerves around the waterfall, and then stoops back in beside me.

I *am* laughing. I clutch my stomach. "Hurts . . . mouth . . . to laugh. My mouth. My mouth and my stomach. And my mouth."

He laughs, too, but it's distracted. His eyes suddenly, pointedly move up to my face, and I realize he'd been looking elsewhere. My smile widens. *Thank you, slutty funnel.*

Josh shifts away, his posture uncomfortable. "Almost there, yeah?"

I gesture toward a row of gabled buildings across the street. "The second one. With the copper-green windows and the tiled roof."

"I've sketched those before." His eyes widen, impressed. "They're gorgeous."

My parents' apartment is located in a line of Flemish-inspired homes built in the late nineteenth century. We live in one of the only neighborhoods that's nice enough for residents to have flowers on their stoops, and passersby won't destroy them.

"Maman likes them, too. She likes pretty things. She's French. That's why I go to our school." My voice drifts as Josh guides me toward the entrance with the climbing pink roses above the door. Home. He removes his hand from the small of my back, and it's only then that I realize it was there in the first place.

"Merci," I say.

"You're welcome."

"Thanks," I say.

"De rien."

The air is heavy with the perfume of rain-dripped roses. I fumble my way inside the building, and he waits on the sidewalk, statuesque. His dark hair is as wet as mine now. A stream of water cascades down his nose. One arm clutches the sketchbook against his chest, underneath his T-shirt.

"Thank you," I say again.

He raises his voice so that I can hear him through the glass door. "Get some rest, Loopy. Sweet dreams."

"Sweet," I echo. "Dream."

chapter two

Ohmygod what the hell did I do last night?????????

chapter three

Andthe whole thing is a blur! And I don't remember anything I said, or anything *he* said, and he must have walked me home because he knew I was so high that I'd get run over by a taxi."

Kurt Donald Cobain Bacon keeps his eyes fixed upon my ceiling. "So Josh paid for your food."

It takes a moment for this statement to register. My best friend and I are lying beside each other on top of my bed. One of my hands slowly reaches out of its own accord and twists the front of his shirt into a tight knot.

"Don't do that." His tone is brusque—as it often is—though not impolite.

I remove my hand, which travels straight to my swollen,

throbbing, worse-than-yesterday gums. And then I emit a rather frightening moan.

"You said he woke you up, and then you left the café," Kurt says. "That means he paid your bill."

"I know. *I know.*" But I'm scrambling out of bed anyway. I grab my purse, dump it upside down, and shake it frantically.

"You won't find it," he says.

A well-loved paperback about a hiking disaster on Mount Everest thunks against my rug. Pens and lipsticks and quarters shower out and roll away. My wallet. An empty pack of tissues, a pair of sunglasses, a crumpled flyer for a new bagel store. Nothing. I shake it harder. Still nothing. I check my wallet even though I already know what I won't find: a receipt from the café.

"Told you," he says.

"I have to apologize for being such a lunatic. I have to pay him back."

"Pay who back?" Hattie asks.

My head whips around to find my younger sister appraising me from the doorway. She's leaning against the frame with crossed arms, but she still looks way too tall. Which she is. Not only did she surpass me in height last year, but she far exceeded me.

"I know what you did last night," she says. "I know you snuck out."

"I didn't *sneak out.* I just left for a few hours."

"But Maman and Dad don't know."

I don't reply, and Hattie smiles. She's as smug as a house

cat. She won't tell. With information this valuable, she'll hold on to it until it's useful. Hattie swipes my wallet from the floor and—staring me down, lording over me with her stupid growth spurt—drops it back into my purse. And then she's gone.

I throw the purse at her vacated space and crawl into bed. I wrap both of my arms around one of Kurt's. "You have to go with me," I say. "To the café. Tonight."

His eyebrows furrow into their familiar V shape. "You think Josh is a regular?"

"Maybe." I have no reason to think this. I just *want* him to be a regular. "Please, I have to explain myself."

His shoulders shrug against me. "Then I'll find the Right Way."

Kurt likes routine, and he always likes to know where he's going ahead of time. He's obsessed with mapping out the best route to get anywhere . . . even a café that's only a few minutes away. He calls these routes the Right Way. The Right Way never involves mass transit, crowded intersections, or streets containing Abercrombie & Fitch–type stores that blast noxious music and/or cologne.

Cartography has fascinated him since he was six, when he discovered *The Times Atlas of the World* weighing down one of my older sister's gluey craft projects. The book became an obsession, and Kurt pored over its pages for years, memorizing names and shapes and distances. When we were young, we'd lie on my floor and draw our own maps. Kurt would make these tidy, detailed, to-scale maps of our neighborhood while I'd create England-shaped islands with Old English–sounding names. They'd have dense woods and spidery rivers and snowcapped peaks, and I'd surround them with shark triangles and sea-monster arches. It drove Kurt crazy that I wouldn't draw anything real.

I've known him forever. Our mothers are also best friends—and they're both Frenchwomen living in New York—so he's just . . . always been around. We went to the same schools in Manhattan, and now we attend the same high school in Paris. He's thirteen months younger than me, so there was only one year when we were apart—when he was in eighth grade, and I was a freshman. Neither of us likes to think about that year.

I blow a lock of his scruffy blond hair from my face. "You don't think . . . "

"You're gonna have to finish that sentence."

"It's just . . . Josh and I *talked*. I remember feeling happy. You don't think it's possible that last night was . . . not some embarrassing mishap, but . . . my way in?"

He frowns again. "Your way into what?"

Kurt isn't good at filling in blanks. And even though he's always known how I feel about Josh, I still hesitate before saying it aloud. This tiny, flickering hope. "A relationship. *Kismet,* you know?"

"Fate doesn't exist." He gives me a dismissive huff. "Catalog last night as another embarrassing mishap. It's been a while since you've had one," he adds.

"Almost a year." I sigh. "Right on schedule."

Josh and I have had exactly one meaningful interaction per

year, none of which have left me looking desirable. When we were freshmen, Josh saw me reading Joann Sfar in the cafeteria. He was excited to find someone else interested in European comics, so he began asking me this rapid string of questions, but I was too overwhelmed to reply. I could only gape at him in silence. He gave me a weird look and then left.

When we were sophomores, our English teacher partnered us up for a fake newspaper article. I was so nervous that I couldn't stop tapping my pen. And then it slipped from my grasp. And *then* it flew into his forehead.

When we were juniors, I caught him and his girlfriend making out in an elevator. It wasn't even at school. It was inside BHV, this massive department store. I bumbled an unintelligible hello, let the doors close, and took the stairs.

"But," I persist, "I have a *reason* to talk to him now. You don't think there's any chance that it might lead to something?"

"Since when is human behavior reasonable?"

"Come on." I widen my eyes like an innocent doe. "Can't you pretend with me? Even for a second?"

"I don't see the point in pretending."

"That was a joke," I explain, because sometimes Kurt needs explanations.

He scowls at himself in frustration. "Noted."

"I dunno." I burrow against the side of his body. "It's not logical, and I can't explain it, but . . . I think Josh will be there tonight. I think we'll see him."

"Before you ask"—Kurt barges into my new dorm room in Paris, three months later, narrowly missing a run-in with an empty suitcase—"no. I didn't see him."

"I wasn't going to ask." Although I was.

My last ember of hope gutters. Over the summer, it faded and faded until it was barely visible at all. The ghost of a hope. Because Kurt was right, human behavior isn't reasonable. Or predictable. Or even satisfying. Josh wasn't there at midnight, nor was he there the *next* night. Nor the following day. I checked the café at all hours for two weeks, and my memories of happiness disintegrated as I was faced with reality: I didn't hear any music. I didn't feel any rain. I didn't even see any Abe.

It was as if that night had never happened.

I looked for Josh online. I pulled his email address from last year's school handbook, but when I tried to send a casual/ friendly explanation/apology—an email that took *four hours* to compose—the server informed me that his account was inactive from disuse.

Then I tried the various social networks. I didn't get far. I don't actually have any accounts, because social networking has always felt like a popularity contest to me. A public record of my own inadequacies. The only thing I found was the same black-and-white, again and again, of Josh standing beside the River Seine, staring somberly at some fixed point in the distance. I confess I'd seen it before. He'd been using the picture online for months. But it was too pathetic to sign up anywhere just to become his so-called friend.

So then I did the thing that I swore to myself I would never do: I Googled his home address. The waves of my shame could be felt across state lines. But it was in this final step toward stalkerdom that I was led to the information I'd been seeking all along. His father's website featured a photo of the family exiting an airport terminal in DC. The picture had been taken two days after Kismet, and the caption explained that they'd remain in the capital until autumn. The senator looked stately and content. Rebecca Wasserstein was waving toward the camera, flashing that toothy, political-spouse smile.

And their only child?

He trailed behind them, head down, sketchbook in arm. I clicked on the picture to make it bigger, and my eyes snagged on a blue sticker shaped like America.

I'm in there. I'm in that sketchbook.

I never saw his drawing. What would it have revealed about me? About him? I wondered if he ever looked at it. I wondered about it all summer long.

Kurt jiggles the handle of my new door, shaking me back into France. "This is catching. You need to get it fixed."

"The more things change, the more they stay the same," I say.

He frowns. "That doesn't make sense. The door you had last year worked fine."

"Never mind." I sigh. Three months is a long time. Any confidence I had in speaking to Josh has crumbled back into shyness and fear. Even if Kurt *had* just seen him in the hallway, it's not like I would've left my room to speak with him.

Kurt pushes his body weight against the door, listens for its telltale click, and then flops down beside me on the bed. "Our doors are supposed to lock automatically. I shouldn't be able to walk in like that."

"And yet—"

"I keep doing it." He grins.

"It's strange, though, right?" My voice is tinged with the same awe that it's had since our arrival two days ago. "*Whose* door that used to be?"

"Statistically unlikely. But not impossible."

I have a lifetime's worth of experience shaking off Kurt's wonder-killing abilities, so his response doesn't bother me. Especially because, despite a summer of disappointments and backtracking . . .

I, Isla Martin, am now living in Joshua Wasserstein's last place of residence.

These were his walls. This was his ceiling. That black grease mark on the baseboards, the one right above the electrical outlet? He probably made that. For the rest of the year, I will have the same view of the same street outside of the same window. I will sit in his chair, bathe in his shower, and sleep in his bed.

His bed.

I trace a finger along the stitching of my quilt. It's an embroidered map of Manhattan. When I'm in Manhattan, I sleep underneath a quilt that's an embroidered map of Paris. But underneath *this* blanket and underneath *these* sheets, there's a sacred space that once belonged to Josh. He dreamed here. I want this to mean something.

My door bursts back open.

"My room is bigger than yours," Hattie says. "This is like a prison cell."

Yeah. I'm gonna have to fix that door.

"True," Kurt says, because the rooms in Résidence Lambert are the size of walk-in closets. "But how many roommates were you assigned? Two? Three?"

This is my sister's first year attending SOAP—the School of America in Paris. When I was a freshman, our older sister, Gen, was a senior. Now I'm the senior, and Hattie is the freshman. She'll be living in the underclass dormitory down the street. Students in Grivois have roommates, tons of supervision, and enforced curfews. Here in Lambert, we have our own rooms, one Résidence Director, and significantly more freedom.

Hattie glowers at Kurt. "At least I don't have to hide from my roommates."

"Don't be an assrabbit," he says.

Last year—when I was in this dorm, and he was still in Grivois—he slept in my bed more often than his own, because he couldn't get along with his roommates. But I didn't mind. We've been sharing beds since before we could talk. And Kurt and I are *strictly* friends. There's none of that he's-my-best-friend-but-we're-secretly-in-love bullshit. A relationship with him would feel incestuous.

Hattie narrows her eyes. "Everyone's waiting in the lobby for dinner." She's referring to both his parents and ours. "Hurry up." She slams my door. It pops back open, but she's already gone.

I haul myself off the bed. "I wish my parents could've sent her to boarding school in Belgium. They speak French there, too."

Kurt sits up. "That's a joke, right?"

It is. It's important to my parents that my sisters and I receive a portion of our education in France. We're dual citizens. We all received our early schooling in the United States, and we've all been sent here for high school. It's our choice where to go next. Gen chose Smith College in Massachusetts. I'm not sure where I want to live, but soon I'll be applying to both la Sorbonne here in Paris and Columbia back in New York.

Kurt pulls up the hood of his favorite charcoal-gray sweatshirt, even though it's warm outside. I grab my room key, and we leave. It takes both of his hands to yank my door closed. "You really do need to talk to Nate about that." He nods to our Résidence Director's apartment, only two doors down.

Okay. So Josh's old room does have its drawbacks. It's also located on the ground floor so it's loud. Extra loud, actually, because it's also-also located beside the stairwell.

"There he is," Kurt says.

I assume he means Nate, but I follow his gaze and grind to a halt.

Him.

Josh is waiting for the elevator in the lobby. In less than a second, an entire summer of daydreaming and planning and rehearsing explodes into nothingness. I close my eyes to steady myself. I'm dizzy. It physically hurts to look at him. "I can't breathe."

"Of course you can breathe," Kurt says. "You're breathing right now."

Josh looks alone.

I mean, he is alone, but . . . he *looks* alone. He's carrying a cloth grocery bag and staring at the elevator, completely detached from the crowd behind him. Kurt drags me toward the lobby. The elevator dings, the door opens, and Josh pushes back its old-fashioned gate. Students and parents bustle in behind him—way too many people for such a small space—and as we pass by, he flinches at being shoved into a corner. But the flinch is just that, one quick moment, before his expression slides back into indifference.

The crowd jostles and smashes buttons and someone's dad forces the gate shut, but that's when an odd thing happens. Josh looks out over the sea of passengers and through the metal cage. And his eyes go from blank to seeing. They see me.

The elevator door closes.

chapter four

The head of school is finishing up her usual first-day, post-breakfast, welcome-back speech. Kurt and I are in the back of the courtyard, nestled between two trees pruned like giant lollipops. The air smells faintly of iron. The school looms over us, all gray stone and cascading vines and heavy doors. Our classmates loom before us.

There are twenty-five students per grade here—always one hundred students total—and it's difficult to get accepted. You have to have excellent grades, high test scores, and several letters of recommendation. It helps to have connections. Gen got in because Maman knew someone in the administration, I got in because of Gen, and Hattie got in because of me. It's cliquey like that.

It's also expensive. You have to come from money to attend.

When my father was only nineteen, he built an overdrive pedal for guitarists called the Cherry Bomb. It was red and revolutionary and turned him from the son of a Nebraskan farmer into a very wealthy man. It's one of the most copied pedals ever, but musicians still pay top dollar for the original. His company's name is Martintone, and even though he still tinkers with pedals, as an adult he works mainly as a studio engineer.

"I have one final announcement." The head's voice is as poised as her snow-white chignon. She's American, but she could easily pass for French.

Kurt studies a map on his phone. "I've found a better route to the Treehouse."

"Oh, yeah? After all this time?" I'm scanning the courtyard for Josh. Either he slept in or he's already skipping. I planned my outfit carefully, because it's the first day in months when I *know* I'll see him. My style tends to be rather feminine, and today I'm wearing a dress patterned with tiny Swiss dots. It has a scoop neck and a short hem, both of which help me look taller, but I've added a pair of edgy Parisian heels to keep me from looking too innocent or vanilla. I can't imagine Josh falling for someone vanilla.

Not that Josh would ever fall for me.

But I wouldn't want to ruin any chance.

Even though I don't have a chance.

But just in case I do.

Even though I don't.

"But I'll let him tell you in his own words," the head says, continuing a sentence whose beginning I did not hear. She moves aside, and a short figure with a shaved head steps forward. It's Nate, our Résidence Director. This is his third year here. He's also American, but he's young, working on his doctorate, and known for being lax with the rules yet firm enough to keep us under control. The kind of person that everybody likes.

"Hey, guys." Nate shifts as if his own skin were the wrong fit. "It's come to the faculty's attention——" He glances at the head of school and changes his story. "It's come to *my* attention that the situation in Lambert got a little out of hand last year. I am, of course, referring to the habit of opposite-sex students hanging out in each other's rooms. As you know, we have a strict policy——"

The student body snickers.

"We have a *strict policy* that ladies and gentlemen are only allowed to visit each other with their doors propped open."

"Isla." Kurt is annoyed. "You're not looking at my phone."

I shake my head and nudge him to pay attention. This can't be good.

"Things will be different this year, upperclassmen. To remind you of the rules——" Nate rubs his head and waits for the gossip to stop. "One. If a member of the opposite sex is in your room, your door must be open. Two. Members of the opposite sex must be gone from your room by nightfall according to the weekday and weekend hours listed in your official school handbook. This means that, three, there will be no *spending the night*. Are we clear? The consequences to breaking these rules are big, you guys. Detention. Suspension. Expulsion."

"So, what, you'll be doing random room checks?" a senior named Mike shouts.

"Yes," Nate says.

"That's unconstitutional!" Mike's sidekick Dave shouts.

"Then it's a good thing we're in France." Nate steps back into the gathered faculty and shoves his hands into his pockets. He's clearly aggravated by this new hassle in his life. The crowd breaks as abruptly as his announcement, and everyone is griping as we make our way toward first period.

"Maybe it won't apply to us," I say, hoping to convince myself. "Nate knows we're just friends. And shouldn't there be exemptions for friends who are in no way interested in each other's bodies?"

Kurt's mouth grows small and tight. "He didn't say anything about exemptions."

Because of our grade difference, our only period together is lunch. I head toward senior English alone and take my usual seat beside the leaded-glass windows. The classroom looks the same—dark wooden trim, empty whiteboards, chairs-attached-to-desks—though it still carries that feeling of summer emptiness.

Where is Josh?

Professeur Cole arrives as she always does, just as the bell is ringing. We have the same *professeurs* for each subject every year. She's loud for a teacher, friendly and approachable. *"Bonjour à tous."* Professeur Cole smacks down her coffee cup on the podium and looks around. "Good. No new students, no need for an introduction. Ah, *pardon.*" She pauses. "One empty desk. Who's missing?"

The door creaks open with her answer.

"Monsieur Wasserstein. Of course the empty desk is yours." But she winks as he slips into the remaining desk beside the door.

Josh looks tired, but . . . even tired looks good on him. He's wearing a dark blue T-shirt with artwork that I don't recognize, no doubt something obscure from the indie comic world. It fits him well—a bit tightly—and when he reaches for a copy of the syllabus, his sleeve creeps up to reveal the tattoo on his upper right arm.

I *love* his tattoo.

It's a skull and crossbones, but it's whimsical and simple and clean. Clearly his own design. He got it our sophomore year, despite the fact that minors in France are required to have parental approval. Which I seriously doubt he had. Which, I'm somewhat ashamed to admit, makes it even sexier. My heart pounds feverishly in my ears. I glance around the room, but the other girls appear to be at ease. Why doesn't he have the same effect on them that he has on me? Don't they *see* him?

Professeur Cole makes us push our desks into a circle. She's the only teacher here who forces us to look at one another during class. I take my seat again, and—suddenly—Josh's desk is opposite my own.

My head jerks down. My hair shields my face. I'll never be able to talk to him about that night in New York.

Halfway through class, the guy beside him asks a question. The temptation is too strong, so I steal the opportunity for another glance. Josh immediately looks up. Our eyes meet, and my cheeks burst into flames. I avert my gaze for the remainder of the hour, but his presence grows larger and larger. I can practically feel it pressing up against me.

Despite the fact that our schedule is, thus far, identical— English, calculus, government—I manage to evade him for the rest of the morning. It helps that he's skilled at both disappearing between classes and arriving late to them. Even when the next class is literally across the hall. When the bell rings for lunch, it's comforting to resume Kurt's company. We take the back staircase, the one less traveled. It's the Right Way.

"Did you speak to him?" he asks.

My sigh is long and forlorn. "No."

"Yeah. That sounds like you."

Kurt launches into something about a freshman in his computer programming class, a girl who is tall and serene and already fluent in several internet languages—totally his type— but I'm only half paying attention. I know it's dumb. I know there are more important things to think about on a first day back to school, including whatever it is my best friend is saying. But I like Josh so much that I actually feel *miserable*.

He has yet to make an appearance in the cafeteria, and it's doubtful that he will now, because I saw him weaving through the crowd in the opposite direction. His friends graduated last year. All of them. If only I were courageous enough to invite him to sit with us at our table, but his friends were so much cooler than us.

Besides, Josh is aloof. Untouchable. We are not.

In the lunch line, Mike Reynard—the senior who was the first to shout during Nate's speech—proves my point when he slams his tray into Kurt's spine. A bowl of onion soup splashes its entire contents onto the back of his hoodie.

Mike pretends to look disgusted. "Watch it, retard."

Kurt stares straight ahead in shock. A slice of baguette covered in melted Gruyère falls from his back to the floor with a *splat*. A soggy onion noiselessly follows.

My cheeks redden. "Jerk."

"Sorry, didn't catch that," Mike says. Even though he did. He's making fun of my soft voice.

I raise it so that he can hear me. "I said you're an asshole."

He smiles, an orthodontic row of unnaturally sharp teeth. "Yeah? And what are you gonna do about it, sweetheart?"

I clench the compass on the end of my necklace. Nothing. I am going to do nothing, and he knows it. Kurt shoves his hands into his hoodie's pockets, which begin to shake. I know his hands are flapping. He makes a low sound, and I link my arm through his and lead him away, abandoning our food trays. Pretending like I don't see Mike's and Dave's pantomimes or hear their cretinous guffaws.

In the quiet of the hall, Kurt races into the men's room. I sit on a bench and listen to the tick of a gilded clock. Count the number of pear-shaped crystals on the chandeliers. Tap my heels against the marble floor. Our school is as grand and ostentatious as anything in Paris, but I wish it weren't filled with such horrible, entitled weasels. And I know I'm just as privileged, but . . . it feels different when you live on the social ladder's bottom rung.

Kurt reappears. His hoodie is balled in his arms, wet from scrubbing.

"Everything okay?" I ask.

He's calm, but he's still frowning with severe agitation. "Now I can't wear it until it's clean."

"No worries." I help him shove it into his bag. "First thing after school."

The lunch line is empty. "I had ze feeling you would return." The jolly, potbellied head chef removes our trays from behind the counter and slides them toward us. "Leek tart for mademoiselle, *un croque-monsieur* for monsieur."

I'm grateful for this gesture of kindness. "*Merci,* Monsieur Boutin."

"Zat boy iz no good." He means Mike. "You do not worry about him."

His concern is simultaneously embarrassing and reassuring. He swipes our meal cards, and then Kurt and I sit at our usual table in the far corner. I glance around. As predicted, Josh isn't here, which is probably a good thing. But Hattie isn't here either. Which is probably not.

This morning I saw her eating *un mille-feuille* and—even though I don't blame her for wanting to start the day with dessert—I tried to stop her. I thought it might be dusted with powdered almonds, and she's allergic to nuts. But my sister always does the opposite of whatever anyone wants her to do, even when it's completely idiotic and potentially life threatening. We're not supposed to have our phones out at school, so I sneak text her: *ARE YOU ALIVE?!*

She doesn't reply.

The day worsens. In physics, Professeur Wakefield pairs us alphabetically to our lab partner for the year. I get Emily Middlestone, who groans when it's announced, because she is popular, and I am not. Sophie Vernet is paired with Josh.

I hate Sophie Vernet.

Actually, I've never given Sophie Vernet much thought, and she seems nice enough, but that's the problem.

My last two classes are electives. I'd like to say that I'm taking art history for my own betterment—not so that I'll have more to hypothetically converse about with Josh—but that would be false. And I'm taking computer science, because it'll look better on my transcripts than La Vie, the class that I wish I could take. La Vie means "life," and it's supposed to teach us basic life skills, but it's better known as the school's only goof-off class. I have zero doubt it's where Josh is currently located.

Professeur Fontaine, the computer science teacher, pauses by my desk while she's handing out our first homework assignment. Her chin is pointy, and her forehead is huge. She looks like a triangle. "I met your sister this morning."

I didn't even know Professeur Fontaine knew *me*. This

school is way too small. I try to keep my voice nonchalant. "Oh, yeah?" When the sister in question is Hattie, whatever follows this statement is generally unpleasant.

"She was in the nurse's office. Very ill."

Hattie! I told you so.

Professeur Fontaine assures me that my sister isn't dying, but she refuses to let me see for myself. When the final bell rings, I shoot a see-you-later text to Kurt, hurry toward the administration wing, push through its extravagantly carved wooden door, and—

My heart seizes.

Josh is slumped on the waiting room couch. His legs are stretched out so far and so low that they're actually *underneath* the coffee table. His arms are crossed, but his eyebrows rise— perhaps involuntarily, for someone sitting with such purposeful displeasure—at the sight of me.

My response is another deep, flaming blush. Why can't I have a normal face? Genetics are so unfair. I hasten toward the desk and ask the receptionist in French about Hattie. Without glancing up, she waves me toward the couch. A bracelet with a monogrammed charm jingles daintily from her wrist.

I can't move. My stomach is in knots.

"Wait there," she says, as if I didn't understand her gesture. Another wave and another jingle.

Move, feet. Come on. Move!

She finally looks at me, more annoyed than concerned. My feet detach, and I plant one in front of the other like a windup doll until I'm sitting on the other side of the couch. The small couch. *Love seat,* really.

Josh is no longer in full recline. He sat up while my back was turned, and now he's leaning forward with his elbows propped against his knees. He's staring straight ahead at an oil painting of a haloed Jeanne d'Arc.

It is now officially more awkward to ignore him than to acknowledge his presence. I search for an opener—something elementary—but my throat remains thick and closed. His silence is a confirmation of my fears. That I was a mess in the café, that his help was given in pity, that he wouldn't actively choose to interact with me and never will again—

Josh clears his throat.

It seems like a good sign. *Good.* "Good first day?" I ask.

A funny expression crosses his face. Was that a dumb question? Did it make me sound like his mother? Hattie is always accusing me of sounding like Maman.

"I've had better." He nods toward the head of school's office door.

"Oh." But *then* I get it. "Oh! Sorry. I'm here for the nurse, so . . . I assumed . . ."

"It's okay." And he says it like it is.

I wonder why he was called to her office. Because he skipped her welcome-back speech? Because he was tardy to his classes? It seems harsh to punish him for these things on our first day. And, great, now we've been silent for at least twenty seconds.

Tell him. Tell him. Just tell him already!

"Listen," I blurt. "I'm really embarrassed about last June. I was taking a lot of medication, and I don't remember much about that night, but I'm pretty sure you paid for my meal so I'd like to pay you back. And I'm sorry. For being weird. And thank you for walking me home. And for paying for my food."

He waits until I'm done. "It's okay," he says again.

And I feel stupid.

But Josh frowns as if he feels stupid, too. He scratches his head, somehow managing to muss his close-cropped hair. "I mean . . . don't worry about it. There's nothing to be embarrassed about. And you don't need to pay me back, it was only a few bucks."

This is the moment. Right here. This is the moment to place a hand on his arm, lean in, and say *the least* I can do is treat him to a meal in return. Instead, I just think it.

"Are you okay?" Josh asks. And then he makes another face.

It takes me a few seconds to figure it out, but that's the third time he's said the word *okay*. His embarrassment gives me a surge of confidence. "What do you mean?" I ask.

"You're here to see the nurse?"

"Oh! No, I'm checking in on my sister. She's sick."

He looks confused. "Geneviève?"

I'm thrown. He remembers Gen, and he remembers that we're related. He knows something about me. I shake my head. "My younger sister, Hattie. It's her first day."

He winces. "That makes more sense."

35

I can actually see Josh beating himself up in his head. The role reversal is fascinating. Somehow, I've made *him* nervous.

"So . . . how are your teeth?" he asks. "Everything heal?"

I smile, more to ease his discomfort than my own. "No problems."

"Good. Glad to hear it."

But I look down at the rug, unable to hold his gaze. *The sketchbook*. It's right there. Poking out of his bag. It's black and it has the blue sticker and it's definitely the same one. I should ask to see the drawing. I should just . . . open my mouth and ask. One question. It's one frigging question!

"You can see your sister now," the receptionist says.

I startle. *"Merci."* I stand hastily and grab my bag. "Good luck," I tell Josh, but then I'm flustered all over again. Just because it's him. I scramble down the hall before he can reply. The nurse's door is open, and Hattie watches me enter from a paper-sheet-covered cot. She tucks her bobbed, choppy hair behind her ears as if preparing for battle.

I tuck my long, wavy hair behind mine. "How do you feel?"

"What are you doing here?" Her question is accusatory.

"I wanted to make sure you're okay. Are you breathing all right?"

"No, I'm dying, and I only have fifteen minutes to live. I want a pony."

The nurse enters from an adjacent room. She's tiny like me but stronger and rounder. "Isla! It's nice to see you, dearie. Your sister gave us quite the scare. But we shot her with epinephrine, and she's been resting all day. The swelling in her throat is gone, and her breathing is back to normal."

"I told you I was fine," Hattie says.

I want to scream. I ask calmly, "Do Maman and Dad know?"

"They're on an airplane back to New York, duh."

My jaw tightens. "Are you going to call them later?"

"Why would I do that when I know you will?"

The nurse steps in. "The school will call your parents tonight." She glances uneasily between us, no doubt wondering how three sisters who look so alike can be so different. We have the same pale white skin and bright red hair, but Gen is ambitious, Hattie is contrary, and I'm . . . the quiet one. Who never causes trouble.

"Is she allowed to go back to her room?" I ask.

Hattie fumes. "God, Isla."

"What?"

"Stop being such a freaking *mom*!"

Her favorite accusation strikes with unexpected force. The shout reverberates around the room. I'm blinking back tears as I turn to the nurse. "I—I'm sorry."

"It's all right." But her eyes remain wary. "Hattie, I'm almost done with your paperwork. You'll be able to leave in just a minute."

It's a dismissal for me, too. I rush toward the exit, head ducked, straight past Josh in the waiting room. There's no doubt that he overheard everything. I'm barreling through the door when he says in a loud and clear voice, "Your sister's kind of a bitch, huh?"

I stop.

My love for him quadruples.

When I turn around, he grimaces. "I shouldn't have said that."

"No!" I say it too quickly. "I mean, she is. Thank you," I add for good measure.

Josh grins. It's wide and relieved and reveals a rarely seen pair of dimples. I could live inside those dimples for the rest of my life. "Do you, uh . . . ," he says. But I don't think he had a question to begin with.

I tilt my head.

The head of school's door opens, and we both jump. She leans out. "Monsieur Wasserstein. Has it already been three months? It's as if you never left." But her voice is droll, almost amused. "Come in."

Josh's expression falls back into that familiar blankness. He stands slowly and hefts his bag over his shoulder. As he disappears into her office, he gives me one last glance. His face is unreadable. The head of school follows his gaze and discovers me by the exit.

"Isla." She's surprised. "Is your sister feeling any better?"

I nod.

"Good. Good," she says again.

She's delaying, searching my face for something, but I don't know what. I hope Josh will be okay. I glance at her office door. When I look back, she's frowning as if she's just found trouble.

chapter five

The next few days are unsettling.

Josh is *aware* of me.

Whenever he enters a room, an unmistakable mass of chaotic energy enters with him. It rattles the air between us. It buzzes and hums. And every time we surrender—every time our eyes meet in a flash of nerve—a shock wave jolts throughout my entire system. I feel frayed. Excited. Unraveled.

And then . . . I'll lose the transmission. His signal will go cold.

I don't understand what's happening.

In calculus and physics, we're separated by alphabetical order. In English, we're stuck where we sat on the first day, on opposite sides of that circle. But our government teacher waited until today, Thursday, to pass out his seating chart. Josh arrived late, saw it being handed around, and sat down beside me. Just like that.

He still hasn't said a word.

Professeur Hansen paces the front of the classroom, lecturing with wild gestures about the US Declaration of Independence and the French *Déclaration des droits de l'homme et du citoyen*. Josh and I are in the back. He opens his bag, and I catch a glimpse of his sketchbook. He removes a cheap spiral notebook instead. In the past, I've watched him create elaborate illustrations related to our lesson plans, but today his work is abstract. Dense patterns and clusters and whorls and—

I let out a quiet—and involuntary—gasp of recognition.

His head jerks up.

My instinct is to pretend that something else caused the exclamation. I fight it. "Kind of conceited, don't you think?" I whisper, and I'm delirious that a good line escapes me.

His eyes widen. But he smiles as he neatly prints the word *CAUGHT!* underneath his sketch of a gnarled, spiny Joshua tree. I let out a snort of laughter that I turn into a cough. Professeur Hansen glances at me, but he doesn't give it another thought. Phew.

Josh turns the page and draws our teacher, a teeny version with flyaway hair and the jaunty gleam of madness. Our classmates' heads begin to fill the space around him. Mike and his bonehead friend, Dave; my snobby lab partner, Emily; and . . . Sanjita Devi. Who was once *my* friend. Who is now Emily's friend.

40

Josh gives Sanjita her own page. He dresses her in a suit of armor without gloves. The suit is as polished as her exposed fingernails, but she's looking down and away, as if she's afraid that we can see through the steel to what's really underneath.

It gives me the chills. He tilts it in my direction for approval.

"Wow," I whisper. "Yes."

Professeur Hansen doesn't hear it, but Sanjita turns around in her seat to glare at me. Her mouth forms a perfect circle of surprise. Few people know about my crush, but she's one of them. In the corner of my eye, Josh discreetly turns the page. I hold Sanjita's gaze. She recedes, battle lost. I clutch my necklace for comfort.

A moment later, Josh extends a slender arm across the aisle. He crooks a finger. I hold out the compass on its long, antique chain, and as he leans forward to take it, his hand carelessly brushes against mine. Or . . . not carelessly? He cradles the compass in his palm, studying it, head mere inches from my own and . . . *citrus*. His shampoo. Oranges, maybe tangerines.

"Ahem."

We startle, and Josh drops the necklace. It swings back against my chest and lands with an audible *thump*. Professeur Hansen has surprised us from behind. The other students laugh, having seen the setup. It's always amusing when he catches someone not paying attention. Except when that someone is you. He comically raps the back of Josh's chair. "As fascinating as Mademoiselle Martin's *neck*lace is, I assure you that the philosophies of Rousseau are far more likely to appear on next week's test."

"Yes, sir." Josh looks apologetic. But not fazed.

"You there." Professeur Hansen smacks my desktop with his fist, eliciting more laughter. "You can do better than this riffraff." He gestures toward Josh.

I've sunk into the deepest depths of my seat. They're waiting for me to reply. The whole class is waiting.

"I know I can." Josh's expression is deadpan. "She's a terrible influence."

Even the *professeur* laughs at that. Satisfied, he pushes up his glasses on his nose and launches back into the lesson. My eyes stay glued to him for the rest of the period. When the bell rings, Josh hands me a sheet of spiral-notebook paper. He's drawn my compass perfectly, down to the filigree on the needle. Underneath it, he's written: *WHY DOES SHE WEAR IT EVERY DAY?*

It shakes me to the core.

I place it beneath the cover of my textbook and try to play it cool, try to swallow the thrill of possessing something that he made. And the absolute wonder that he noticed. I move toward the exit, glancing over my shoulder with a smile. I hope it looks flirtatious. "I wear it so that I won't get lost, of course."

"Is that something that happens often?" he asks.

There's a traffic jam at the door. Josh is directly behind me, and when I turn my head to reply, his own smile is lopsided—*unquestionably* flirtatious—and I can no longer remember my name or my country or even my place in the universe.

"I'm over here," Kurt says.

Not only am I still staring at Josh, but I've also turned the wrong way down the hall. The stupidity blush is immediate. I lower my head and double back.

Amazingly, Josh follows.

"We're going to the cafeteria," Kurt tells him. "You're never there. Where do you eat?" It sounds like an interrogation.

Josh's smile wavers. "Uh, my room. Usually. Not always."

"You'll get detention. We aren't allowed to leave campus while school is in session."

Josh's smile disappears altogether.

"You should join us sometime." I say it quickly, because I'm embarrassed about Kurt. He's so rigid. And awkward. But the shame that follows these traitorous thoughts is instantaneous. "Or now. Or, you know, whenever."

As if I'm any *less* awkward.

My best friend frowns. It's not that he doesn't like Josh. But this invitation would mean a change in our routine, and Kurt is a creature of habit.

Unfortunately, Josh catches the expression. He crosses his arms—uneasiness in every line of his body—and turns back to me. "Yeah, maybe. Sometime."

My blood ices.

Sébastien.

He was my first, last, and only boyfriend. He attends another school nearby. We dated last winter, and I thought he was a decent guy until I introduced him to Kurt. Sébastien was uncomfortable around Kurt. This made Sébastien aggressive, which intensified Kurt's nervous habits, which turned Sébastien cruel. Which made me dump Sébastien.

Josh knows that Kurt has high-functioning autism. Everyone here knows. When a stranger misinterprets Kurt's behavior as rudeness and reacts poorly, I can usually forgive them. But when someone who knows him doesn't even want to *try* to understand him?

No. I can't forgive that.

My heart plummets with dead weight. "Well. Thanks for the drawing."

Kurt pulls down his hoodie—laundered the evening of the soup incident, no longer stained—and his sandy hair sticks out in a hundred directions. "You finally saw your portrait? The one from summer?"

I glance at Josh, and he takes a step backward. "No," I tell Kurt. "It was a drawing he made in class. Just now."

Josh rubs the side of his neck. "I should get going."

"But I wanna see the drawing of you." Kurt turns toward Josh. They're both tall, about the same height, but Kurt is broader, and his stare is forceful. "Do you have it?"

"N—no," Josh says. "No, I'm sorry. I don't."

"It's okay. Maybe some other time." I press my lips together.

Josh crosses his arms again, and his muscles tighten. "It's just that I don't have that sketchbook here. In France. That's all. Otherwise I'd show you." And then he rushes away. We watch him until he disappears from view.

"Was that weird?" Kurt asks. "I think that turned weird."

"Yeah. It was weird."

But it wasn't. It was a moment of truth buried inside a lie. I saw Josh's sketchbook less than an hour ago. He wanted to get away from us. Or, more likely, he wanted to get away from Kurt. My chest constricts. It's sudden and painful, but I hold back my tears. I don't want to have to explain them.

After lunch, I resume the habit of not looking at Josh. It's easier now.

It's also not easier.

I think he likes me. I don't even know how that's possible, but I do know that it doesn't matter anymore. It *can't* matter. In physics, I feel his stare—a string as delicate and gossamer as a spider's web, gently tugging at the back of my skull. I imagine snipping it loose with a pair of sharp scissors. I don't know if he'll try to talk to me after class, and I don't know what I should say if he does. When the bell rings, I bolt.

He's not at school the next day. I don't know why.

I don't see Josh over the weekend. I remove his drawing from my government textbook and carefully place it inside the top drawer of my desk. I open the drawer. Shut it. Open it. Shut it. Open it, and touch it, and worship it.

Slam it shut and feel so disloyal to Kurt.

Open it again.

Josh is back on Monday. In English, I feel him glancing at me repeatedly. When I finally lift my eyes and look across the circle, he gives me the softest smile.

Oh, it melts me.

The rest of the day is filled with these tiny moments. Another warm smile here, a friendly wave there. Something has changed . . . but what? On Tuesday, he asks me if I've read the new Joann Sfar. I haven't, but I'm stunned that he remembers our freshman-year, one-sided conversation. And then he's gone again.

Wednesday.

Thursday.

Friday.

Where is he?

chapter six

An old man with a busted piano is playing *"La Vie en rose"* on the street outside my window. He hauls it around this part of the city, from one corner to another, but I've never seen how he moves it. It's early evening on Friday, and the tinkly, fractured music is a bizarre contrast to the rough, powerful memoir I'm reading about being lost at sea.

There are two knocks against my door.

"Just kick it," I shout from bed. "I haven't gotten it fixed yet."

I turn the page of my book, and the door gently swings open, sans kick. I glance up. A double take, and I'm scrambling to my feet. "I'm sorry, I thought you were—"

"Kurt," Josh says.

"Yeah."

We stare at each other.

Ohdeargod, he's attractive. He looks recently showered, and his clothes seem even more carefully put together than usual. Behind his casual American attire, I can always still spot his artist's eye. His T-shirts and jeans fit, he wears the right colors, the right shoes, the right belt. It's subtle. But he never just throws something on.

"How did you know this was my room?" I finally ask.

"I saw you come in here the other day while I was waiting for the elevator. It caught my attention, because . . . this used to be mine." Josh glances around, taking everything in. This must be strange for him.

It's strange for *me*.

Along with the quilt of Manhattan, my bed is mounded with soft pillows and cozy blankets. I've squeezed in a skinny, antique bookcase that overflows with adventure books of all kinds—novels, nonfiction, comics. I have a curvy glass lamp and sheer lace curtains and, instead of posters on my walls, I've hung scarves and jewelry. My closet is jam-packed with clothing, and I have an additional chest of drawers stacked on top of the school's chest of drawers. Indulgent bath products line the corners of my tiny sink and equally tiny shower. My desk is organized with special nooks for homework, and my pens, pencils, and highlighters are arranged like bouquets in matching vases.

"I knew that," I admit. "That this was yours."

Josh raises his dark eyebrows."Why didn't you say something?"

I can only shrug, but he nods as if he understands. And I think he does. He places his hands in his pockets, nervous and unsure.

"You're still in the hallway." I shake my head. "Come in."

He does, and the door swings shut behind him.

"Careful!" I grab a textbook and shove it underneath to prop it back open. "Nate's enforcing the new rules, you know."

Immediately, I feel like a dork.

But Josh looks confused, and I realize he doesn't understand because he missed Nate's speech. I fill him in. "And I don't want to get in trouble," I add. "Because then he might not allow Kurt in here anymore, and we've already been caught once." It happened during a room check on the second day. We got off with a warning, but we've spent most of our afternoons since at the Treehouse, our secret refuge across the river.

Josh rubs the back of his neck. "Yeah. Of course."

He wants to leave.

I flush with panic. I don't know why he's here, but I do know that my heart will break if he goes. I gesture toward the desk chair. He takes it. I can barely contain my exhale of relief. I sit across from him on the edge of the bed. I smooth my wrinkled skirt. I stare at my coral-painted toenails.

"It's prettier in your hands," he says at last. "The room. Mine always gets messy."

I tuck a loose strand of hair behind my ear, and then I look down and let it fall forward again. "Thanks." I force my eyes to meet his. *Hazel.* My stomach twists. "My mother is a window dresser. She always tells me that small spaces can still be beautiful."

"Hard to get smaller than these rooms."

"You know those crazy holiday department-store displays that people actually wait in line to see? She does them for Bergdorf Goodman."

"Those are a big deal." He leans forward, impressed. "Your mom is French, right?"

My heart skips as it does every time he remembers something about me. "Yeah. She started working here, moved there for a better internship, met my dad, and . . . stayed."

Josh smiles. "I like that."

"How did your parents meet?"

"Law school. Yale. Boring story."

"I'm sure it's not boring to them."

He laughs, but my own smile fades. "Where have you been this week?" I ask. "Were you sick?"

"No. I'm fine." But he sits back again, and his expression becomes impenetrable. "It's Sukkoth."

Sue-coat. "Sorry?"

"The Jewish holiday?"

The humiliation blush is instant. Ohmygod.

"I'm off from school until next Thursday," he continues.

I search for something intelligent to say, something I've picked up from living in New York, but my mind is blank. *Sukkoth.* That's not a holiday people take off, is it? It can't be. As my brow furrows, Josh's eyes brighten. They look . . . almost hopeful. He shakes his head as if I'd asked the question aloud. "Nope. Most American Jews don't take it off. And even then, it's only the first two days."

"But you're taking an entire week?"

"I also took off last Friday, even though Yom Kippur didn't start until sundown. Same thing, the day before Sukkoth."

"But . . . *why?*"

He leans forward. "Because you're the first person to question it."

I'm not sure whether I'm more stunned by his deception or by being singled out. I laugh, but even to my ears, it sounds apprehensive. "Exactly how many holidays are you planning to take off?"

Josh grins. "All of them."

"And you think you'll get away with it?"

"I did last year. As the only student here of the Hebrew persuasion, the faculty feels *uncomfortable* questioning my religious observance."

I laugh, but this time it's for real. "You're going to hell."

"Then it's a good thing I don't believe in hell."

"Right. That whole Jewish thing."

"More like that whole atheist thing." Josh sees my surprise and adds a verbal asterisk. "Don't tell the press. My father can't afford to lose the Jewish vote." But he rolls his eyes as he says it.

"Your dad doesn't practice, either?"

"No, he does. My parents both do, in that whole go-to-temple-twice-a-year way. But politics and media, can't be too careful." His tone suggests that he's quoting something they've told him at least a thousand times.

I pause. And then I decide to push the subject one step further. "Your dad is running for reelection this year. That must be weird."

"Not really. In our house, there's always something that needs campaigning. It's just a pain in the ass, that's all."

I expected this reaction. I've always assumed that the dark shadow he carries—the one that defies the rules and manipulates the system, the one that's inked into the very skin of his arm—has something to do with his parents. But I know better than to keep questioning him. Kurt has given me both practice and patience when it comes to getting someone to open up. Because of this, I'm also skilled at subject changes.

"You know," I tease, "you still haven't told me why you're here. You were . . . passing by? Wanted to brag about getting a week off from school?"

"Oh. Uh, right." Josh sort of laughs and glances out my window. "I was just wondering if you wanted to go out."

Holy.

Shit.

"I'm on my way to Album," he continues, referring to a nearby comics shop. "Since we were talking about that new Sfar earlier, I thought if you weren't busy, you might want to come along."

. . . *oh*.

My heart beats like a cracked-out drummer. Josh, don't *do*

that to a lady. I'm still clutching the book about the shipwreck, so I set it down to wipe my sweaty palms. "Sure. I'm meeting Kurt in two hours for dinner, but yeah. Sure."

At the mention of Kurt, Josh winces slightly. Which makes *me* wince. But then, as if he'd been waiting for the opportunity, he leans over and nabs my book. Reads the back cover. And then holds it up along with a single raised eyebrow.

"I like stories about adventure. Especially if there's some kind of disaster involved."

The eyebrow remains arched.

I laugh. "I read the ones with happy endings, too."

Josh gestures toward my shelves. "You read a lot."

"Safer than going on a real adventure."

Now he's the one who laughs. "Maybe."

Leave it to me to admit cowardice to the object of my longtime infatuation. I jump to my feet in embarrassment. "Speaking of adventure."

Josh watches me remove a pair of platform sandals from underneath my bed. I turn my head to smile at him and catch his eyes dart from my cleavage to the ceiling. He closes them as if cursing himself. My pulse quickens, but I feign ignorance. I slide into my shoes. "Ready?"

He nods without meeting my gaze. I grab my purse, and we head for the door. He pulls out the textbook, pushes it across my floor, and shuts the door behind us.

It pops open.

He slams it again.

It pops open.

I yank it closed while tugging the handle down just so. We watch it. It stays.

"Sorry. My door sucks."

"Um, actually." Josh's hands are in his pockets again. His shoulders are practically up to his ears as we head toward the exit. "I should be the one apologizing. It's my fault that your door sucks."

"It is?" I'm not sure why, but this delights me. "What'd you do?"

He glances at me. "I might have kicked it."

"On purpose?"

"Yeah."

"Were you angry?"

"No." His face scrunches up. "It was a stupid reason."

"Oh, come on. You can't hold out on me now."

Josh groans with good nature. "Fine. I kicked the lock last winter to break it so that my ex-girlfriend—girlfriend at the time—could come and go as she pleased. And before you ask, yes, I did try to get a duplicate key made first."

I can't help but laugh. "That's . . . kind of ingenious. Kurt and I just trade ours around. Sometimes I forget to get mine back, and I get locked out of my own room. Well. I *used* to. Oddly enough, it hasn't happened this year."

He snorts as he holds open the main door for me.

"Using your hands this time," I say. "A novel approach."

As if on cue, he flinches and looks at his right hand. But it's a moment of genuine pain. My smile disappears. "Are you okay?"

"It's nothing." But my expression must be so *bullshit* that he laughs. "Really, I'm fine. I've been drawing more than usual—"

"Because of the holidays?"

"Exactly." He grins. "It's just a little tendinitis."

"*Tendinitis?* Don't you have to be old to get that?"

Josh glances over his shoulder. "Can you keep a secret?" He lowers his voice. "You have to promise not to tell anyone, okay?"

"Okay . . ."

"I'm eighty-seven years old. I have terrible hands but *amazing* skin."

I burst into laughter. "Scientists should study you."

"Why do you think I'm in France? Because it's the home of the world's best dermatological universities, that's why."

His straight face only makes me laugh harder. He glances at me, pleased, and then smiles to himself. We cross the narrow street. Somehow, our strides are in sync despite our difference in height. His entire body is lean and lovely. I want to lace his long, gorgeous fingers through mine. I want to bury my nose against his long, gorgeous neck.

Josh is overly focused on the cobblestones.

Something is happening between us. Is it friendship? It doesn't *feel* like friendship, but it's possible that I'm projecting my own desires. And I'm ashamed for even thinking about him like this after what happened last week. Because I'm not thinking. I'm *hoping*. People aren't supposed to be able to change, but . . . I've never bought that. Maybe Josh could learn to like Kurt. Maybe I misinterpreted his actions. There could have been any number of reasons for him to want to escape from Kurt so quickly. Maybe.

"So tell me what you're working on," I say.

"Oh, man." Josh rubs his neck. This seems to be his most frequently used gesture of unease. "It's always sort of embarrassing to tell someone new."

"What is it? I promise I won't laugh."

"You say that now." He grimaces and keeps his eyes on the jumble of bicycles and scooters parked alongside the road. "I'm making a graphic novel about my life here at school. A graphic memoir, I guess. There's not a phrase for it that makes it sound any less egotistical. Unfortunately."

So it's true. "How big is it?"

"Um, about three hundred pages. So far."

My jaw actually drops.

"I *really* like myself."

"You don't have to turn it into a joke." I shake my head. "That's incredible. I've never done anything like it, that's for sure."

"Well, I'm not done yet. One more year of school."

The colossal white dome of the Panthéon appears before us, illuminated like a beacon. We live on the Left Bank in the bottom of the Latin Quarter, along the edge of a residential neighborhood. It's peaceful but—because there are several other schools nearby—it's not very quiet during the day. But it *is* magnificent at dusk. Sometimes I forget how lucky I am to live here.

"Have you always been this passionate about drawing? I mean, a lot of kids are, but then we're sort of taught to stop." I look up at him. "You never stopped, did you?"

"Never." Josh finally meets my eyes, but his expression has turned mischievous. He points at my necklace. "Tell me the real story."

I stop walking. "Try flipping it over this time."

"Oh?"

I smile and hold it out on its chain. He takes the compass, angles it into the light, and reads the engraving on the back—first silently and then aloud. His voice is deep, clear but quiet. "Isla. May you always find the Right Way. Love, Kurt."

"It's the only sentimental gift he's ever given me. I suspect his mom helped, but it doesn't matter. He has this thing about maps and directions and finding the best route. But I like that the words have more than one meaning."

Josh places it back into my hands. "It's beautiful."

He turns contemplative as we trek up the rue Saint-Jacques. Perhaps he *is* reconsidering Kurt. There has to be a way to approach the subject. I'll *find* a way. A siren wails past with its French *ooo-WEE ooo-WEE*, but it only heightens the return of our silence. I'm relieved when we emerge into a bustling district of retail.

Album is a chain, but this particular location is split into two stores that sit across a busy intersection from each other. One sells American superhero-type imports and figurines. The other sells Franco-Belgian books called *les BD*, *les bandes dessinées*.

French comics tend to have a better presentation than their American counterparts. They're hardcover, taller, glossier. They have a wider range of stories and, because of it, they're also more widely read. Comic shops are everywhere here, and it's not uncommon to find businessmen and women browsing their aisles in expensive haute couture.

Without having to discuss it, Josh and I enter the location with *les BD*. We're greeted by the heavenly perfume of freshly printed text, and a youngish man with a trim beard gives us an amiable *salut* from behind the counter. I nod a greeting in return.

"Isla."

It startles me to hear Josh speak my name. I turn around, and he holds up a book from the edge of the first display table. It's the new Sfar, of course. I take it, and it opens with the delicious crack of a hard spine being tested for the first time. I'm thrilled to discover that it's one of his *fantastique* titles— the pages are filled with woods and monsters and swords and royalty and love. Adventure.

"Yeah?" Josh asks.

I beam. "Yeah."

He looks happy, and then sad, and then he turns so that I can't see his face. It worries me. I want to know what's wrong, but his body language tells me not to ask. But then he turns back around—as if he'd made up his mind about a conversation that I didn't even know we were having—and blurts, "Does your boyfriend like comics?"

For a moment, I think he's joking.

The word was a *joke*. But his expression is serious, and it looks like he expects a serious reply, and I am very, very thrown.

I swallow. "Excuse me?"

"Sorry." He frowns at the table of new releases. "I don't know why that sounded so harsh."

My heart hammers against my chest, but I speak the words slowly. "Kurt. Isn't. My boyfriend."

Josh freezes. Several seconds pass. His eyes are fixed on a Tintin reissue. "He's not?"

"No." I pause. "*No.*"

"But . . . you're always together. You're so close."

"We *are* close. Best friends close. Practically brother and sister close. Not—*not*—boyfriend and girlfriend close."

"But . . . the necklace. You share keys . . . "

"Because we're *friends*. Who *hang out*."

His ears have turned a deep crimson. "So . . . you've never gone out with him?"

"No! I've known him since we were in diapers." My mind is reeling. "I can't believe you thought we were dating. For how long?"

"I—I guess this whole time."

A new and terrible panic stirs within me. "This whole time as in this year or this whole time as in since Kurt was a freshman?"

Josh seems to have a lump in his throat. "Since he was a freshman?"

"Does *everyone* think we're a couple?" Our classmates joke about it, but I never thought that they were serious.

"I don't know." Josh shakes his head vigorously, but he says, "Probably?"

"Ohmygod." I'm finding it difficult to breathe.

He lets out a strange laugh. It's near hysterical, but it stops as abruptly as it starts. "So *are* you dating anyone? Someone else?"

"No. No one since last year."

"Cool." His fingers tap rapidly against the stack of Tintins.

I fight to keep my voice steady. "And you? Are you seeing anyone?"

"Nope. No one since last year."

I want to weep with joy. He liked me, but he thought he *couldn't* like me. It's difficult to wrap my mind around this idea. I suspected his attraction, but the full truth of the situation is unbelievable. How is it possible that my crush—my three-year-long crush—has a crush on *me*? This doesn't happen in real life.

Josh is equally thrown. He's grasping for something to say when his eyes catch on the Sfar. "There's more downstairs, right? Should we go down there?"

"No." I hug the book with both arms. "This is exactly what I wanted."

chapter seven

I'm still clutching the book—now through a blue Album bag—
as we wander toward the Seine. We have another hour before
I'm supposed to meet Kurt for sushi in the Marais. Nighttime
has officially arrived, and the streets are abuzz. I feel as if I'm
floating. Glancing, smiling, blushing. Both of us. My voice has
abandoned me. Josh's left hand grasps his right elbow, an anchor
to keep him in one place.

How does one proceed in a situation like this? If only the
discovery of mutual admiration could lead promptly into making
out. If only I could say, "Listen. I like you, and you like me, so
let's go find a secluded park and touch each other."

We steer around a group of tourists pawing through bins of
miniature Notre-Dames. Josh swallows. "Just so we're clear,"

he says, "I wasn't, like, trying to steal you away from Kurt when I asked if you wanted to go to the store with me. I was trying to, you know . . . be your friend. I don't want you to think I'm a creep."

I smile up at him. "I don't think you're a creep."

But Josh looks at an ornate iron balcony, a carved stone archway, an enormous poster for the Winter Olympics in Chambéry. Anything but me. "It's just that last weekend I realized that even if you were, um, taken, I still wanted to hang out with you."

He wanted me as *more* than a friend first. My chest tightens happily. "Last weekend?"

"Yom Kippur?" Josh glances at me to see if I'm following his train of thought. I'm not, and I'm grateful when he launches into it without me having to ask. He seems relieved for the new topic. "Okay, so the period of time between Rosh Hashanah— which was the day before we came back to school—"

"That's the Jewish New Year?"

He nods. "Yeah. So the period between Rosh Hashanah and Yom Kippur is for reflection. You're supposed to think about mistakes, ask forgiveness, make resolutions. That sort of thing. And then Yom Kippur is, essentially, the deadline."

We split apart to pass a gentleman walking a basset hound, and when we reunite, the distance between us halves. "So. Wait. You contemplated your life and . . . resolved to become my friend? Even though you're no longer a practicing Jew?"

Josh gives me a wicked smile. "Is that a requirement for your friendship?"

I give him a look.

He laughs, but he follows it with a wistful shrug. "I don't know. There's something . . . poetic about this time of year. And it's not like I've figured out everything spiritually or whatever, but I do think it's still okay to make resolutions. On my own terms."

"Sure it's okay. My family is Catholic, both sides, but they never go to Mass. I don't even know if my parents believe in God. But we still put up a Christmas tree, and it still gives us a sense of peace. Traditions can be nice."

"Do you believe in God?" he asks.

For some reason, his directness doesn't surprise me. The real Notre-Dame is ahead of us, gigantic and humbling, and its reflection shimmers in the dark river below. I stare at it for a while before answering. "I don't know what I believe. I guess that makes me a Christmas Tree Agnostic."

He smiles. "I like it."

"And you're a Yom Kippur Atheist."

"I am."

I've never had a conversation like this before, where something so sensitive was discussed with such ease. We cross a bridge toward the cathedral. It's on the Île de la Cité, the larger of the two islands that comprise the center of Paris.

"I have a question," Josh says. "But I'm not sure how to ask it."

I wish that I could give him a playful nudge. "I'm sure you'll do fine."

There's an excruciating pause as he searches for the right phrasing. "Kurt has . . . autism?"

Internally, I cringe. But I spare him as he spared my own ignorance. "Yeah. What the DSM *used* to call Asperger's, and what they now call high-functioning autism. It's the same thing. But it's not a problem, it's not like it's something that needs to be cured. His brain just works a little differently from ours. That's all."

Josh gestures toward a bench in the cathedral's small park, and I reply by moving toward it. We sit down about two feet apart.

"So how *does* his brain work?"

"Well." I take a deep breath. "He's superrational and literal. So sarcasm, metaphor? Not his strengths."

Josh nods. "What else?"

"It's difficult for him to read faces. He's worked on it a lot, so he's way better than he used to be. But he still has to remember to make eye contact and smile. I mean, obviously he smiles, but he only does it when he means it. Unlike the rest of us." I'm rambling, because I'm struck *again* by the fact that I'm sitting on a bench—a bench not even on school property—beside Joshua Wasserstein.

"So he's honest."

"Even when you don't want him to be." I laugh, but it immediately turns into worry. I don't want Josh to get the wrong idea. "He doesn't *mean* to be rude, though. Whenever he finds out that he's accidentally hurt someone's feelings, he's devastated."

"It's kind of French, you know? Not the hurting-people's-feelings thing. Only smiling when it's sincere. Americans will smile at anyone, for any reason."

"You don't." The words leave my mouth before I can stop them.

Josh is taken aback. It takes him a moment to gather his thoughts. "Yeah, I've been told that I have a hard time . . . concealing my displeasure."

"I know." I hesitate. "I like that about you."

His eyebrows shoot up. "You do?"

I stare at the bench's wooden slats. Somehow, the two feet between our bodies has halved into one. "It means that when you do smile? I know it's not false. You're not just smiling to make me"—I shake my head, and my hair bounces—"*whomever,* feel better. If they're saying stupid things. And can't seem to stop talking."

His mouth spreads into a slow smile.

"Yeah." I laugh. "Like that."

"What else?"

I tilt my head. "What else what?"

"What else do I need to know about Kurt?"

His phrasing implies that we'll be spending more time together. The happy tightness returns to my chest. "Not much else to know. It's not like he's a card-counting savant or a mathematical genius or anything. I mean, don't get me wrong. He's brilliant. But those stereotypes are the worst. Though he *does* love routine."

Josh smiles again. "Let me guess. Sushi?"

"Same day, same time, same restaurant." Kurt and I meet after his weekly therapy session, but Josh doesn't need to know that.

"Same entrée?"

"Shrimp nigiri and miso soup. But I get the special, whatever it is. I ask the server to surprise me."

The bells of Notre-Dame peal out from the towers. We startle, covering our ears and laughing. The bells are loud—a cacophony of chimes crashing over one another. From this close, it's hard to even make out a pattern. They ring and ring and ring, and we're helpless, completely bowled over with laughter, until they cease their clanging.

The distance between us has disappeared.

His jeans rub softly against my bare legs. I'm too aware of my movements, too aware of my nerves, too aware of everything. All five senses are overloading. I jerk my head toward the cathedral. "That was my cue."

"Mind if I walk with you?" Josh's question sounds anxious, like he's trying to catch his breath. "I need to pick up a brush. At Graphigro." It's an art supply store a few blocks away from the restaurant. I don't know whether he really does need a new brush or whether this is an excuse to spend a few more minutes with me. But I'll take it either way.

This entire evening has been surreal. We cross another bridge, the Pont d'Arcole, onto the Right Bank. The scent of metal and urine wafts up from the Seine, but even this barely registers. We're in a two-person bubble. The noises that I should be hearing—cars speeding, pedestrians rushing, construction clattering—are muffled. Instead, I hear my heart thumping against my rib cage. Josh's steady footsteps against the pavement. The occasional swish of his pant legs catching against each other.

Ask me out. I chant it like a mantra. *Ask me out, ask me out, ask me out.*

"What are you doing this weekend?" It ruptures from my mouth, far less casual than I'd hoped. "I mean, you don't have detention, do you?"

Aaaaaand way to make it worse.

But Josh glances at me with a smile. "The head called me into her office, because she wanted to make sure that we 'get off to the right start' this year. But she didn't give me detention. Not yet."

I have no idea how I'm supposed to respond.

"Actually," he says, "I'm going to Munich."

I freeze, midstep. It's against school rules to leave the city without permission, never mind the entire *country*. Someone bumps into me from behind. I stumble forward, and Josh reaches out to grab me, but I've already steadied myself. His hand hesitates in the space between us. And then it returns to his pocket.

I kind of wish that I'd fallen.

"So, um. Munich. This weekend?"

Josh is studying me, making sure that I'm really okay. "Yeah. Oktoberfest."

I frown. "Even though it's still September?"

"Ah, but most of the festival happens this month. Misleading, I know." He grins, and there's an enticing flash of dimples. My insides go wobbly. "But I want to visit as many countries as possible before graduation. And I've never been to Germany."

"And you're traveling alone?" I'm impressed. Maybe even awed.

"Yep. My train leaves in the morning."

Kurt appears on the opposite side of the street. He's checking his phone, no doubt preparing to text because I'm a full minute late. I shout his name. He pulls down his hoodie and brushes the hair from his eyes, thrown to discover me with Josh.

I shuffle my feet against the curb. "Well. This is my stop."

Josh kicks the curb once, too. "Maybe sometime I can join you guys for dinner?"

Ohmygod. "I am *such* an assweed."

He bursts into laughter.

"Sorry. I'm so sorry! Would you like to have dinner with us?"

He's still laughing. "I was only teasing."

"Please." I clasp a hand around my compass. "Eat with us."

"It's okay. I really do need to pick up a brush before tomorrow. Besides"—he glances at Kurt—"I wouldn't want to impose."

"You wouldn't be imposing."

But Josh is already walking backward down the side street. He's still facing me. "See you in a few days," he shouts. "Enjoy your raw fish."

"Enjoy your schnitzel!"

I laugh at the unexpected perverseness of our final exchange as Kurt pops up over my shoulder. His brow wrinkles. "Why was he here? How did *that* happen?"

Josh turns around. I admire the back side of his physique as the streetlamps illuminate him, one after another. His figure grows smaller. He reaches a curve in the road and looks over his shoulder. One hand raises in a wave. I mirror the gesture, and he vanishes.

"I don't know." I'm mystified. "I was alone in my room. And then he was there."

It's Sunday—just before midnight—and I'm curled in bed with Joann Sfar, when there are two knocks against my door. The sound is so soft that I'm not sure I actually heard it. My mind races to Josh, but I push it away as improbable. Kurt? No, he'd text. Maybe it was next door. Or maybe it was a practical joke; it wouldn't be the first.

I wait for a voice.

Nothing.

I settle back into my book, warily, when I hear it again. *Knock-knock.* Low to the ground. I'm still gripping the hardcover, which might make a serviceable weapon, as I climb out of bed and tiptoe forward. "Hello?" I whisper.

"It's me," the other side says. "Josh."

He adds his name, because he does not yet realize that I'd

recognize his voice anywhere, under any circumstance. I've had this fantasy before: Midnight. Him. Here. My heartbeat accelerates. I shake out my pillow-limp hair and take a steadying breath. It doesn't work. I turn the handle silently, but my hand trembles.

"Hi," he says. His face is close to mine, as if his cheek, or maybe his ear, had been pressed against the wood.

"Hi," I reply.

Josh leans against the doorframe. His body is several inches lower to the ground, which makes our eyes nearly level. We study each other in silence. He looks different this close. He looks *real*. Complete, somehow. I glance down the hallway. It's dark and empty. This fantasy is *definitely* familiar . . . until he holds up a beer stein.

I frown, but it clicks only a second later. "You went! You really did go."

Josh lifts the stein in a mock cheers. "I did."

I smile. "How was it?"

"Crowded. Loud." He sounds depleted. "A fairground with wall-to-wall frat boys and drunken parents trying to escape from their own bratty children. Mike and Dave would've fit right in."

"Yikes. That bad, huh?"

"It's safe to say that I'll be selecting a new destination next weekend."

"Germany's loss."

The corner of his mouth lifts into a smile. He holds out the stein, and I tuck my book underneath my arm to accept it. The stein is made out of traditional earthenware, heavy and gaudy and carved, with a pointed tin lid.

I laugh. "This is really, really hideous."

"They all were. And the ones in the beer tents were even worse, plain glass with this badly designed Oktoberfest logo. At least this one has a sword fight. See the tiny knights in front of the Bavarian castle? It was the most *adventurous* one I could find."

And that's when I realize . . . this is a gift. Josh picked this out for *me*. Suddenly, the stein is beautiful. I clutch it against my chest. "Thank you."

He nods at my book. "How is it?"

"Good. You can borrow it. If you want."

Josh looks down at his sneakers, and then back up, and then back down. "You know that I like you. Right?"

My heart pounds so hard that he can probably feel the reverberations. But—for once—the words fall easily from my lips. "So stay here next weekend. Go out with me."

chapter eight

Josh isn't in school the next day. He has three more days off for a holiday that he doesn't celebrate. I wish I could get away with it, but the idea of potentially missing an important class or being late on an assignment makes me break out in hives. But I understand that his priorities are elsewhere—his art. So I'm shocked when I enter first period on Tuesday, and he's slouched at his desk . . . a full five minutes before the bell rings.

A rush of adrenaline removes any last trace of morning sleepiness. "What are you doing here?" I hug a notebook to my chest, glowing with happiness.

"H—hey." He sits up straighter. "Yeah. Funny story."

I raise my eyebrows.

"Perhaps the head of school grew suspicious about the length of my absence. Perhaps she called my parents. Perhaps my parents confirmed that we don't celebrate Sukkoth."

My shoulders fall. "Perhaps you have a shit-ton of detention?"

Josh shrugs, but it's a shrug of affirmation.

"That sucks. I'm sorry."

He clasps his hands on top of his desk. "Actually." Josh lowers his voice and leans in. "The situation isn't all bad."

I crinkle my nose. "It's not?"

He stares at me. He stares harder.

"Oh." My gaze drops in a sheepish sort of pleasure. "Um. How much detention did you receive?"

Josh sits back again, resuming his slouch. "Only three weeks, but—"

That snaps my head back up.

"Including Saturdays." Another shrug. "It's not a big deal, I can use the time to work. But I'm also on my final warning. Didn't take long," he adds.

My heart stops—literally stops—for a full beat. "Final warning? As in *expulsion*?"

"Seriously. Not a big deal." But my panic must be showing, because he scoots forward in his seat. "Let's just say that for a 'final' warning? It's not my first."

I wait. I have no idea how he can be so calm about this.

"Last year," he explains. "In fact, I was on my final warning once in the winter and once in the spring. So, somehow, I got two. This is number three."

"Well . . . be careful." It sounds so lame. "I mean, the leaves haven't even changed, and you wouldn't want to miss that. Though they *are* prettier in New York—"

"I'll be careful." His voice is deliberate. He smiles.

I fiddle with a curl in my hair.

Two desks away, Emily Middlestone leans over. She's wearing a pair of designer eyeglasses that I'm sure are fake. "You know, that'd be really stupid if you got kicked out in your last year of school."

Josh's expression wipes blank. "Yeah, Emily. That *would* be stupid."

Professeur Cole bursts into the room and grinds to a halt. "Am I late?" she asks Josh.

He shakes his head once. "Nope."

"Well. How fortunate that you've finally learned how to tell time." But her smile is sly. She marches up to her podium, and I take my seat.

The one directly across from Josh.

We glance at each other with more openness throughout the week, but there's still a shyness between us, an unwillingness to look or talk for too long. Our relationship has yet to be solidified. Anticipation—of *something*—hovers in the air. At night, it takes me hours to fall asleep. I place the beer stein on top of my mini-fridge, beside my bed, so that I can see it from my pillow. Proof that he's thinking about me, too.

He doesn't visit my room. His afternoon detention runs

until dinner, and he still isn't eating in the cafeteria. And then, after dinner, opposite-sex visitation hours are over. He's cut back on rule breaking, and apparently that's one he's not willing to risk anymore. So I continue my usual schedule of homework and studying, and I try to bite back the analyzing. Kurt has been giving me dirty looks.

On Thursday, before government, Josh removes a pen from between his teeth. "So. Saturday. I'm out of detention at eighteen hours. Anytime you want to meet after that . . ."

Paris runs on a twenty-four-hour clock. Eighteen hours is six p.m. My stomach butterflies emerge from their chrysalises. "Yeah?"

He points the pen at me. "You know that because you asked me out, you're the one who has to pick the place, right?"

Throat. Dry.

Dry throat.

All of the dryness in my throat.

Josh places the pen back between his teeth and then immediately takes it out again. "Whatever you suggest." He grins. "I'll say yes. You'll definitely get a yes. If that helps."

My response is another hot blush.

The rest of my school week is spent in freak-out mode, a situation that leaves me with a newfound respect for guys. Sébastien planned and organized most of our dates. It's an alarmingly high-pressure job. Kurt reminds me that it'll be Nuit Blanche. White Night. A night that never grows dark. The first Saturday of every October, museums and galleries open their doors for free until dawn. The tradition started in Saint Petersburg, Russia, traveled here, and has continued to spread around the world. But—even speaking as someone used to its decadence—there's still no greater city than Paris for an all-night festival.

I'm not the only one watching the clock. At precisely *vingt et une heures*—just as the numbers on my phone tick from 20:59 to 21:00—I hear a sound that's instantly recognizable: two light knocks, down low. My nerve endings jolt. Yesterday, I told Josh *when* to arrive but not *where* we're going. Mainly because I hadn't figured it out yet.

Three years of anxiety flood throughout my body. What if I'm wrong? What if this isn't what I've always wanted?

What if it is?

I open the door.

Josh is knee-bucklingly sexy. It's the first cool night of autumn, and he's dressed in a striking wool coat. The collar is turned up in that self-confident yet unkempt way that only artists can pull off. I've seen him wear this coat before, this beautiful going-on-a-date coat, but this is the first time that he has worn this coat for *me*.

"Youlookamazing."

But the words tumble from his lips, not mine.

I'm wearing a swishy dress, and my hair is in neat, pretty waves. My mouth is painted red. Maman once told me to place the boldest color where I want people to look. I bite my bottom lip. "Thanks. You do, too."

Josh tucks his hands into his pockets. His shoulders rise nervously.

My breathing is shallow. Like I can't get enough oxygen. "So I thought we'd go to the Pompidou? They have an exhibition of this weird photographer from Finland. He's supposed to be totally nuts, and I thought it might be interesting, but I don't know, maybe that's stupid, we can do something else if you want—"

"No."

Blood rises to my cheeks. "No?"

"I meant we should go. That sounds cool."

"Oh." I swallow the goose egg that's been stuck in my throat. "Okay. Good."

There's a long pause. Josh takes an exaggerated step to the side. "Unfortunately, you *will* have to leave your room."

I laugh, and it sounds like I've been sucking helium. "Right. Been a while since I've been on one of these. A date. I forgot how they worked." I close the door behind me, internally exploding with humiliation. We're only two steps down the hall before my door jack-in-the-boxes back open.

Josh slams it shut with a move that's both calculated and knowing. "Oh, man. It really is too bad that some asshole broke your lock."

Finally, I laugh. Genuine and normal sounding. And then my date says the best thing that he could possibly say: "It's okay. I haven't been on one of these in a while either."

My smile triples in size.

Josh grins. "Just give me your hand."

"W—what?"

"Your hand," he repeats. "Give it to me."

I extend my shaking right hand. And—in a moment that is a hundred dreams come true—Joshua Wasserstein laces his fingers through mine. A staggering shock of energy shoots straight into my veins. Straight into my heart.

"There," he says. "I've been waiting a long time to do that."

Not nearly as long as I've been waiting.

chapter nine

The Centre Pompidou is the modern-art museum, a huge box of a building that looks as if it's been turned inside out. Its inner structure is exposed and color-coded: green pipes for plumbing; blue for heating and cooling; yellow for electricity; and red for safety. The bold primary colors clash with the noble gray elegance of the rest of the city. For some reason, that makes me like it even more.

I wouldn't have minded the walk here—my sushi place is right around the corner, not to mention the Treehouse—but Josh took one look at my heels and led me straight to the nearest taxi stand. I *am* wearing my tallest pair. He's still over half a foot taller than I am, but I know I can reach his lips if he tries. I hope he tries.

The museum's lobby is silver metal and blinding neon. As we pass the information desk, Josh takes my hand again. Our palms are sweaty. It's heaven. We ride the crowded escalators up, up, up beside a wall of steel and glass. The glittering streets of Paris stretch all the way to the horizon. We talk about the shiny little nothings we see—people and cars and cathedrals, even la Tour Eiffel—but it's not that we don't have anything meaningful to say. The feeling is that we have *everything* to say.

And where do you begin with everything?

We switch escalators from level four to five, and I ride backward on the stair above him. Our eyes are level. We're laughing, I'm not even sure why, and he's holding both of my hands now, and—suddenly—he's leaning in.

This is the moment.

Josh hesitates. He second-guesses himself and pulls back. I lean forward to say the timing is right, I'm ready, let's do this thing, and his smile returns and our eyes are closing and his nose is bumping against mine and—*blip!*

We jump. His pocket blips again.

"Sorry," he says, flustered. "Sorry." Our hands unclasp, and he pulls out his phone to silence it. And then he bursts into an unexpected laugh.

Everything inside of me is throbbing. "What is it?"

"He got a job." Josh shakes his head. "He really got one." He holds up the screen, and a snapshot of a guy with mussed hair and a polyester vest grins back at me. He's giving the V sign, the English finger. It's his best friend, Étienne St. Clair.

I smile, despite our thwarted kiss. "Where's St. Clair going to school now?" For reasons unknown to me, Josh's friend goes by his last name.

"California. Berkeley. He said he was getting a job at a movie theater, but I didn't believe him." Josh shakes his head again as we grab the final escalator. "He's never worked a day in his life."

"Have you?" Because not many people who've been to our school have.

Josh frowns. He's ashamed of his answer, and it comes out like a one-word confession. "No."

"Me neither." We both hold the guilt of privilege.

Josh glances at his phone again. I lean in and examine the picture closer. "Oof. That's one seriously ugly uniform. Does anyone look good in maroon polyester?"

He cracks a smile.

The escalator ends. Josh types a quick reply, silences his phone, and returns it to his pocket. I wonder if he told St. Clair about our date. I wonder if I'm newsworthy.

We head toward the galleries, but the mob inside the top-floor restaurant gives us pause. The tables have been removed, and an army of svelte models in frizzy white wigs, white lipstick, and marionette circles of white blush are maneuvering trays of champagne through the swarm of bodies. Josh turns to me and cocks his head. "Shall we?"

"Why, yes." I respond with a matching twinkle. "I believe we shall."

We slip inside, and he grabs two flutes as the first tray whizzes by. We're the youngest people here, by far. It must be a private party. The clamor of excited voices and the outlandish, kaleidoscopic music make the room unusually loud for Paris. "It's like New Year's Eve in here," I shout.

He bends down to shout back. "But not the real one. That glamorous, fake one you see in films. I always spend the real one watching television alone in my bedroom."

"Yes! Exactly!"

Josh hands me a glass and nods toward one of the restaurant's giant decorative-aluminum shells. We duck underneath it. The noise becomes somewhat muffled, and I raise my glass. "To the new year? Our new school year?"

He places a dramatic hand across his heart. "I'm sorry. But I simply *cannot* toast that place."

I laugh. "Okay, how about . . . comics? Or Joann Sfar?"

"I propose a toast"—Josh raises his glass with mock gravitas—"to new *beginnings*."

"To new beginnings."

"*And* Joann Sfar."

I laugh again. "And Joann Sfar." Our glasses clink, and his eyes stay carefully fixed upon mine in the French tradition. My smile widens into a grin. "Ha! I knew it."

"Knew what?"

"You held eye contact with me. I've seen you pretend like you don't know how things go around here, but you do know. I *knew* you knew. You're too good of an observer." I take a triumphant sip of champagne. The pristine fizz tickles the tip of my tongue, and my smile grows so enormous that he breaks into laughter.

Thank you, France, for allowing alcohol to be legal for teenagers.

Well, eighteen-year-olds. And we're close enough.

Josh is amused. "How do you know I wasn't looking at you simply because I *want* to look at you?"

"I'll bet you speak French better than you let on, too. You never use it at school, but I bet you're fluent. People can play dumb all they want, but they always give themselves away in their actions. In the small moments, like that."

The bubbles seem to go down the wrong hole. He coughs and sputters. "Play dumb?"

"I'm right, right? You're fluent."

Josh shakes his head. "Not all of us grew up in a half-French household."

"But I'll bet you're still good."

"Maybe. Maybe not." Thankfully, he's amused again.

"So why do you pretend not to know things?" My fingers play with the stem of my glass. "Or not to care?"

"I *don't* care. About most things," he adds.

"But why play dumb?"

He takes another sizable gulp of champagne. "You know, you ask really tough questions for a first date."

A painful blush erupts across my face and neck. "I'm sorry."

"It's okay. I like girls who challenge me."

"I didn't mean to be challen—"

"You aren't."

I raise an eyebrow, and he laughs.

"Really," he says. "I like smart girls."

My blush deepens. I wonder if he knows that I'm the top student in our class. I never talk about it, because I don't want people to judge me. But it's true that his ex-girlfriend was smart, too. Rashmi was last year's salutatorian.

Josh says something else, but the noise level in the restaurant has been increasing, and it's finally reached its maximum volume. I shake my head. He tries again, but I still can't hear him so he takes my hand. We down the rest of our drinks as we squeeze through the revelry. He plunks the empty glasses on a passing tray, leads me past a final throng of partygoers, and we emerge gasping and laughing into the hall.

"Well," Josh says. "Now that *that's* done."

I gesture toward the galleries. We stroll through them hand in hand. But the air here is cold, almost reminiscent of mortuaries, and the sparsely furnished rooms grow stranger and stranger. Miniature sculptures of mundane objects that you have to get on your knees to see. A short film of a fast-food joint being purposefully flooded with water. A collection of puppets with crayons shoved up their asses.

"That looks . . ."

"Uncomfortable?" Josh finishes.

"I was going to say like a very colorful suppository."

He bursts into laughter, and an elderly woman with a dead fox around her shoulders glares at us. The fox has been dyed an alarming shade of purple. Josh whispers into my ear, "That's how it became such a vibrant color. Crayons. Up its butt."

I cover my giggling, but it's no use. She glares again, and we scurry into the next room. "Ohmygod. This whole thing is . . . not what I'd hoped."

"Don't say that." But he's still laughing.

I shake my head. "I wanted weird, but maybe it's *too* weird?"

"It doesn't matter. I'm with you. I'm happy to be anywhere with you."

My heart puddles. "Me too."

Josh squeezes my hand. "Come on." He pulls me closer as we walk, and our bodies bump against each other. It's amazing how *solid* he is. How real. Muscle and skin and bone. "We still haven't seen your Finnish artist. Maybe he's over here?"

We find the exhibit hidden away in a back corner of the museum. The walls are collaged with hundreds, maybe thousands, of grainy, unframed photographs. We peer closer at one of a crumpled single-serving potato-chip bag. The artist had laid a scribbled note beside the object as some kind of label before snapping the picture. It's written in Finnish, but it's also been marked with a date.

"Huh." We say it together.

Josh points to another photograph. It's an empty bus seat, also labeled. "So he's cataloging his day-to-day life? I guess?"

I look around for a sign in French and find it beside the door. I walk over to read it. "These aren't his things. They're some woman's."

Josh gives a low whistle. "No wonder this looks like a stalker's bedroom." He bends over. "Oh, shit! Look at this one. Yeah, I think that's *actually* shit."

I race back to his side. "How did he get her shit?!"

"Maybe he went into a public restroom after her? He was probably gonna take a picture of the seat and got lucky. Maybe it wouldn't flush."

I snort loudly.

"I mean, I've been waiting for *you* to leave something behind for ages, but you keep picking all of these working toilets."

I fake-gasp and shove him. He laughs and shoves me back, and I squeal as the purple-fox lady enters the room. She shoots us *daggers*. We straighten up, but our snickering is barely contained as we attempt to focus our attention on a picture of a discarded Coke can. "This guy's lady love is kind of a slob, don't you think?" he whispers.

I cover my mouth with my hands again.

"A reaaaaaaaal litterbug."

"Stop it," I hiss. My eyes are watering. "Ohmygod, look at this one! How did he get her toenail clippings?"

"If you were my girl," he whispers, "I'd take creepy pictures of your trash when I knew you weren't looking."

"If you were *my* girl," I whisper back, "I'd put the creepy pictures in a foreign museum so you wouldn't know that I take creepy pictures."

A single belly laugh escapes from Josh, and the woman spins around and actually stomps her foot. Like a cartoon character. It's the last straw. We lose control, cracking up hysterically, as we run from the room and toward the escalators.

"If you were my girl," I say, barely able to catch my breath, "I'd remove your skin, dye it purple, and wear you like a scarf at fancy gatherings!"

He stops and bends at the waist, he's laughing so hard. "Oh, fuck." He wipes a tear from his eye. Two museum guards whip around the corner. "Go, go, go, go, go!"

We tear down the hall, and the guards take off after us. We hit the escalators, and—for some reason—they give up. After, like, ten whole yards. They cluck their tongues as we disappear from view. "So much for security." Josh is cheerfully dismayed. "Maybe we should steal a painting?"

I laugh, and he watches me from the step below. Beaming. The current between us is so intense that it's almost visible. He takes my hand and turns it over, examining it. It's so much tinier than his. "If you were my girl?" he says. "I'd steal you away from the fancy gathering and take you somewhere less pretentious."

I rest my thumb against an ink stain on his index finger. "And if you were mine, I'd tell you that I know a good place just up the street."

He lifts his head. His eyebrows rise.

I smile.

"If you were my girl," he says, but there's an explosion outside in the courtyard, and I miss the punch line. Fireworks crackle in showers of pink, green, blue, white, green, pink, orange. The museumgoers on the escalators heading upward erupt in a frenzy of applause as we continue heading down. "If you were my girl," Josh says, pressing his nose against my ear. I turn my head, and the lights and the noise and the people disappear. The distance between us disappears.

Our kiss is anything but shy.

His lips press deeply against mine, and mine press deeply back. Our mouths open. Our tongues meet. We're hungry, deliriously so. Even with my eyes closed, the shape of his body flashes before me, lit by the spectacle outside. Light, dark, light, dark. He tastes like champagne. He tastes like desire. He tastes like my deepest craving fulfilled.

chapter ten

Our mouths are still attached when Josh hits the ground floor. A number of things follow in rapid succession: His chin smacks my nose on its upward trajectory as he quickly reclaims his height over me; I lose my balance, stumble forward, and take both of us crashing to the museum's polished concrete floor.

"Holy shit." Josh looks up at me, and his eyes widen. "Holy shit!"

Blood is pouring from my nose.

"Is it broken? Did I break your nose?"

I touch it and wince, but I shake my head like it's not a big deal. I shove my dress back down over my indecently exposed upper thighs. "I'm fine." *Imb fimb.*

Josh pulls me up and out of the escalator's path. He pats his coat frantically, searching for something, but he's coming up empty. A concerned observer whisks out a stylish floral pocket square and hands it to me.

"Merci," I tell the dapper man. *Mbear-see.* I hold it to my nose for a few seconds, and it comes down looking like a crime scene.

"No. No." Josh can't stop repeating himself. "I'm sorry. I am *so sorry.*"

"It's okay!" I hope he can understand my voice. "It's only a bloody nose." I hold out the pocket square, unsure, and the man furiously waves his hand. *Thatsokaykeepit.* I nod another thanks to him as Josh leads me to the closest restroom. "Really, I'm fine," I assure him. But he touches his forehead in horror as I disappear inside.

Damage inspection. My nose is still running, my chin is stained like a tomato, and tomorrow I'll be sporting a vicious bruise. At least my dress is still clean? A woman with flawless ebony skin and to-die-for cheekbones emerges from a stall. She gasps. "What happened?" she asks in French. She's already producing an entire pack of tissues from her purse. She pushes them into my hands.

"I get these all of the time," I say. "It's so embarrassing."

Only the first half is a lie.

I hold up a tissue, carefully pinch the bridge of my nose, and wait for the bleeding to stop. And wait. And wait. I urge her to leave, because it's weird to have a stranger, even a well-meaning one, stare at me for this long. She finally does. Immediately, I hear Josh ask her in manic—but word-perfect—French if I'm okay.

Aha! I *knew* it.

When the blood comes to a standstill, I reappear with a whopping smile. Josh wrings his hands. "Isla, I am so sorry. Are you sure it's not broken?"

My smile turns into a full-blown grin. "Positive."

His discomfort eases, but only momentarily. His brow refurrows in confusion.

"*Un nouveau record,*" I say. "*Combien de temps ça t'a pris? Une heure?*" A new record. How long did that take? An hour?

Josh's eyes narrow. He realizes that I caught him speaking in fluent French, even though he implied upstairs that he can't. "*Au moins quatre-vingt-dix minutes,*" he admits grudgingly. *At least ninety minutes.* It only took this long for me to learn the truth.

I stare at him. I stare harder.

Finally, he shakes his head and laughs. I smile—sweetly, this time—to let him know that his secret is safe. Josh rubs the back of his neck. "I don't suppose you'd still want to show me that other place? That less pretentious, date-continuing place?"

"I don't know," I tease. "It's a secret place. Can I trust you?"

"I'm *great* at keeping secrets."

I nudge him gently. "I know you are."

The air outside is gusty and crisp, and it adds to my feeling of recklessness. I don't know if I'll be able to tell Kurt what I'm about to do, if this is breaking some sort of friendship code. It might be. But I don't care.

We're radiant, the thrill of the evening having been

returned, as we hurry up the next four blocks. I take a left on rue Chapon and lead him to a building with white peeling paint and red wooden shutters. I stop at the keypad. Josh looks surprised, maybe even shocked. "Don't tell me you have an *apartment*."

I punch in the code, and the door buzzes. I give him a mischievous smile. "Come in."

"I figured we were going to a bar or club or something. Color me intrigued, Martin."

I wrinkle my nose.

Josh cringes. "Yeah. That doesn't really work with a male surname, does it?"

I head upstairs, smiling to myself, and he follows quietly. After we've passed several floors, he shoots me a curious look. "All the way up," I say. We spiral and spiral until we reach the top landing. Josh glances at the purple door with the leopard-print mat, expectantly. Nervously. "Not that one." I steer him around a hidden corner toward a second, smaller door. "*This* one."

He tugs on the knob and discovers that it's locked. I fish out the skeleton key from the bottom of my purse. It's heavy and iron. "You know," he says, "if you weren't tiny, cute, and remarkably innocent looking, I'd be running away right now. This feels like the setup to some torture porn."

"Never trust a girl because she *looks* innocent." I wag the key at him, but my heart pounds faster. *He said I'm cute.* I turn the key, the lock thunks, and the door creaks open.

Josh squints into the darkness. "Ah. More stairs. Of course."

"Last set, I promise."

He follows me inside, and I gesture for him to shut the door.

We're enveloped in pitch black. "Wait here," I whisper.

"Are you getting your ax?"

"Handcuffs."

"Kinky. But, okay, I'll try it."

I laugh as I climb the final set of stairs. They're narrow, rough, and steep, so I ascend with caution. I raise an arm above my head until my fingers hit the trapdoor. One more turn of the key, a powerful shove with the heel of my hand, and it pops open. The stairwell illuminates. I look down. Josh looks up at me, bathed in starlight and wonder.

He steps onto the rooftop balcony with silent reverence. I close the trapdoor, and we're surrounded by a sparkling, winking cityscape.

"You can see everything from here," he says. It's the first time I've heard him speak with awe. The serpentine river and crumbling cathedrals and sprawling palaces and everything, yes, *everything* is visible from here. The view is even better than the Pompidou's. The City of Light pulses with life, Nuit Blanche celebrations in full swing.

"Welcome to the Treehouse." I shine with a buoyant pride. "I've never had a real one, but it makes for a good substitute. The only part that requires an imagination is the tree itself."

"I can't believe it. This is yours?"

"My aunt's. Tante Juliette lives in the apartment with the purple door. I used to play up here when I was a little girl, but then she gave me the key during my sophomore year. Kurt and I need somewhere . . . to escape."

Josh is taking in the space, lingering on and processing each item. The balcony is square, snug, and crammed with a variety of worn objects: a wooden ladder, two mismatched cane chairs, a mossy terracotta pot holding a miniature rosebush, stacked piles of round stones, a cracked mirror with a gilt frame, a collection of pale green soda bottles, a steamer trunk with a broken lock, and the head of a white carousel horse. A low concrete wall holds everything in.

"They're all found objects," I explain. "We pick them up off the street. We have a rule that none of our *décor*"—I say this word somewhat jokingly, somewhat seriously—"can be purchased."

Josh squats down and delicately touches the horse's mane. "People leave things like this on the street?"

"In front of their houses. They set them out for the garbage-men to take away."

"What about this?" He points to a chipped porcelain bowl that's filled to the top with fresh water.

"That's for Jacque. He's the stray cat who sometimes hangs out with us."

Josh shakes his head. "This . . . yeah. This is incredible. You must bring all of your *paramours* here."

It's a tease, but as he stands back up, I sense a real question underneath. "There's only been one. And, no, he didn't receive an invitation." I bend over to remove a thick, plaid blanket from the steamer trunk. "Okay. I lied."

"You did bring him here?"

I hold up the blanket and laugh. "No. I bought this. I didn't find it on the street."

Josh emits a barely discernible but clearly relieved breath of held air. It makes me smile. I lay down the blanket. We sit, facing each other with crossed legs. "So tell me about him," he says. "Tell me who I should be jealous of."

"Well. His name is Jacque, he's about yea-high, and he has the most *delightful* little paws."

"Come on."

"The guy isn't important. It's not like I dated him for two years," I add pointedly.

"Ugh, don't remind me." But after a few seconds, he nudges my knee. "Go on."

I sigh. "His name was Sébastien. He's French. He attends a school ten minutes away from ours. And my *aunt* set us up."

"Oy." Josh winces. "The same aunt who lives below?"

"The very one. Tante Juliette is friends with his *maman,* and they invited us both to brunch last winter, not telling us that the other one would also be there. It was humiliating. But, oddly enough . . . we clicked. We dated quietly for a few months."

"Dated quietly?"

"We didn't want to tell our nosy families that their plan worked." I pause for a well-timed grin. "So we didn't."

"Did anyone know?"

"Of course. Kurt knew. And Sébastien's friends."

"So . . . what happened?"

My gaze lowers. "Turns out, he wasn't a nice guy. He didn't really like Kurt."

"I'm sorry." Josh winces again. "How serious were you guys? Before that?"

"You mean did we have sex."

He's taken aback by my bluntness. He ducks his head, abashed.

"Yes," I say.

He tries to cover his surprise. Again. I suppose everyone at school assumes that I'm a virgin—that is, if they don't already think I'm banging my best friend.

"But we were never serious-serious," I explain. "I mean, when you grow up half French, it's not like sex is this big taboo. And, yeah, you have to be careful and you need protection and blah blah blah, but it's not that American Puritanical be-all, end-all. You know? Sébastien was the only one, though. I don't want you to get the wrong—"

"No." He shakes his head rapidly. "I know."

A long pause. "How about you?"

"The same. Just the one."

The wind picks up, and I rub my bare arms. "But you loved her."

"I thought I did." Josh stares out over the city. "And then I knew I didn't, and *she* knew she didn't, but we stayed together, because . . . I don't know why. Maybe because we thought we *should* be in love. At least I did. I wanted to be in love." He looks back at me. "Have you ever been in love?"

"No." *Yes. With you.*

A motorcycle passes on the road below. We listen until its

guttural roar fades away. Josh glances at me, and then he double-takes. "You're shivering."

"Oh, I'm fine. I like the chill."

But he's already on his knees, removing his coat. He swings it up and around my shoulders, and the weight of it stuns me in more ways than one. My body weakens with lust. The coat smells like citrus and ink and *him*.

"I saw you that next night," he says.

"Huh?" My eyes open. "What night?"

"Last summer. I went back to the café at midnight the next night, and I saw you there. I knew it was a long shot, but . . . I had this feeling you might be there. And you were."

I know that feeling. I *had* that feeling. "Why didn't I see you?"

"I never went inside. I saw you through the window, and you . . ."

"I was with Kurt," I finish.

"So I kept walking. I felt like such an idiot. If only I'd known, I *wish* I'd known. You'd been so funny and flirty, and—"

"Flirty?"

"Yeah." He grins. "I could kinda tell you liked me."

"Ohmygod." I'm mortified.

"No! It was cute. Trust me, it was really, really cute."

"Yeah, nope. I want to die now, thanks."

"No. I'm serious. I always liked you, but I thought you didn't like me. You would never talk to me. So I didn't think you were even an option, and then I got together with Rashmi, and that was that. But I realized last summer that you're just shy."

Back up, back up, back up. "You always liked me?"

"A supersmart hot girl who reads comics? Are you kidding? You were definitely on my radar."

Hot. I've been upgraded to hot. No one has *ever* called me hot. Cute? Yes. Adorable? Yes, often, and it makes me want to punch them. I didn't know short girls could even *be* hot. I thought I'd been permanently relegated to elfin-pixie-child status.

"Well, bloody noses." I hug his coat tighter. "Those are definitely hot."

Josh buries his head in his hands. He moans. "I can't believe I did that."

"I believe the laws of physics did that."

"And my chin."

I laugh. "But until that last part, it was pretty great, right? I mean, we had actual *fireworks.* Talk about a credits-rolling, happily-ever-after kind of a kiss."

"If only I could take credit for those."

"You know . . . you can always try again."

He raises his head. "Setting off fireworks?"

"A second first kiss."

"I think that's just called a second kiss."

I bump my knees against his. "Are you seriously going to make me ask again?"

"Um. No." Josh quickly leans forward.

"Unless." I put a hand on his chest. "Are you sure? Because. If you don't want?"

He smiles. "You're ruining our second first kiss."

"I just . . . wanted to make sure," I say.

"I'm sure." But he stops before he reaches me. "Wait. Are *you* sure?"

"Of course I'm sure."

"Okay. So we're both sure." Josh smiles again. He places one hand on each side of my face. His fingers are cold, but I warm beneath their touch. We stare at each other for several seconds. His smile fades, and then, slowly, he leans over and kisses me.

It's a gentle kiss, lips slightly parted. Soft.

Josh pulls back a few inches. He studies my forehead. My cheeks. My chin, my ears, my nose, my lips.

"What are you doing?" I ask.

"I wanted to know what you look like up close."

"*Oh.*" It comes out like a breath.

"You have freckles on your eyelids," he says.

I close my eyes, and he kisses them—one delicate kiss on each lid. His nose trails down the side of mine, and his mouth comes to a rest above my own. My arms wrap around the back of his neck. Our lips meet with more urgency. More exploration. We kiss until it can no longer be called kissing, it's definitely making out, as his hands slide underneath the coat and around my waist.

We sink into the blanket.

Our fingers are in each other's hair, and his breath is in the hollow of my neck, and I wish the world would swallow us here, whole, in this moment. And that's when it hits me that this—*this*—is falling in love.

chapter eleven

We kiss on the stairs, on the streets of the Right Bank, on the bridge over the Seine, on the streets of the Left Bank. We kiss until our mouths are sore and our lips are numb. It's so intense that I don't realize my feet are blistered until we're only a few blocks away from the dorm. I pop off my heels on the steps of Saint-Étienne-du-Mont, a church across from the Panthéon, and release a pained hiss of relief.

"Blisters and a bloody nose." Josh sits down beside me. "This went well."

I smile and kiss him again.

"Those shoes are insane," he says.

I wiggle my red feet. "Maybe they were a *bit* much."

"Your footwear tends to run on the exceedingly tall side. You know we all know you're short, right? It's not, like, a secret."

"Hush."

"I like that you're tiny. I like that I could carry you around in my pocket."

I shove his arm with my shoulder. "I said hush."

"And if we ever vacation together, you can sit on my lap to save airfare."

I shove him harder, and he laughs. He tries to push me back, but I'm faster, and he tumbles against the steps. He laughs even harder. I do, too. "You deserve that," I say.

"And now I'll pay my penance." Josh jumps to the ground and faces his backside toward me. "Get on."

"What?"

"You can't walk in those shoes, and the streets are covered in broken glass."

"I'm sorry. Are you offering me a *piggyback ride*?"

He sighs in fake exasperation. "Will you just get on already?"

"Just because I'm short doesn't mean that I don't weigh anything."

"Just because I'm skinny doesn't mean that I can't carry someone short. You're what, five one?"

"Yeah." I'm surprised that he guessed it exactly. "What are you?"

"Six one. So there."

"Freak."

He grins at me over his shoulder. "Get on."

I stand, my heels in hand. "Okay. You asked for it."

Josh squats down, and I climb on. It's like trying to mount a thoroughbred. He hops in a way that bounces me up higher, above his waist, and I settle into him. My arms wrap around his shoulders. His hands rest above my dress, holding on to my lower thighs.

"Ah, I see. This was all a clever ruse."

He heads toward our dormitory. "A ruse?"

"To get under my dress on our first date."

The back of his neck instantly warms. "I promise it wasn't."

"Mm-hm."

His neck grows even hotter. I breathe in his scent deeply, delirious with happiness. In the distance, Paris is still celebrating, but our own neighborhood is quiet—the only sound, his footfalls. "You know my friend St. Clair?" he says after a few minutes. "He's only a few inches taller than you, and his girlfriend, Anna? She's taller than he is."

"Kurt only likes tall girls. Maybe it's made me paranoid that all guys might prefer partners closer to their own mouth height." It feels strange to confess this aloud.

"I'd like to point out that we've had zero problem reaching each other's mouths." There's a smile in his voice. I smile back against his neck.

Josh walks the next few blocks in silence. Unfortunately, it's not *actually* comfortable to sit like this, and—judging by his labored breath—it's not comfortable to carry me, either. But he gallantly piggybacks me all the way to our dorm, through the empty lobby, and straight to my door. The dismount is awkward, and we're both in at least moderate pain, but it doesn't matter. Our lips find each other again. He's out of breath, but he pushes me against my door until it bursts open. We collapse into the room.

Kurt blinks at us from my bed. "You really do need to fix that door."

Sunday is Josh's only detention-free day, and he texts me right as I'm waking up. I'm glad we remembered to exchange numbers. I squeeze my phone and roll over in bed.

"Watch it," Kurt mumbles.

"He says *good morning.*"

"It's the afternoon. Tell him he's wrong."

I text Josh a good morning in return and suggest that he ask for next Saturday off, too. After all, that's *his* Sabbath. Winking smiley face. He texts me back a long line of exclamation points followed by a WHY DIDN'T I THINK OF THAT??

I hug Kurt. "He likes me. He liiiiiiikes me."

"Duh." But he settles into my hug. "I've missed this."

"Me too."

Last night we cheated on the rules. Nate was out for Nuit Blanche so Kurt decided to stay in. Which worked out perfectly, because it meant that I got to rehash every detail of every second of my date. Until I was told to shut up.

His eyes widen. "Half of your nose is purple."

I scramble out of bed and lunge toward the mirror. Damn. I

gently prod my nose, wince at the tenderness, and sigh. "At least it's proof that yesterday really happened?"

But Kurt is already thinking about today. "I have a history essay due tomorrow, and you need to study for that calculus test. Do you want to work here or in my room?" And then he grins. His room is disgusting, and I refuse to hang out in it. Tidiness— in his bedroom, in his school bag, in his appearance—is *never* on Kurt's agenda.

I lean in closer to my reflection. "I don't know. Josh and I didn't make plans, but it seemed kinda understood that we'd hang out."

Kurt clambers off my bed and puts on his hoodie. "That sucks."

"You suck."

"I'm about to bring you breakfast. I'm so far from sucking that you can't even handle it." And he slams my door shut behind him. I wait for it to pop open, but—for once—it doesn't. He kicks it back open. We laugh.

"Back in ten," he says.

Every Sunday, we have fresh baguettes from the *boulangerie* two streets over. I remove a jar of Nutella, a knife, and two antique jade mugs from their designated drawer and turn on the electric kettle. A heaping spoonful of instant coffee mix— Kurt's favorite, unpalatable American brand—is added to each cup. And then I return to the mirror. My nose resembles a small eggplant. Even with a thick layer of concealer, the proof of our date will last for at least a week.

Kurt returns as the kettle *dings*. Our routine is meticulously orchestrated. He's pouring the water into our mugs when there are two knocks, low on my door. The sound gives me an instant jolt. A hit stronger than caffeine. But Kurt looks at me in confusion as if to say, *I'm already here?*

"I could let myself in," Josh says, in cheerful spirits. "But I won't, because that'd be rude. Also, you might be getting dressed, and that'd be—"

"She's dressed," Kurt says. "Come in."

I yank open the door before Josh gets the wrong idea.

"Hey," he says. There's an uneasy pause. "So I guess you've stopped propping this open?"

I actually, literally smack my forehead. "We forgot! I can't believe we forgot."

Kurt slides over my physics textbook with his foot, and I shove it underneath the door. "Nate was out last night," he says, "so I stayed over."

Josh enters the room, but his arms are crossed. Unsure. "You slept here?"

"Yes," Kurt says.

I smile grimly. "Not to be a cliché? But it's *really* not what it sounds like."

Josh uncrosses his arms. "No, I know." He shakes his head and starts to cross them again, but he catches himself. His hands move to his pockets. "I should've called. I thought you might want to get some breakfast. Lunch. Whatever it is. I'll come back—"

"No!" I say. "Join us. We have bread and terrible coffee. Yeah? Huh, huh?"

"You do make it sound tempting."

My smile softens. "Come on. Stay."

Josh returns the smile, at last. "Fine. But only because I feel sorry for you. Clearly an angry gangbanger punched you in the face last night."

"It's astounding what one chin can do."

Kurt studies us from the bed as if he'd chanced upon a pair of wild beasts in their natural habitat.

Josh's expression falls. "I'm sorry. Does it hurt?"

"Stop apologizing." My smile widens as I drop a spoonful of powdered coffee into the Oktoberfest stein. "I only have two mugs. Sorry."

Josh sits in my desk chair. "*You* stop apologizing."

I add the hot water and give him the stein. He grins. I take a seat beside Kurt and thrust half of my baguette at Josh, who protests with a waved hand. I insist. He accepts. We're bordering on uncomfortable silence territory.

I'm relieved when Josh turns to Kurt. "You know, there's something I've always been curious about. I once saw your name written down on a list in the head's office. Your *full* name."

Kurt sighs. Heavily. "I was born the week Kurt Cobain died. My parents were friends with him, so they named me in his honor."

Josh freezes, Nutella-smeared knife midair. "They were *friends* with him?"

"My dad is Scott Bacon. He was the lead guitarist for Dreck."

"The early nineties grunge band," I say. "They had that one hit, 'No One Saw Me'?"

"Yeah." Josh shakes his head. "Yeah, I know who they are."

"The song made him rich and famous, and that attracted my mother. She was a runway model here in Paris," Kurt says matter-of-factly.

Josh freezes again.

I always forget how surprising it is for people to learn about Kurt's parents. It seems like he should come from a family of neurosurgeons or astronautical engineers, but the giveaway is that—underneath the unkempt hair and messy wardrobe—Kurt is handsome. Strangers often mistake him for an athlete, because he's tall and angular and muscular. But he's only in shape because he hates mass transit and walks everywhere. I wonder if his appearance is another reason why Josh thought we were dating.

"But their relationship isn't like that," I explain. "Kurt's mom had her own money. They married for love, they're still together."

Josh takes a huge bite of bread and talks before swallowing. "I can't believe they knew Kurt Cobain. That's so cool."

I used to watch Josh in the cafeteria, and he's always been a sloppy eater. I feel oddly pleased to see this bad habit up close. Maybe because it reminds me of the Josh that his friends knew—the relaxed, barriers-down, inner-circle Josh. Or maybe because it reminds me of Kurt, and Kurt is safe.

"No," Kurt says. "It blows. I was named after a guy who committed suicide. Also, people assume I'm this huge Nirvana fan, which isn't even logical, because it's not like I named myself."

"Do you like them at all?" Josh asks.

"No. We can switch names, if you want."

"Kurt Cobain Wasserstein." Josh says it slowly and laughs. "Nah. Doesn't have the same ring."

"Kurt *Donald* Cobain Wasserstein. You can't forget his middle name. I can't."

"Which would make you . . . Joshua Elvis Aron Presley Bacon."

Kurt startles. "Are you serious? That's your middle name?"

Josh's stone countenance makes me snort with laughter.

"Isla, is he serious?" Kurt asks again, but then he reads my own expression correctly. "Oh." He wilts. "Never mind. You were just . . ."

But then a perfect moment occurs as Kurt straightens back up. He grins.

Josh points a finger. "You are *not* going to say it."

". . . *joshing* me."

Josh clutches his chest in agony as Kurt explodes into loud belly laughter. My heart might burst from happiness. Josh shakes his head. "I'm only letting you get away with that because I'm trying to make a good impression on your lady friend, okay? My real middle name is David."

Kurt considers it for several seconds. "Deal. I'll take it."

Josh takes his first sip of coffee. "Oh, man. You weren't kidding. This *is* terrible."

"So what should we call Isla?" Kurt asks.

Josh sets down the stein to properly examine me. He gazes into my eyes as I think, *David*. Josh's middle name is *David*. Thanks to sleepless nights on Wikipedia, I know it's also his father's middle name.

"Isla is a good name," he finally says. "The right name."

Kurt isn't impressed. "Isla was named after something, too, you know."

"Don't you dare," I say.

Josh sits forward. His eyes shine. "Do tell."

"Prince. Edward. Island," Kurt says.

There's a long pause. And then I'm the one sighing. "Yeah, so my parents did that horrible thing where they named me and my sisters after where we were conceived."

Another pause.

"They did not," Josh says.

"Alas. Geneviève was named after the patron saint of Paris. 'Hattie' is short for Manhattan, and, yeah . . . Prince Edward Island. My parents were on vacation. I mean, don't get me wrong, I'm glad my name isn't Prince or Edward. But the notion of island travel? *Completely* ruined for me."

Their laughter is interrupted as the stairwell door opens with a booming metallic *clang*. A swarm of girls peer in at us as they pass by my open door. More than one eyebrow is raised. I hear my name murmured down the hall and into the lobby, accompanied by laughter that's not nearly so friendly.

"You know," Josh says, with a glance toward me. "I'd almost

forgotten how annoying this room is. Those stairs drove me nuts."

"I don't like the window," Kurt says.

"Seriously. Those prisonlike bars, the traffic. Do you remember that opera singer who used to perform out there?"

"So what are you doing today?" I ask, pushing the girls from my mind.

My question catches Josh off guard. "Um, working. Drawing. By myself. In my room. On the top floor?"

"Oh. Cool!" I try to sound chipper. How naive for me to assume that we'd be hanging out. Of course he's busy. "We'll be working down here. On homework. Like usual."

But Josh seems . . . confused. Disappointed.

It takes me a moment. And then I realize that he's just told me that he'll be alone in his room *and* where his room is located. And *I* told him that I'll be here with Kurt. The guy who slept in my bed last night.

"Unless you wanted to hang out?" The words spill from my lips. "I'll come up. To your room. If you want."

Josh's entire body brightens. "Yeah?" He glances at Kurt. "You're invited, too, of course."

"I don't think you mean that." Kurt drains the last of his coffee. "And I'd pass, anyway. I'd rather not watch you guys feel each other up."

chapter twelve

The sixth floor isn't a regular floor. True, it has the same peculiar contrast of crystalline fixtures and fluorescent bulbs, antique wallpaper and industrial rugs, but it's what the French call *les chambres de bonne*. The maids of the aristocracy used to live up here. The ceilings are lower, and there are fewer rooms. It's also silent. No voices, no music. Eerie.

I pass a door that's been plastered with a dozen images of the same boy band, another with a small whiteboard that has a phone number scribbled on it, and another with a large whiteboard that's been tagged with the words *DAVE HAS TINY BALLS!*

Room 604's door is blank.

In previous years, Josh would tack up silly illustrations of himself in various costumes—cowboy, pirate, clown, robot, bear. My heart tugs at yet another reminder of his current state of unhappiness at our school.

I smooth the front of my dress. It's been an hour since breakfast, because I needed to take a shower. I also needed to apply some serious bruise-covering makeup. I take a deep breath and copy his signature knock.

Josh opens the door with a knowing smile.

I return it shyly.

He steps aside, and I enter. I expect him to close the door behind me, because, well, *he's Josh,* but he props it open with a book about Parisian architecture. I'm touched by this gesture of respect . . . even though I wouldn't mind the privacy right now.

"Sorry, it's such a mess." He shoves his hands into his pockets. "I cleared off the bed, though, and the sheets are clean."

My eyebrows practically hit my hairline.

"To sit on." His accusation is made jokingly, but his skin turns melon pink. "Nice shoes, by the way."

I'm wearing flats. "Nice deflection, by the way."

"Nice to see you, by the way."

"Nice save, by the way."

Josh grins as I drop my homework-stuffed bag to the floor. In theory, I'm going to study, and he's going to draw. In reality? I hope we make out.

His bedroom is spectacular. The small space feels extra small, because of the sheer volume of artwork, which is everywhere. But the room doesn't feel cramped. It feels like a cocoon. His drawings are on his desk—which isn't even our standard-issue desk, it's some kind of drafting desk—on his dresser, on the floor, on top of his fridge. And they cover nearly every inch of his ceiling and walls.

"I feel like I'm inside of your head." And then I regret saying it. Because, creepy.

But Josh seems to relax. "My friends used to say that, too."

I examine his work closer. The illustrations are in black ink, and I recognize locations from all across the city: the rose window and spires of la Sainte-Chapelle, the hedge maze inside le Jardin des Plantes, a wall of human skulls and femurs inside les Catacombes, a caged bird in the le Marché aux Fleurs, the opulent exterior of le Palais Garnier—the phantom's famous opera house.

And the faces. So many faces.

St. Clair; his girlfriend, Anna; his ex-girlfriend, Ellie; St. Clair and Josh's mutual friend Meredith; and of course . . . Rashmi. My eyes fall on a drawing beside Josh's window. Rashmi is lounging across a lobby sofa—her head on one armrest, her feet on the other—reading a novel. Her long hair is draped over the back of the armrest in rich, black waves.

"Wow," I say quietly. "Rashmi looks really pretty."

Josh swallows. "I did that one a long time ago. Did you see this?" He points to a funny picture of St. Clair poking Anna's back with someone else's arm, but now I'm distracted and disoriented. I'm *surrounded*. Rashmi alone. Rashmi with friends.

Rashmi with Josh.

"She's my friend, Isla. Or she was. I haven't even talked to her in months."

"No, I know." And I shake my head, because I *do* know. I'm not sure why this caught me by surprise. I sit on his bed and smile to show him that I'm fine. She's his friend, and he clearly misses his friends, so it's good that these drawings are here. Sure. If I can convince him, maybe I can convince myself.

Josh stares at me for a long time. I keep my eyes on his bedspread—blue-and-white plaid, very male—and try to remember how Isla-of-the-past would have fainted if she could see Isla-of-the-present. "If I show you something," he finally says, "you have to promise me that you'll take it as a compliment. No judging."

I tilt my head in question.

"I'm serious. You have to promise."

"Why? Is it bad?"

"No, I just . . . wasn't planning on showing it to you. At least not yet."

"And now you're worrying me." I'm only half joking. "Is this the part where you confess that you've been taking pictures of my discarded yogurt cups?"

"I lied," Josh says.

My worry becomes whole as he slides open a drawer, removes a battered sketchbook, and places it in my hands. I turn it over. *WELCOME*, the blue sticker says. "That's the one I was using last June," he says. "I didn't leave it in New York. Obviously."

"This is it?" My relief is profound. "Yeah, I know. I've seen it in your bag."

He blanches. "You have?"

"It's okay. I understand. I mean, the drawing isn't flattering, right? I was so out of it. I understand why you wouldn't want to show me."

"Uh, no." He's squirming. "That's not it. Not even a little bit. Not even at all."

Consider my curiosity *way* more than piqued.

Josh sits down beside me. He sighs. I open the book, and it flips right to it. As if he looks at it. A lot.

I stare at the page. *Pages.* There are *two* drawings of me. In the first, my elbow is propped up against the table in Kismet. My head rests in my hand, and my hair tumbles loosely around my face. My eyes are closed in reverie. In the second, my head rests on my arms, which I'm using as a pillow. My hair spreads across the table in sweeping waves and curls. My lips are oh-so-slightly parted.

The pictures are . . . *sexy.* His brushstrokes are all curves.

Josh reaches over and turns the page.

There's a third drawing.

This one is from memory. I'm standing in the rain. My hair is wet. My sundress is soaked. More curves—*mine*—are exposed. A giant garden rose floats behind my head like a halo, and I'm staring straight ahead at the viewer. The artist.

My heartbeat pounds in my ears. I look up at Josh, eyes wide.

"Kurt asked to see it," he says. "When I thought you were dating. I thought he'd kick my ass."

"My dress *is* rather clingy."

Josh groans. "And now you think I'm a pervert."

I smile. "Only if the rest of the book is like this." I bump his shoulder softly as I proceed to thumb through it. At first I don't realize what's happening, but . . . I *am* looking for others. There are plenty of women, of all ages, inside—even some pretty ones—but as I continue to search, it's clear that mine are unique. They're the only drawings that look like *that*.

Josh bumps my shoulder in return. "Feel better? Or am I still on par with that Finnish photographer?"

"No." I'm still smiling as I set down the book. "Definitely not. For sure not."

"Good." His voice is deeper, quieter.

I stare at him. He stares back. His fingers comb through my hair, and he cradles my head in his hands. My eyes close. I slide my own hands up the nape of his neck, and then farther upward, nails raking against his scalp. Our mouths hover, a murmur apart. Our breathing is fast and warm. He parts my lips with his.

And then we clash together like the ravenous animals we are.

I climb onto his lap, *needing* closeness, pushing my hips against his. The skirt of my dress rides upward. I feel desperate, in agony. A ragged sound escapes from between his lips. Our kisses grow frantic, and his mouth is assertive and his hands are strong and—

"*Ah hem.*"

We bolt upright. Nate is standing in the doorway. I tumble

off Josh, and he grabs the sketchbook and lunges into his desk chair, strategically planting the book on his lap. Every square inch of my skin is on fire.

"Have a nice day," Nate says wearily. He trudges away.

I groan. "I can't decide if the new rules suck more for him or for us."

Josh bangs his forehead once against his desk. "Definitely us." Before I can reply, his phone rings. He lifts his head to peek at the screen. And then he swears under his breath. "I have to take this, or she'll never stop calling." He picks it up. "Hey, Mom."

Don't think about the sketchbook. Do not *think about what it is covering.*

"Yep. Everything's fine." Pause. "I'm doing homework." Pause. "No." Pause. "No, I'm not." Pause. "Yeah. I know." Josh rolls his eyes as he tosses the sketchbook back to the bed, a twofold message that the mood is beyond repair, and I'm welcome to look at anything inside. "No. I know." Their conversation continues like this for five minutes until he cuts her off. "Oh, man, fire drill. Gotta run, bye." He hangs up. And then he slings his phone across the desk and drops his head into his hands.

I give him a moment before asking. "Fire drill?"

Josh lifts his head. "Usually I come up with a better excuse." He stretches out a leg and taps one of my shoes with his. "Hard to think with you sitting there."

I tap back. "I take it you aren't close with your parents?"

"No. I'm not."

I wonder how often they talk. I only talk to mine about once a week, but our calls always last for at least an hour. "Is that why you're here? In France? I have to admit, I've always thought it was kind of odd that a senator would send his kid to a foreign country to be educated."

"Paris wasn't exactly their first choice." And then he gets this strange expression, as if he's surprised by his own words.

"What do you mean?"

"I . . . I've never admitted that to anyone before."

My brow furrows.

Josh stares at his hands, massaging his left thumb into his right palm. "My friends were aware that I don't get along with my parents, so . . . they sort of *assumed* that I was shipped here because I'm *difficult*. Or whatever. And I never corrected them. I guess I wanted them to believe it, because . . . it's less embarrassing than the truth." He looks back up at me and holds my gaze. "I chose this. Being stuck here is my own fault."

My eyes widen. I wait for him to explain.

"When my parents started looking at private high schools in New York and DC, I talked them into believing that sending me overseas would be better for my education. And I was immature, and I was dumb, and Paris sounded romantic and artistic and all of that bullshit, but the moment I got here, I realized . . . it's just a city. You know? And, yeah, it's beautiful and cultured and everything the cliché says it is. But, I don't know. It's always felt like I'm killing time here until my real life can begin."

Killing time. I don't think he counts me as a part of this, but the words are still wounding. I try not to let it show. "So where would you like to be? New York? DC?"

"No. And *definitely* no. I'm going to Vermont next year."

I frown. "Vermont? What's in Vermont?"

"The Center for Cartoon Studies." Josh perks up at my confusion. He scoots closer in his chair. "It's the only one of its kind—it completely focuses on sequential art. And it has this insane faculty, all of the best cartoonists visit to teach there."

"Cartoonists? Like, what? The guy who draws *Calvin and Hobbes?*"

He shakes his head. "No. Anyone who draws sequential art is a cartoonist. Superhero stuff, graphic novels, graphic nonfiction. It doesn't just apply to the people who draw comic strips."

"Oh." And now I feel dumb. "How big is the school?"

"It's not big. It's about half the size of SOAP." He picks up a pencil and rocks it between two fingers. "So what's next for you?"

The nerve is struck. Just like that. "I . . . I don't know."

His pencil stops.

I should have seen the question coming, but it blindsides me. I'm humiliated to find myself fighting back tears. "I'm applying to both la Sorbonne and Columbia, but I don't know where I want to go. I don't know where I belong."

Josh moves onto the bed, beside me again. "Hey. It's okay. You still have plenty of time to decide."

"No. I don't. And you wanna know the worst part? I kind of *hope* one of them will reject me so that I won't have to make the decision myself."

His eyebrows raise. He's silent for a long time, debating something in his head. "I've seen the charts in the head's office." He's choosing his words carefully. "You're the best student in our class. Both schools are going to accept you."

So he *does* know. I scratch at my peachy-pink nail polish. Chip it away, bit by bit.

"What do you want to study?"

The pit in my stomach grows deeper. "Nothing."

"Nothing?"

"I mean . . . I don't know. I don't know what I want to do, or who I want to be, or where I want to live. It's like everyone else has their entire future mapped out except for me."

Josh's expression falls. "You know that's not true."

"Maybe at other schools, but at ours? People have plans. *You* have plans."

"Well. Which city do you like better?"

I tug on my compass. "They both feel like home. When I was young, my family spent summers here and the rest of the year there. Now it's the reverse. I'm a citizen of both countries, I'm fluent in both languages, and I'm comfortable in both cities."

"Comfortable."

Something about the way he says it. "What?" I ask.

"It's just . . . don't you want to try something new? What about all of those adventure stories weighing down your bookshelves?"

I don't know. *I don't know.* I like reading about adventure, sure, but I also like doing it from the safety of home. But what *is* home, besides a quilt-covered bed? Where is it?

Josh sees that I'm getting upset with myself, so he tries to lighten the mood. "You know where I think you should go? Dartmouth."

"Yeah. I don't even know where that is."

"It's in New Hampshire, on the Vermont border. And the Center for Cartoon Studies? Just so happens to be on the other side. And I've heard that Dartmouth has an amazing program in Nothing. The best Nothing program in the world. That's what people say."

I finally crack a smile. He's teasing, but it's still nice to know that he wouldn't mind me living nearby. Or, at least, that he likes me enough to joke about it. I nod at his drafting table. "So show me your real work. Show me what you do in here all day."

Josh is surprised and happy to give me a tour through his workspace: dozens upon dozens of brushes, pens, and pencils, India ink, oil paints, watercolors, nibs, erasers, reference photographs, a hair dryer for speeding up ink-drying time, several different-size pads of what he calls his semiprecious paper, and an elephantine box where he keeps his best. Like me, he's crammed a skinny bookcase into his room, but his shelves are packed with bound sketchbooks, art books, reference books, and what appears to be every graphic memoir ever written—Jeffrey Brown, Craig Thompson, Alison Bechdel, James Kochalka, Lucy Knisley, and tons of others I've never seen before.

There is a distinct absence of school-related work. The strap of his bag pokes out from underneath his bed, so I assume the rest has been shoved down there, as well. And below his dresser—where I've placed a second dresser for more clothing—he's placed a large metal flat-file. His own graphic memoir has been divided between its drawers. They're labeled: BSB FRESHMAN, BSB SOPHOMORE, and BSB JUNIOR.

"Do you have a senior drawer?" I ask.

"Not yet." Josh taps his temple with a finger. "I'm still storyboarding last summer." He shows me what he's been working on—blue-penciled thumbnails of his annoyed self in DC, attempting to block out the sound of his father recording an attack ad about Terry Robb. Terry is his opponent in the upcoming election. "It's easier to start like this. It keeps me from making bigger mistakes later."

"What do your parents think about you writing about this? About your private lives?"

He shrugs. "They don't *know* I write about our private lives."

I wonder if that's actually true. "What does 'BSB' stand for?"

"*Boarding School Boy.* That's the title."

I glance at the top drawer, his junior year, and then at him. He nods. I slide it open and find a stack of thick paper with fully inked illustrations. The top sheet is a drawing of his friends in graduation caps, smiling, arms around one another. Josh stands apart from them, small and distant. I lift it up, delicately, to peer at what's below. It's a multipaneled page of Josh wandering around a city that is unmistakably Venice, Italy.

Cartoon Josh is familiar. It's the same Josh that I used to see wearing silly costumes on his door. It's an accurate—though

121

exaggerated—portrait of who he really is. His nose is more prominent, his frame skinnier. But he's still beautiful. He looks sad and angry and tender and lonely. I lower the top illustration and slide the drawer shut. His work is so personal. I don't feel as if I've earned the right to look at it. Not yet.

"I hope I get to read this someday."

I know he'd let me, right here and right now, but he looks relieved that I've chosen not to. "You will," he says.

The rest of our day is spent in companionable silence—Josh with his sketches, myself with my textbooks. When the sun begins to set, he turns on his desk lamp and scrounges for food. His fridge is packed tight with ready-made items.

"Aha!" Josh yanks out something from behind the orange juice.

I cap my highlighter. "You do remember where the cafeteria is located, yes?"

"And *you* remember that I saw your electric kettle? The one against school rules?"

"As if you don't have one."

"I have two." He grins. "And a hot plate."

"The cafeteria serves food. Fresh food. Made by actual chefs! If it wasn't closed for dinner on Sundays, I'd prove it to you right now."

Josh holds up a plastic cup. "Crème brûlée?"

I smile. "Please don't ruin my favorite dessert."

"Really?" He pauses, mid–foil removal. "It's mine, too."

My heartbeat picks up, pleased by this tiny discovery, as if it's more evidence for the case of *us*. But I don't speak of it. I only release a sigh. "Lavender crème brûlée. Ginger crème brûlée. Espresso crème brûlée."

"I had rosemary once. Unbelievable."

I grip his comforter with both hands. "No."

Josh consumes his dessert in two bites. He tosses the empty cup into his trash can and hops once. "I'll take you there right now. Come on, come on!"

I laugh. "Sorry. Sunday night is pizza night."

He deflates. "Damn."

"Join us."

Josh plops down beside me on the bed. "That's . . . actually kinda weird. My friends and I used to have pizza on Sunday nights, too."

"I know. I used to see you guys at our restaurant."

"Seriously? Pizza Pellino?"

I nod. It wasn't a coincidence.

"Hey." Josh grows uneasy. "About Kurt. About *your* bed." He bounces twice to demonstrate where he found the subject change.

"Yeah. He sleeps in it."

I've correctly identified his question *and* given him the wrong answer. He tries to act as if it doesn't matter, but his expression resembles what mine must have looked like when I realized I was surrounded by the likeness of his ex-girlfriend.

"We've slept in the same beds our entire lives," I say. "There's nothing sexual about it. I promise."

"That's not how *I'd* feel lying beside you." But before I can enjoy this thrilling and perfect response, an even more alarming question has popped into his head. "Have you ever woken up and seen . . . you know. In the morning?"

"If you expect me to answer that, you have to say it."

"I am not saying it."

I pause. "Fine. Yes."

Josh balks.

"But it's not like it's, ugh, *aimed at me* or anything. And it's not like we sleep naked. I mean, we've been friends forever, so, yeah, we've seen stuff, but—"

"Has he seen *you* naked?" he blurts. And then he notices my expression and instantly regrets it. "Sorry. That's none of my business."

I'm opening my mouth to agree when I'm struck by a startling new truth. The situation has changed. Or maybe it's *about* to change. "No," I say. "It is your business. If you want it to be."

"I do."

I swallow. "Me too."

His brow lifts.

"Does this . . . does this mean you want to be my boyfriend?" My question sounds both immature and momentous. But Josh doesn't flinch.

"Yes," he says. "I want."

chapter thirteen

Josh is my boyfriend.

Josh is my *boyfriend.*

It's a miracle that after only a single weekend, we are a real-life, not-just-in-my-dreams couple. Every morning, he arrives at my door before Kurt so that we can have a few minutes alone before breakfast. And then he joins us in the cafeteria. I think, maybe, he needed reassurance that he wouldn't be sitting at an empty table. It's strange to realize that Josh—detached Josh, composed Josh—worries about these things, too.

It might even explain the detachment.

We're inseparable until our schedules split apart in fifth period. But we reunite after school, and I walk him to detention. If Kurt is the expert of roads less traveled, Josh is the expert of

125

rooms long forgotten. All day long, he sneaks me into spaces that are cramped and hidden and neglected, and we kiss through the darkness until the warning bells ring.

I work on homework while he's in detention, and when it ends, we all have dinner in the cafeteria. And then we re-separate from Kurt. We leave campus for the privacy that our dormitory no longer allows. It means that I usually visit the Treehouse twice—once with Kurt in the afternoon and once with Josh in the evening. We spend our nights in liplocks, sweet and earnest, while fumbling sublimely around things less innocent.

When Josh dated Rashmi, they were notorious for their public displays of affection. It was torturous. I was both envious and repulsed. With me, he's quiet. He holds my hand and steals my kisses, but he saves most of his affection for when we're alone. I think he understands that I don't enjoy drawing attention to myself. I also think, perhaps, he's placed a higher value on his own privacy.

Even so, our relationship hasn't escaped the notice of our classmates. But I'm happy. Despite my shyness, I want to parade him in front of the entire school. I want to shout, *Look! Look at this perfect boy who wants to hold my hand.*

On Friday, Hattie startles us from behind in the hall. "So you're the guy who busted my sister's nose. Either you have the best aim or the worst. Which is it?"

"Pleasure to meet you," Josh says.

"Whatever. Isla, I need forty-six euros."

"Why?" I touch my nose self-consciously.

"Because I want to buy a weasel skull and put it on this one girl's pillow."

I try not to sigh. I'm not successful.

"She's my friend," Hattie says.

"No," I say.

"Ugh, fine. *Maman*."

We watch her stalk away. "Was she for real?" Josh asks.

"I'm never sure."

He shakes his head, mystified. "Your older sister isn't like that, is she? We had studio art together my freshman year. She always *seemed* cool—"

"She is."

"Yeah. She always seemed like . . . she had things figured out. Like she had the motivation and confidence to do anything."

I smile. "That's Gen, all right. Last summer? She shaved her head and came out as bi. My parents love her new girlfriend. But my mother is *pissed* about her hair."

Josh laughs. When I drop him off at detention that afternoon, I run into another opinionated force. The head of school stops me. "I'd be concerned," she says, "but Monsieur Wasserstein has been remarkably punctual, as of late. You must be the reason."

I'm not sure how to respond.

The head looks down at me through her glasses, which are perched on the tip of her nose. "You're a bright girl. Be careful there." And then she strides away.

I don't appreciate her tone. Or her presumption that hormones might be getting in the way of my intelligence. Is she afraid that Josh's attitude will rub off on me? That I'll stop caring about my education? Well, she can take her concern and shove it up her ass. But when I open my bedroom door a few hours later, Josh is also unusually cross.

"It backfired," he says. "You know that whole detention-on-the-Sabbath idea? I asked the head about it, and she went straight to my parents."

I wince.

"Yeah. And even though this time the excuse is—in theory—legitimate, my parents agreed that I'm being *impudent,* and now I have two additional weeks of detention."

I'm shocked. "Two *weeks?* But that means—"

"Detention through the end of October."

"That's insane! What the hell is the head's problem?"

He kicks off his shoes and flops onto my bed. "Welcome to the latest attempt at trying to get me to take this school more seriously."

"I'm sorry. The Sabbath thing was my idea. My stupid, stupid—"

"Hey." Josh sits up on his elbows. "Only because I didn't think of it first."

There's a commotion in the hallway. "Look who's on Iz-la's bed," Mike says. "Give us a show, girlie girl! Give us a sneak peek."

Emily hoots. "Is Kurt jealous?"

Dave pushes his shaggy hair away from his eyes. "Nah. They're getting ready for a threesome."

I want to punch them all in the throat. But Josh is staring

down Mike. "Her name is Eye-la. It must be difficult to remember when your brain is smaller than your penis. Which, rumor has it, isn't that big in the first place."

"Fuck you, Wasserstein."

"Good one."

The stairwell door *clangs* open, and Sanjita appears behind them. Her gaze is fixed on something ahead in the lobby. It's an unnatural position that tells me she already knows this is my room. "Come on, Mike." She tugs on his arm. "I'm hungry."

He's still puffed up like an angry baby owl. He points a finger at Josh. "I'll get you."

They swagger away, and Josh scowls at the doorway with supreme irritation. "Has there ever been an emptier threat?"

"What is *with* people today?"

"I don't know. But I hate them. I hate everyone in the world but you."

"And Kurt."

"And Kurt," he agrees. "Where *is* Kurt?"

"It's sushi night. Remember?"

He sinks into my pillows. "Oh. Right."

We discussed it earlier and decided that Kurt and I should keep Friday nights, and then Saturday nights will be ours. But I'm disappointed, too. The schedules, the rules, the people.

As soon as his Sabbath detention is over, he's back at my door. "I want to draw you again," he says. "Before dinner. While there's still light."

My bloodstream courses with euphoria as he hurries me

toward the Arènes de Lutèce, an amphitheater long abandoned by the Romans. Once, it was immense and crowded and used for gladiatorial combat. Now, it's smallish and empty and parklike. It's only a few blocks away from our school, but it's wholly concealed behind its surrounding apartments. No matter how many times I visit, I'm always still surprised to find an *entire ancient arena* hidden back here.

The park tends to stay quiet. Today, a father is teaching his young son how to dribble a football in its large and dusty center. Josh and I climb the stairs to the original stone niches above the field. Each niche contains a modern bench, and we pick the one with the best view. Against his knees, Josh props up a sketch pad (one with thick, removable pages) and immediately commences drawing with his favorite brush pen (a capped pen with a brush tip). He works as he always does, with his thumb tucked underneath his index finger. I love watching his hand.

"What should I do?" I ask. "How should I sit?"

"Sit however you want. But try not to move *too* much," he adds with a smile.

There's nothing like being openly stared at by an attractive member of the opposite sex to make me feel as if all of my limbs were in the wrong place. I search for a distraction. "So . . . what's the story behind your sticker?"

Josh flips over the pad, expecting something to have appeared.

"The one on your sketchbook. The American WELCOME one."

"Oh." He snorts. "There's no story. My dad had a huge

stack of them in his office, and I just took one. There were a lot of assholes on Capitol Hill ragging on Mexican immigration that week, so I drew the word I *wished* they were talking about instead. But it wasn't an original idea. I saw an Australian sticker like it once."

"You know what I like about you?" I ask, after a few minutes.

"My dynamite moves on the dance floor."

"You've crafted this bored veneer, but you're always giving yourself away in moments like that. In the moments that really matter."

"I *don't* care about anything," he says. "But I care about you."

"Nope. You have a mushy heart, Joshua Wasserstein. I can see it."

He smiles to himself and keeps drawing. There's a fragrant gust of wind, and the first leaves of the season rain down upon us. A nip pierces the air. I watch the tiny boy in the arena dart between his father's legs and listen to the faint crunch of gravel as an elderly couple walks the footpath behind us. The sun grows lower on the horizon. There's a new stillness, and I realize that Josh has stopped working.

He's staring at me. Spellbound.

"What is it?" I'm afraid to move. "What's wrong?"

"I've never seen the sun shine directly through your hair before."

"*Oh.*" I glance down at the glowing curtain. "It never looks the same, does it? Inside, it's auburn. Outside, it's more of a red."

"No." Josh reaches out. He softly touches one of the waves. "Red isn't the right word. It's not auburn or orange or copper or bronze. It's *fire*. It's like being mesmerized by the flames of a burning building. I can't look away."

I've blushed far less around him lately, but—at this—my cheeks warm.

"And *that*," he says as I look down at my lap. "That rosy blush. And your rose-scented perfume. God, it drives me mad."

I lift my eyes in surprise. "You've noticed? I don't wear much."

"Trust me. You wear exactly the right amount."

"You smell like tangerines." I say it before I can take it back.

"Satsuma." He pauses. "You have a good nose."

"Yours is better. At least, the shape of it is."

"My nose is huge." He laughs, and it makes his throat bob. "Yours is like a bunny rabbit's. What the hell are you talking about?"

I laugh, too. "It's not huge. But it *is* interesting."

"Interesting." He raises a teasing eyebrow.

I smile. "Yes."

Josh smiles back. His ink-stained fingers thread through my hair, and he leans in toward my lips. But then he pauses to smell my neck. A shiver runs through me. He kisses my neck softly and slowly, and my eyes close.

I want him to kiss me there forever. But he pulls back, languid, letting his fingers fall back out gently through my hair. He smiles at me again. "Roses," he says.

My head and heart are in full swoon. "Thank you. And thanks for saying such nice things about my hair," I add. "Not everyone is that nice."

"Who wouldn't say nice things about it?"

"Ha-ha," I say.

But he appears to be genuinely confused.

"Really?" I take a deep breath. "Well, okay. When I was little? Every grandmother would stop me on the street to tell me how much I looked like one of her grandchildren. 'She has hair *just like yours*,' they'd always say. 'Except hers is more orange' or 'hers is more auburn.' It was so uncomfortable, especially for someone as shy as me. Hattie's the only one who ever talked back. 'Then it's not *just like mine*, is it?' she'd say."

Josh laughs.

"And when a redhead hits puberty? You become this magnet for gross men. A month doesn't pass without one telling me that I must be good in bed because all redheads are sex fiends, or I must be a bitch because all redheads have fiery tempers. Or they'll tell me that they *only* date redheads, or that they *never* date redheads, because we're all ugly."

Josh is stunned. "They say those things to you? Strangers?"

"At least a dozen men have asked if 'my carpet matches my drapes.' And now there's the ginger insult—thank you, England—and some cultures think we're unlucky, and ohmygod, you know what the French say about redheads, right? They think we *smell*."

"Like roses?"

"Then there's the crap that comes with it naturally. The sunburn, the freckles—"

"I love the freckles." Josh taps his sketch pad with an index finger. "I have plans to hang these on my walls, you know."

He does?

He does. The next day, my face appears in all of his prime-viewing locations—above his desk, beside his bed, on his fridge. Drawings with leaves in my hair and my eyes closed in rapture. Drawings with delicately exposed collarbones and neatly tucked legs. Drawings with a stare as direct as it is vulnerable.

I feel like his muse. Maybe I am.

"It's still so surreal," I tell Kurt, one afternoon in the Treehouse, "to be the object upon which *his* eyes are focused."

"Object," Kurt says.

"I don't mean *object* object."

"It's wrong to objectify people."

"You're right. I used the wrong word." It's easier to agree than to explain the perplexing and disconcerting truth. When it's Josh looking at me . . . I don't mind.

Kurt is petting Jacque. He scratches underneath his chin, Jacque's favorite place, and the gray tabby purrs accordingly. "Where'd you find that?" He inclines his head toward a heart-shaped stone.

"Oh. Um, near the Arènes de Lutèce?"

"So your boyfriend found it."

"We found it together."

"And you brought it here together?"

I pause. And then I nod.

Jacque jumps onto his lap, but Kurt pushes him off. "I have to work." He yanks out his chemistry textbook, and someone else's ballpoint-pen-drawn map of underground Paris flies out of his bag and hits my arm.

I hand it back to him. "I'm sorry I didn't tell you. We come here sometimes at night."

"*Mm,*" Kurt mumbles. We work until dinnertime, but the next day, when I ask if he wants to study at the Treehouse, he declines.

The following Sunday at the Treehouse, Josh surprises me with three brushes and a large plastic jar of cheap dark-green tempera paint. "The brushes are my own, but the paint was found. And free."

"Where'd you find it?"

His expression turns devilish. "The art room."

"Cheater." But I return his smile. "What are you gonna paint?"

"I like that. Not what *do* you want to paint, but what *are* you going to paint."

"I trust you, if that's what you mean." I tug out the plaid blanket from its trunk. "Not that I should. Art thief."

"Paint thief, thankyouverymuch. The art will be my own." He helps me arrange the blanket, folding it over an additional time so there's more space than usual around the rooftop's perimeter. "I'll need the space to work."

I shrug happily. It's sunny, probably one of the last warm days of the year, so I'm already slathered in SPF. I slip out of my wedge sandals and wiggle my toes in the air.

He studies the concrete wall. "Where will we go when the weather turns?"

"I tough it out here through mid-November. And some winter days aren't so bad, you know? But Kurt and I usually hole up in the dorm, sometimes the library."

Josh glances at me. It's so sexy that my heart misses a beat. "But where will *we* go?"

"Everywhere," I reply. "We'll go everywhere together."

"I want to show you my favorite portraits. The Van Gogh self-portrait at the d'Orsay. And there's this Van Dyck that I've always loved at the Louvre. *Le Roi à la chasse.* I don't even know why I love it so much. Maybe you could tell me."

I close my eyes to feel the sunshine against my lids. "I'd like to take you to the restaurant inside the mosque. We'll have mint tea and honeyed desserts."

"We'll ride the Ferris wheel at the Place de la Concorde."

"And then we'll walk through the Tuileries and drink *vin chaud* to stay warm."

"The flea market in Montmartre," he says. "We'll shop for rusted bicycles and broken mirrors."

"We'll ride the *métro* to its farthest stops, just to see what's at the end of each line."

"Those," Josh says to the wall, "are *perfect* days." I open my eyes. He dips a small brush into the paint and pauses midair.

And then . . . he comes alive.

His plan unfolds quickly. He's painting a mural on the inside of the rooftop's wall. He begins with a sketch, an outline, and moves around the interior in a complete circle. It's already clear what this mural will be.

I smile and let him work in silence.

Josh switches to a larger brush and bolder strokes. Fat green leaves and thick green branches appear across the wall's peeling white paint. I lose myself in a book about the search for an ancient lost city in the Amazon, glancing up occasionally to watch the tree grow. But when he circles around again, unexpected shapes appear between the leaves. He's creating a mock-up of the surrounding skyline. It's precise but with his usual touch of whimsy—certain buildings rounder, others more square.

Jacque visits. He purrs against Josh's leg.

When Josh doesn't notice—which is a first, Josh adores Jacque—he scowls and saunters toward me. I feed him scraps of duck gizzard from the salad I had for lunch, and he allows me to pet him for a few minutes before disappearing back over the rooftops.

The sun beats down. Josh takes off his shirt. He's so deep into his work that he's forgotten I'm here. He's a work of art himself. The lines of his back and arms are strong, more so than his slender body would suggest. He has a small mole on his right shoulder blade and a faded scar on his lower back. The skull-

and-crossbones on his arm looks even more *him* against this backdrop of similar brushstrokes.

And . . . his hips. They jut out skeletally from the top of his jeans, and I find my eyes returning to this area again and again. This right-above-the-pants area.

Christ.

Josh removes a second jar of paint from his shoulder bag. As he circles a fourth time, yet another unexpected layer appears behind Paris. Towering skyscrapers. Suspension bridges. Statues of lions. He paints a Flemish building with climbing garden roses and a tiled roof, and then a brownstone with ivy window boxes and an American flag. What surely must be *his* house.

I was wrong. Josh didn't just turn my rooftop into an actual tree house. He turned it into a tree house with a view of the world. *Our* world. Paris and New York.

He circles around one last time, sprinkling in a few birds among the tree branches. Some look almost real. Others are so fantastical that they must exist exclusively in his imagination. The complete mural takes less than six hours.

When Josh emerges from his trance, he is dazed and art-drunk. He blinks at me. Inexplicably, I burst into tears. He continues to stare at me without expression, and I continue to sob—embarrassingly fat tears. He tilts his head. Another blink. And then he drops to the blanket. His eyes are wild with fear.

"It's . . . it's *beautiful*," I say.

Every muscle in his body relaxes. He laughs so hard that he

collapses backward. His paint-covered hands clutch the blanket, and his body shakes with uncontrollable laughter.

"It's not funny." I dab at my face with the blanket.

He doubles up even harder.

"I'll have to wash this blanket now anyway." I gesture toward his paint smears.

Josh slowly stops laughing. He smiles up at me—a beatific, godlike smile—and holds out his long arms. I nestle into them, green paint and all. He hugs me tightly. My ear is pressed against his naked chest, and his heart is beating a thousand times a minute. I run my hands down his body. He closes his eyes. I kiss his skin and the paint and his sweat. He lifts my face toward his and kisses away my tears. "Thank you," he says. "That was the best reaction that anyone has ever given me. For anything."

chapter fourteen

My heart reacts to his news by shattering. A heap of fragile glass shards. "You're going home? Why didn't you tell me this could happen?"

It's been exactly one week since Josh turned the Treehouse into a *tree house*. But tonight is too chilly for an open-air rooftop, so we're slumped against each other on the top of my bed. At least he looks miserable, too. "I don't know," he says, tossing aside his phone. "I guess I hoped that maybe, somehow, they might . . . forget about me."

"Your parents wouldn't *forget* about you."

"You'd be amazed at how many minutes we've spoken to each other since school began. Twenty? Maybe? And most of them just now?"

I sigh. "Happy birthday to you."

Josh's parents chose today—of all days—to inform him that they're flying him home for the entire week of elections. He'll be an interest story for the news: the eighteen-year-old who gets to vote for his father for the first time. His parents want footage at the polls, a gushing post-vote interview, the whole charade. "It's so sleazy," he says. "They're bringing me into their world of sleaziness, and they want me to sleaze for their cameras."

"Voting for your dad isn't sleazy."

"Everything else is."

"Agreed." The worst part is the timing. He's leaving right after his run of detention ends, just as we'd be gaining full-time access to each other. "But," I continue. "At least there's cake."

His brow raises hopefully. "Cake?"

I smile and slide off the bed.

"You've already done too much," he protests, though it's clear he's okay with it. "The crème brûlée. The gifts."

I laugh. "Only one of those gifts counted."

"But I like them equally."

After lunch, I gave him a—poorly made, by myself—papier-mâché fox with purple crayons glued into its butt. And then I gave him his real present, original artwork by one of his favorite cartoonists. I had it shipped overseas the week we started dating, right after he offhandedly mentioned his October 24th birthday. I've been worried that it's too much too soon, but he seemed genuinely delighted by both.

My birthday is in late June. I won't be able to vote until the next election.

I'm heading toward the mini-fridge for his cake, when . . . something stops me. The quiet. I peer into the hall. For once, it's empty. Nate's door is closed. There's not a single person in sight. A wave of recklessness washes over me. Or maybe it's desperation, the impending separation pounding throughout my body. My hand hovers above my door handle. And then I take action.

I shut my door.

Josh swallows. We've been so careful to follow the rules. "Are you sure?"

"Positive."

"My birthday is looking *much* better."

I flick off the overhead light.

"Also much darker," he says.

I fumble toward my desk, turn on a lamp, and remove something small and round from the fridge—a glossy chocolate mousse and hazelnut cake. I light a perfect ring of candles around the edge and softly sing *"Joyeux anniversaire."* It has the same tune as its English counterpart. Josh grins at my singing voice, which he's never heard before.

"Sultry," he says.

I can tell he approves. It's embarrassing, but pleasing. Josh closes his eyes and all eighteen candles are extinguished in a single blow.

"You got your wish!"

Josh nods at my door. "I did."

I swat him with our forks. He grabs them and uses them to

pull me down beside him. We're laughing as we dig into the cake, but it doesn't take long before I'm dizzy with sugar. I fall backward into the bed. Josh makes it a few more minutes before shoving away the platter and collapsing beside me. He groans a happy groan. I lace my fingers through his right hand, and he winces in the lamplight.

I immediately let go. "Tendinitis?"

"It's fine."

I give him a look.

"Okay," he admits. "It's kind of bad right now."

We stare at his hand. It twitches.

"Oh-oh," I say sadly. *"Mon petit chou."*

Josh's head shoots up in surprise. It's the first time I've called him by a term of endearment. *My little cabbage.* It's like calling someone "sweet pea." His expression melts, but he looks down and away. "You still make me nervous, you know."

"I do?"

"I feel like this . . . awkward giant around you. You're like this perfect porcelain doll. Delicate and sweet and pretty."

I smile. "I won't break."

Josh returns the smile. "No?"

"No. And neither will you." I take his hand back into mine and massage his fingers gently. The tendons are so tight that they feel like cords of rope beneath his skin. He grimaces. I pause, but his expression turns weak. Pleading. I press harder, and he closes his eyes. Harder still. He moans. I rub each finger slowly, up and down, one after the other. The muscles loosen, but they never relax. They're too overworked.

"I should do this more often. Your poor hand needs help."

Josh cracks one eye. "I'm all right."

"Are you kidding? At this rate, you'll be crippled by twenty." I continue massaging. "Have you been to a doctor?"

He takes his hand back from me. "It feels better now."

"I'm sorry." The rebuke stings.

But Josh gives me a teasing smile. "That's not what I meant." He bends over, reaches into his bag on my floor, and removes . . . his brush pen.

"Oh." My shoulders sag. "You want to draw."

"Yes. You."

That perks me up. I try to hand him a sketchbook, but he refuses it.

"No," he says. "I want to draw *on* you."

The air is charged. I swallow. Josh notices the movement and kisses my throat. My eyes close. He trails faint kisses around my neck, over my jawline. Onto my lips. I respond with a deeper kiss, harder, starved for his taste. A hand slides across my bare legs, touching the line where my skirt meets my thighs. The other hand tugs on the bottom of my sweater. A question.

Our eyes open. His pupils are dark and dilated.

I don't drop his gaze as I pull off the sweater. Underneath, I'm wearing a silk camisole. I reach down to take it off, too, but he places a hand on my arm to stop me.

"I want to start here," he says.

Josh pulls me to my feet. His head tilts as he studies his canvas—my milky white skin. I don't blush. He moves in. The tip of his brush touches my shoulder first. His strokes are long and careful, delicate and swift. My eyes close. The ink sweeps smoothly across my skin. The brush tickles the top of my chest, my neck, my arms, my hands. My feet, my calves, and the back of my knees. My thighs.

My breath catches.

"*There,*" he whispers.

I open my eyes before a full-length mirror. I'm covered in garden roses, spinning compasses, falling leaves, desert islands, Joshua trees, and intricate geometric patterns. It's beautiful. *I'm* beautiful. I turn to him in wonder, and he holds out the pen.

"Your turn," he says.

My stomach clenches. "You know I can't draw."

"That's not true. Everyone can draw."

I shake my head, gesturing down my body. "Not like this."

Josh removes his shirt. Heavenly gods. He's so gorgeous I could weep.

"I don't know where to begin," I say.

He clasps my hand around his pen, and he kisses one side of my mouth. And then the other. "I'll get you started." Together, we draw a simple heart over his real heart. I laugh, which makes him laugh. "See?" he says. "It's easy."

So . . . I draw.

My lines are not as confident, and my illustrations are not as recognizable. I decide to stick with circles and swirls. Josh watches me work. I cover his chest, his neck, his back, his arms, his fingers. His abdomen.

"There," I say. "I'm out of skin."

He stares into the mirror for a long time. I sit on the edge of the bed. At last, he turns to me. "Thank you."

For some reason, *now* is the moment I blush. "You like?"

"I love."

His words hang in the air. The atmosphere begins to shake. Does he mean . . . ?

Josh sits beside me. He touches his forehead to mine. He closes his eyes and says, "Isla Martin. I'm in love with you."

My universe explodes.

"I love you, too, Josh. I love you *so much*."

Our bodies press against each other, and the ink on his chest stamps a reverse image onto my camisole. His heart over mine. I fall backward and pull him down with me. His hips arch away as he tries to hide what this is doing to him, but that only makes me press against him harder. We kiss with abandon. Together, we remove my camisole. The ink smears. It spreads from his chest onto mine. It spreads across our bodies in handprints, across my blankets in smeared limbs. I undo his belt buckle and unzip his jeans, and we roll into the cake, and there's hazelnut glaze and chocolate mousse and black ink—

The fluorescent light is blinding. "You really should fix—"

"Jesus, Kurt!" I say.

Josh blocks my body with his. "Shut the fucking door!"

But Kurt is frozen.

"Shut the door!" we shout.

He does. The stairwell beside my door *clangs* open, and his feet race upward. My heart slams against my chest. I throw Josh's shirt at him. "Nate will have heard that."

Josh yanks it on. "Shit. Shit, shit, shit."

"I'm sorry. He didn't mean it. Kurt."

My boyfriend kisses me, quick as a dart, and he's gone. Another *clang* and Nate's door *fwoomps* open as the stairwell door *clangs* shut again. Maybe Nate didn't see Josh. Maybe he doesn't know the shouting came from my room. Maybe.

There's a sharp rap on my door.

"Hnngh?" I say in my best I-was-asleep voice.

"That was the second time," Nate says from the hall. "If it happens again, I have to report you to the head of school, and she *will* suspend you both." He waits. "Just say 'okay,' Isla."

"Okay." It barely leaves my throat. I'm dying. The junior in the room beside mine shifts around in her bed. I pray that she's still asleep.

"What was that?" Nate calls out.

"OKAY."

"Thank you. Good night." Nate pads away, his door *fwoomps*, and the world is silent. I exhale. I'm shaking. And then I'm crying, but it's not because I'm scared or humiliated. It's because the most amazing moment of my entire life has just happened.

Josh loves me.

I trace the ink on my body. His beautiful illustrations are smeared with streaks of gooey chocolate. Reluctantly, I turn on my shower. The steam is already billowing when I climb in. The hot water hits me, and purple-black ink floods down my body.

It touches everything.

He is everywhere.

chapter fifteen

Josh appears over my shoulder. "I thought we'd agreed you're going to Dartmouth."

His detention must have just ended. I'm working on an essay for Columbia University, so I finish my sentence, look up at him, and smile from my desk chair. "Remind me again where that's located?"

"Four-point-nine miles from the Center for Cartoon Studies. Maybe. I'm not sure. I'd have to check."

"She's already filled out the application," Kurt says, spoiling my surprise.

Josh freezes. And then he drops to his knees. "Is he serious? Are you serious?"

I slide out the hidden paperwork from Dartmouth. "We're serious."

He rips away the Columbia papers and throws them to my floor. "You don't need those, you really don't need those."

I laugh as I pick them back up. "I do."

"You don't."

"These are tough schools." My smile fades as I gesture to the folders on my desk labeled LA SORBONNE, COLUMBIA, and DARTMOUTH. "You know I have to apply to them all."

"And you'll get into them all. But you'll *accept* Dartmouth. And we'll get a studio on the river—which will still be bigger than this—and a cat that looks like Jacque, but we'll call him Jack. And we'll get a crappy car, something that doesn't even have AC, but it'll have a great radio, and we'll drive someplace new every weekend."

"I want that," I say.

"Me too."

Kurt shakes his head in disgust. He's sitting on my bed. "I still don't understand why you'd alter your plans after all these years."

I swivel around in my chair to stare him down. "My plans were never that planned."

But it's too late. Josh's face has already fallen. "I'm sorry," he says. "I'd never ask you to do this if it's not what you wanted."

That makes me laugh again. "Yes, you would."

His frown deepens. "No. I wouldn't."

"I *do* want it. You know I don't know what I want to do with my life. So I might as well do whatever it is I'm going to do . . . there."

Kurt groans as if in physical pain. "Your parents will be furious."

"*If* I get accepted"—my gaze is still locked upon Josh—
"they'll be fine with it."

"No, they won't." Kurt clenches his entire body in
frustration. "They'll be worried that you're throwing your life
away for some guy."

Now he has my attention. "Hey. Don't say that."

"You've been dating him for less than a month."

"We wouldn't even be attending the same college. And
neither of us has gotten in yet, so just stop it, okay?"

Kurt glares at me. "I'm the one trying to finish my homework.
You're the one bringing *him* in here."

"Actually, I brought myself in here. And I'm still here." Josh
points at himself. "Hi."

"This is *my* room," I say to Kurt.

"So I don't have a say in it anymore?" he asks.

"No!" I say.

"I'm gonna go," Josh says.

"Don't," I say as Kurt says, "Good."

I get up to follow Josh, but he stops me. "You should stay,"
he says quietly. I start to protest, and he cuts me off. "I refuse
to be the person who messes things up between the two of you.
Work it out." He kisses my cheek. And then he's gone.

I scowl at Kurt. "Well? Do you wanna talk about it?"

"Talk about what?" he says testily.

I lower my voice, because my door is still open. "Last night?"

"When you screamed at me?"

"When you came in here and found something you weren't
expecting."

Kurt slams shut his textbook so hard that it makes me jump. "You're the one person who's never supposed to talk to me like that," he says. "Like I don't understand. You've wanted to screw him for three years. Why wouldn't you now that you're dating? I'm not the idiot that you think I am."

I'm stung. "I don't think that. You *know* I don't think that."

"You do."

There's truth to what he's saying. It shames me.

"Listen. I don't want to tag along on your dates, and I don't want you to stop going out, but it'd be nice to know if you still gave a shit about me."

I crumple down beside him onto the bed. "I'm sorry."

"Don't say you're sorry. Say you're still my friend."

"I'm still your *best* friend." I lean against his shoulder and sigh. "What can I do to make it up to you?"

"For starters, you can fix your lock. I never want to see your breasts again."

"Ohmygod, Kurt."

He snorts with laughter. "They're bigger than the last time I saw them."

I shove him away. "Do you want me to leave my own room? Because I'm seriously about to vomit."

"No." His expression becomes solemn again. "I don't ever want you to leave."

"Come with me this weekend," Josh says. "Out of the country."

It's Friday, and we're making out in a custodial closet

between second and third period. It's been a long, tension-filled week. Today is Josh's last day of detention, and this will be our final weekend before he has to fly to New York for the election.

I think he's kidding until I see his expression. "Josh. We can't just *go*."

"Why not? I went to Germany last month."

"Yeah, but." A broom falls against my back, and I shove it aside. "That's different."

"The only difference is that it'd be better, because you'd be with me."

I want to go. I want to go with him so badly.

The broom falls on me again, and Josh throws it into the corner. "Stay," he tells it.

"I hate this closet."

"Come on. Let's go someplace where we won't have to prop open our doors and hide between mops."

"I want to, I really do. But it's too risky." I pause. "Isn't it?"

"No, you see. Because here's what we'd do: We'd catch a train early tomorrow morning, spend the afternoon and evening wherever, crash in a hotel, and then catch the train back on Sunday morning. We'd only be gone for one night."

"And . . . how many times have you done this?"

He shrugs. "A bunch of times last year. Just the once this year."

"And you've never been caught."

"Never." Josh squeezes my hands. "Nate practically *expects* us to be out all night on the weekends. He doesn't freak out if we aren't in our rooms. This stratagem has only two rules: One, we limit ourselves to a single night away. Anything can happen in a night, and excuses are easy to make. And, two, we tell our plan to the people we're in regular contact with so that they won't go asking around for us."

"So . . . Kurt." This bothers me. He'd keep our secret, but he'd also be disappointed in my rash behavior.

"He's the only person who'd notice our absence."

I bite my lower lip.

"Where would you go?" he asks. "Name a place that you've never been before."

"Barcelona." I'm surprised at how fast I answer.

Josh is less surprised. "Why?"

"Gaudí."

"The architect?" Of course my boyfriend knows about Antoni Gaudí. He was a Modernista revered by artists of all kinds.

"I saw his work in an old *National Geographic.* It looked almost magical. I've never seen anything like it, not in real life. But maybe that's stupid, maybe it's too touristy—"

"No. It's perfect. It'd be my first time, too." Josh stops. His words have accidentally triggered the real subject beneath the surface of this conversation. He swallows a lump in his throat. "It'd be our first time together."

And now we're discussing something else. Something we both ache for.

The thought of Josh returning to America is unbearable. It's only a week—I know this—but whenever I imagine his plane touching down at JFK, I feel . . . not just *ill,* but *wrong.* As if our impending separation were something so much worse. I want to be alone with him. No detention, no election. No Kurt, no Nate. Just the two of us, together, in all of the ways that two people in love can be together.

The bell rings. Our time in the closet is over.

"Let's do it," I say. "Let's go."

Our train is already speeding through the countryside when dawn breaks across France. The car is nearly empty, and we've selected a pair of seats with a table. Josh sits beside the window, because he needs the light to draw. He pencils thumbnails into a new sketchbook while I read about a cannibalistic plane crash in the Andes. One of his shoes rubs gently against mine. I rub it back. I've always thought the best relationships are those that are as happy and content in silence as they are in action, but until Josh, I'd only ever experienced it with Kurt.

My eyes grow heavy as the sun grows brighter. I lean against Josh's shoulder only to feel his hand stop moving. "Oh. Sorry." I sit up so that he can resume drawing.

But Josh removes his dark blue hoodie, places it on his lap, and guides me onto the makeshift pillow. I breathe deeply, inhaling his comforting scent. I'm lucky. I am so, so lucky. I feel his arm moving again as I drift into a half-awake slumber. A dreamlet. An image of one bed and two bodies, his curled protectively around my own. At some point, I fall into a real sleep, because soon he's brushing my hair away from my face.

"This is our change," he whispers.

We're in Figueres, Spain. Catalonia. It's the birthplace of Salvador Dalí and just across the border from France. I clamber into a sitting position as our train approaches the station. Josh grabs his sketchbook and flips back the tabletop. He groans as he stands. His limbs are crunched and stiff.

"You should have woken me up. You were in that position for hours."

He slips back into his hoodie. "But *you* needed the rest."

We've packed light—a backpack each—and we shove our books into them. The train comes to a stop, we hop out, and I shiver at an unexpectedly strong wind. The brilliant dawn has turned into a dusky morning. The sky continues to darken as our connecting train rattles toward Barcelona. The French countryside was green and gray, and the Spanish countryside is green and golden. But the threatening clouds deaden its warmth.

"I don't suppose you brought an umbrella?" I ask.

"I don't even own an umbrella."

"Ah, that's right. I forgot that your skin is water-repellent."

Josh laughs in amusement. "I like you."

I smile at my lap. An entire month of making out, and he can still do that to me. Who cares if it might rain?

Two hours later, we exit the Barcelona Sants railway station. The neighborhood is urban and sort of . . . grubby. We pass a group of skaters, and the *clack* of a board hitting the cement is echoed by a much louder *clack* from the sky. The downpour erupts. The skaters shoot off across the street, and—on instinct—we chase after them into the closest café.

"Ohthankgod." Josh weakens at the sight of lunch. "That worked out well."

Our wet shoes squeak against an orangey-red tiled floor. Behind the glass counter, slender baguettes are stuffed with spicy pork, buttery cheeses, and thick slices of potato. I order three different *bocadillos*—*chorizo, un jamón serrano y queso manchego, y una tortilla de patatas*—and we split them at a counter overlooking the congested cars.

Josh rips off an enormous hunk of the chorizo sandwich. "You know what's great? We've never had to discuss it, but we share the same philosophy when it comes to food."

"Variety?"

"And lots of it." He points an accusing finger. "So, hey. You speak Spanish."

"Spanish, *sí*. Catalán, no." Catalán is the native language of Barcelona, though both are spoken here. "Taking a French class would've been cheating."

"Any other languages I should know about?"

"Only Mandarin. Oh, and a little Russian."

Josh freezes, mid-bite.

I smile. "Kidding."

"Maybe that's what you could do someday. You could be an interpreter."

My nose wrinkles.

"Sandwich artist? Professional skateboarder? Train conductor?"

I laugh. "Keep trying."

Our spontaneous lunch is delicious, because Spanish pork is beyond belief. It's like fish in Japan or beef in Argentina. Or *anything* in France. Though admittedly, I'm biased. I study the custom map that Kurt drew for us last night. He stopped being disappointed in me when he realized I'd given him the perfect excuse to play cartographer. "Should we take a cab to La Pedrera?" I ask. It's the first landmark that Kurt has marked. "Or should we check into our hotel first?"

Josh lifts away a lock of my wet hair. "This reminds me of last June."

I raise my head and find him absorbed in memories. He wraps the lock around an ink-stained index finger. He uses it to gently pull me closer into a deep, open-mouthed kiss.

The hotel.

Definitely the hotel.

chapter sixteen

The hotel that Josh reserved online is gorgeous. It has mosaicked columns and a babbling courtyard fountain and dozens of succulents dangling from planters on the walls.

Unfortunately, it was too early to check in.

The tension inside our cab is heavy. Tangible. I don't know how we're supposed to wait, but we've been left with no choice but to explore the city first.

We're splashing toward the heart of Barcelona. Red-and-yellow-striped flags—some with the blue triangle and star of independence, some without—hang everywhere from apartment balconies, soaked with storm. The city's appearance is distinctly Western European, but it's also filled with colorful architecture and steep hills. Palm trees and leafy trees.

Purple vines and red flowers.

"It's almost like a Parisian San Francisco," Josh says.

Either he's trying to change the subject from the obvious one, or he's thinking about his friends in California. Probably best to change the subject. "Speaking of, how are St. Clair and Anna doing these days?" I ask.

"Good." He sits up straighter. "They're pretty much living together now."

"Wow. Already? Do you think they'll last?"

Josh frowns. "Yeah, of course." And then he sees my expression. "Sorry. Sometimes I forget that you don't really know them."

I don't forget.

They watch me, stare back at me, every time I'm in his room. The wall-to-wall drawings make his friends a constant, unspoken presence. I wish I knew them better. I want them to know that *I* exist, that I'm a part of Josh's life now, too.

"St. Clair and Anna are one of those couples that seem like they were made for each other," he says. "Instant friendship, instant chemistry. He was obsessed with her from the moment they met. She was the only thing he ever wanted to talk about. Still is, actually."

"I like Anna. I mean, I like St. Clair, too—he was always friendly to me—but I don't know him as well. Not that Anna and I ever hung out." I don't know why I'm babbling. Maybe so I won't feel untethered from this part of his life. "But she did live on my floor. And the first week of school, she told off Amanda Spitterton-Watts on my behalf."

Josh grins. "She punched her, too. Last spring."

"I know. That was weird." I laugh. "But also awesome."

Amanda was the Emily Middlestone of last year—the school's most popular mean girl. I saw Anna throw the unexpected punch, and it was my testimony that kept her from being suspended. I felt like I owed her. And not just for sticking up for me in the past, but. . . she knew about my crush on Josh. She once caught me absentmindedly doodling his tattoo. I thought for sure she'd tell him, but she never did. He never side-eyed me with that particular brand of I-know-you-like-me weirdness.

Anyway. I was grateful.

Our cabbie pulls over on Passeig de Gràcia, a large thoroughfare where every shop is emblazoned with an expensive name. Dolce & Gabbana. Salvatore Ferragamo. Yves Saint Laurent. But amid this luxury shines an actual jewel: Casa Milà, aka La Pedrera.

We dash below an awning and squint through the rain, across an intersection, at its curious stone facade. Over a century ago, a wealthy man named Milà commissioned Gaudí to design the building. Its grandiose structure is made entirely of waves and curves. There's not a single straight line of construction. It was the home of Milà's family, as well as several renters, but most of the locals despised it as an eyesore—exactly how the same generation of Parisians felt about their own recently built Eiffel Tower.

I wonder how I would have felt about it back then. I'd like to think I would have been one of the people who understood that it was special. That being singular is the exact thing that makes something—or someone—amazing.

"Nice roof," Josh says. "But your Treehouse is better."

I nudge him, my own singular and amazing someone, and he nudges me back. La Pedrera's rooftop terrace is famous. It's covered in strange, bulky chimneys. Some of them look like giant soft-serve ice-cream cones, others like soldiers in medieval helmets. Tourists march up and down Escher-esque staircases, around and around the chimneys, bumping umbrellas. They're like boats adrift at sea.

"It's like an ocean." Josh's voice is filled with admiration. "The wavy limestone, the iron railings." And the balconies look like twists of tentacles and seaweed. Though it's possible that the weather is adding to our overall perception. Our eyes travel toward the unsheltered line of people waiting to get inside.

"That's, uh, some crowd," I say.

"And some rain."

I glance at him and give a tentative shrug. "Next?"

He grins with relief. "I don't want to waste a single minute of this day."

I feel the same way, I think, staring at his dimples.

Kurt's map walks us down the street toward a second Gaudí-designed house. We affix ourselves to the sides of buildings for protection from the rain, but it doesn't matter. It soaks us anyway. "It's your turn," Josh says. "Tell me about your friends. Sanjita. What happened there?"

"So . . . you remember."

"I remember that you were friends with her our freshman year. Did you split because she wanted to be popular? I asked Rashmi once, but she said her sister refused to talk about you."

The stab to my heart is sharp and unexpected. "You asked your *ex-girlfriend* about my friendship with her sister?"

"Whoa. No. Not recently. While we were dating."

"Oh." Though I'm still confused.

Josh guides me below a neon-green cross, the sheltered entrance of a *farmàcia*. "Isla. I would never do that to you. I've had exactly one exchange with her since school began. About three weeks ago, she texted me to ask how I was doing. I told her I'm great, because I'm seeing you. She wished us well. She's dating some dude at Brown."

I wish this knowledge wasn't as welcome as it is. I try not to think about Rashmi. I try not to think about her and Josh in my room last year. I try not to think about how they probably had sex in my bed. And maybe my shower. And maybe my floor, too.

I try.

Josh interprets my silence as a need for further explanation. "I spent some time with her family one summer. Sanjita was acting out, and I could tell she was depressed. That's why I asked Rashmi about you guys. So what happened?"

I've never told anyone this story before. It takes me a minute to gather my courage. "She's the only female friend that I've ever had, apart from my sisters. When I showed up at our school . . . I didn't even know *how* to make friends."

Josh removes my hands from my coat pockets. He pulls me closer.

"I mean, Kurt and I were friends before we even knew what the word meant. So it felt like a miracle when Sanjita wanted to hang out with me. And we had fun. And we could talk about boys, and she was interested in fashion, and she was emotional. She was the anti-Kurt. So I should've known what would happen when he joined us the following year, but I didn't. I thought my friends would automatically become friends with each other through . . . I don't know. The divine egotistical magic of me."

Josh winces. "I'm sorry."

"So he comes to Paris, and she's embarrassed by him. And I can tell that she wants me to ditch him, and he keeps asking me why she doesn't like him, and . . . I'm just *stuck* between the two of them."

"Like you were with Sébastien."

"Worse, because this came first. I wasn't expecting it." My voice catches. "Sh—she made me choose. *She actually said it.* She said Kurt was holding us back."

He squeezes my hands. "Kurt would never ask you to choose."

"I know." Tears spill over my eyes. "And that's why I chose him."

Josh looks for something to dry my tears, but we're already so wet that it's pointless. We laugh as he tries to dry them with the inner sleeve of his hoodie.

"I'm sorry that happened," he says. "I'm sorry she hurt you."

I shrug at my boots.

"If it makes you feel any better? Sanjita was miserable for, like, a full year after you guys stopped hanging out. Even after her social-climbing aspirations had been met, and she'd become friends with Emily. I think she still has regrets about what she did."

"I know she does. When I look at her, I see them, too."

"Do you have any regrets?"

"Only that I stopped trying to make new friends. Between her and Sébastien? Ugh." I give our connected hands a single swing. "But *someone* recently taught me that not everyone is so judgmental."

Josh shakes his head. "I don't know. I can be pretty judgmental."

"Yeah, but . . . it's like you're on the right side of the law."

He smiles.

I poke his chest. "You wanna see something cool?"

"I'm looking at it."

"Shut up." I laugh. "Turn around."

We're standing across the street from Casa Batlló, another Gaudí masterpiece. The surface is covered in ceramic-shard mosaics—aqua and cobalt, rust and gold—in rough, skinlike patterns. And it has another spectacular rooftop, an animalistic arch of metallic tiles that's curved like the back of a mighty dragon. I like this building even more.

Josh's eyes widen with speechlessness.

"See that turret with the cross?" I point to the roof. "Some people think it's supposed to be the lance of Saint George who's just slayed the dragon."

"Architecture. Maybe *this* is your future."

"It's more art than architecture."

"Same thing," he says.

I ponder this, but if my interest was that strong, I'd want to rummage around through its insides. I'd want to inspect every angle from as close a vantage point as possible. "Nah," I finally say. "I just like the story. And the way it looks."

Josh places an arm around me. "Every art needs its connoisseurs."

I happily burrow into his wet side.

"What's next?" he asks, glancing at the clock on his phone.

I look at him in question.

He shakes his head, and we try not to be disappointed. It's still too early to check in.

Sagrada Família is next. The map easily leads us to the closest transit station. The *métro* is an unaccented *metro,* but apart from that, it's identical to its brethren in Paris. When we exit the station, the rain has slowed to a drizzle. And then we see it. Casa Batlló may be a dragon, but Sagrada Família?

It's a monster.

It wants me to cower. It wants me to weep. It wants to save my soul from hell. Gaudí started work on this church in the late nineteenth century, but it won't be finished for at least another decade. It stretches twice as high as the tallest cathedrals of France. It looks like a fantasyland castle—wet sand dripped through fingers, both sharp and soft. Bright construction lights are everywhere, and workers are tinkering around its massive spires in dangerously tall cranes.

We circle the entire structure, shading our eyes from the

rain, as we look skyward toward the figures that are carved into every inch of its facade. So much is happening, everywhere, that the overall style defies categorization. Some of the spires are topped with mounds of rainbow-colored grapes, while the west side is austere and tormented, drawing the eyes to an emaciated Jesus on an iron cross. Stone women wail beside a pile of skulls at his feet. But then the east side is an abundance of life—humans and angels and animals and wheat—and topped by a green tree covered in white doves.

"It's beautiful," Josh says. "*Fuck,* that's beautiful."

Something occurs to me. I'm off running. "Hold that thought!"

"Where are you going?" he shouts.

"I'll be right back! Don't move!" I dart across the street and down two blocks until I find a convenience store with a display of umbrellas beside their entrance. I grab the first one, pay for it, and race back with a clear kiddie umbrella.

Josh is confused and upset. "Don't you think it's too late for that?"

I hold it above his head as I dig into his backpack. I toss him tomorrow's T-shirt. "Dry your hands." He obeys, and then I replace the shirt with his sketchbook and pen. "You have to draw it. When will you get another chance?"

"Isla, I . . ."

I zip up his bag, step aside, and hold the tiny shelter above his body.

He watches the rain roll down my face. "Thank you," he says quietly.

I beam back at him. He kisses my cheek and then bends over his pages, further protecting them, as he uncaps his pen with his teeth. He draws quickly, and I have to urge him to slow down. I don't mind the rain. He focuses on the dove-covered tree. "We have maybe two hours until sundown," he says, after nearly twenty minutes of silence. "How are you doing? Are you cold?"

"A bit, but I'm okay. There's only one more destination marked on our map."

"Do we win a prize if we check off every box?"

"The grand prize."

He raises an eyebrow as he caps his pen. "Then we'd better do it."

We admire his drawing together. I like it even better than the real thing. I only see the beauty, not the accompanying fear. Everything Josh touches is beautiful to me.

He puts his sketchbook away as I search for our map. "Oh, no!" I glance in the direction of the convenience store. "I must have dropped it while I was running."

"Do you remember its name?" He takes the umbrella and holds it over my head. "Not the convenience store. The name of our final destination?"

"Yeah, of course."

Josh smiles. He unbuttons my coat, places his fingers against my collarbone, and fishes out my necklace from below my dress.

It's *incredibly* sexy.

He holds up the compass. "Then we'll find the Right Way."

chapter seventeen

We take the metro north and emerge into a neighborhood that's emptier and dirtier. No one exits the station with us, and there are no street signs for our last destination.

"Is this the right place?" I ask.

Josh scratches his head. "I think so. Let's try up there."

He points toward an area that looks less barren. We hike up the street, sharing the umbrella as best we can. The drizzle has turned into a fine mist. Weeds spill out through ruptures in the sidewalk. Everything feels abandoned. We finally chance upon a long hill with several grouped sets of stairs and escalators. *Escalators.* I've never seen them outside like this, sandwiched between residential apartments and souvenir shops. But despite these promising signs . . . the street is still deserted.

As we ride the rickety escalators, the mist gets lighter and lighter. And as we reach the top of the hill, it evaporates into a clear sky. Sunshine.

We tilt our heads backward and marvel at the heavens.

There's another, smaller hill across the street. "Looks like it's right up there," I say.

With a burst of energy, Josh scoops me over his shoulder and runs toward it. I scream with laughter. He shouts with mad glee. I pound on his back with my fists, but he doesn't set me down until we're through the gates and on the summit. He throws up his arms in triumph. "I win!" And then he buckles like a weak hinge. "I'm dying."

I grin. "Serves you right."

Josh lifts his head. "Oh, yeah?" And then he sees my expression change as I notice what lies behind him. He turns to look. His entire body straightens in astonishment.

We're not just at the top of the final hill. We're at the top of Barcelona.

The jumble of the city stretches to every corner of the horizon, sharp rectangles of brown and gray and yellow and red. Towering above it all are the spires and construction cranes of Sagrada Família, but directly below us, there's a seemingly endless path winding its way down through a landscape of Mediterranean greens.

Parc Güell.

In the far distance, we can see the turrets and sculptures that Gaudí designed for this park—and its accompanying crowds—but, up here, everything is trees and serenity. The air is so fresh and clean that my lungs are *surprised*. For the first time in months, the world stills. Since before Paris, since before New York . . . actually, I can't remember the last time I felt such an overwhelming sense of calm.

"We must've come up the back way," I say.

"We should lose the map more often."

We wander down the main path in silence, our hands clasped together. I'm in awe. Several minutes pass before we see anyone else. It's a young vendor with a blanket on the ground, attempting to sell feathery earrings to two Japanese women. Josh nods toward a narrow side-path through the trees. We take it.

I squeeze the water from my hair as we stroll, and he rubs a hand briskly through his scalp. Droplets fly everywhere. "Hey, now," I say. "Watch where you aim that thing."

Josh points his head in my direction and rubs harder.

"You are such a boy."

"You love me."

I smile. "I do."

The air smells of mountains and pines. There are *so* many trees here. Cypress trees and olive trees and palm trees and mystery trees with plump red berries.

Josh holds out a hand to stop me.

And then I hear it. Behind a covering of bushes, a couple is having sex. My mouth opens in delighted shock. Josh laughs silently. We move ahead so as not to disturb them. There's a good chance that they're our age. Most European teenagers don't have cars, and they often live with their parents through the end of college. Parks are somewhat notorious for amorous pursuits.

Josh gestures toward a secluded area, off path. He's suddenly nervous.

But I was about to point it out, too.

It didn't take long for the thought of the other couple to transfer onto us. We sneak through the foliage. I lean up on my tiptoes, our lips meet, and our bodies sink to the ground. Our hearts pound like crazy against each other. He unbuttons my coat, and his hands are around my back and under my dress. I wish I wasn't wearing tights. But as quickly as our making out begins, he pulls away, gasping. "Never mind. Can't do this. If we go any further, the stopping part will be excruciating. It already is."

"I'm sorry." I reach out to touch him, but he rolls away.

"No, it's fine. Just . . . give me a minute."

The other couple appears between the leaves on the nearby path. They sense our presence and giggle, exactly the reason why we're waiting until our hotel room. I drape my coat over a thick branch to dry. I unzip my boots and strip off my wet tights.

Josh covers his face. "You're killing me."

I smile at him as I wring out the bottom of my dress.

He moans. "Unfair. Girls are so mean."

I laugh. "Give me your hoodie. I'll hang it up."

Obediently, he takes it off. His T-shirt rises with it, and my eyes lock on the lowest portion of his abdomen until he readjusts it. My boyfriend doesn't realize that he's killing me, too. I hang up his hoodie and lie down beside him. We stare at the sky. His head rests against his backpack, and my head rests against his chest. The wind rustles, swirling the scent of pine around our temporary campsite.

"Your eyes remind me of pine trees," Josh says.

"I always wished they were a brighter green. They're so dull."

"Don't say that." He kisses the top of my head. "Have I ever told you about the cabin?"

"Uh-uh." I'm listening to his heartbeat.

"There was this cabin upstate that my family used to rent in the autumn—rough walls, stone fireplace, beds with patchwork quilts. The works. And when we were there, my dad would forget to be worried about politics, and my mom would forget to be worried about my dad. And we'd go hiking, and we'd pick apples from this abandoned orchard. And there'd be so many that we'd throw them into the creek just to watch them float downstream. And we'd play board games at night—"

"What games?"

"My favorite was Pictionary."

I snuggle into him. "Of course."

"My mom's favorite was Clue, and my dad's was Risk. And my parents would cook these home-style dinners like pot roast with mashed potatoes and baked apples—"

"From the orchard?"

"Yeah. And while they'd cook, I'd be spread out on the rug

in front of the fireplace with these giant stacks of paper, and I'd draw. And . . . I'd look up, and my parents would be in the kitchen with this perfectly round window behind them. And all I could see outside of that window—from my position on the floor—were those pine trees.

"So I like pine trees," he finishes. "A lot."

I curl my hand around his thumb and squeeze it.

"What about you? Where were you the happiest?"

I have to think about it for a while. "Well, there was this one trip to Disney World—"

"Did you have mouse ears? Please tell me you had those mouse ears with your name stitched on underneath."

I poke him. "No."

"I'm gonna picture you with the mouse ears anyway. Continue."

I poke him harder. "So Gen was ten, I was seven, and Hattie was four. Gen was adorable. She has those perfect corkscrew curls, you know? Plus, she was always in charge of everything. And Hattie was . . . Hattie. So they were getting all of the attention, like always, but then my parents surprised me with this Disney Princess breakfast. Just for me. And Belle and Snow White and Cinderella were there, and Jasmine told me that my dress was pretty, and that *I* was pretty, and it was amazing. My parents . . . they *knew*. They knew I was the one who needed it."

"This," Josh says, "is my new favorite story."

"Of course, the whole thing was supposed to be a secret. But the second I saw my sisters, I was like, 'Princess Jasmine thinks I'm prettier than you!' Which wasn't even true, but it *felt* true. Mom wanted to kill me, and Hattie threw this massive tantrum that lasted the rest of the trip, but it was worth it. Best day ever."

"You *are* prettier than your sisters. You're way prettier than your sisters."

"That is . . . the most romantic thing that you've ever said to me."

He laughs again. "It's true."

An unseen bird warbles, and another unseen bird answers its call. "You know," I say, "I can't remember the last time I was in a place where I couldn't hear any traffic."

"Ah, you're a nature girl at heart. You've just never been given the opportunity."

"And you're a nature boy?"

"Definitely. See, if you come with me to New England, we can learn how to do all of those outdoorsy things you read about in your books. Exploring, camping, rock-climbing, rafting, stargazing, building fires—"

"Building fires?" I smile.

"That's right. Fires. Plural."

The sun dips below the tree line, and suddenly, Josh is backlit by a stunning golden light. He looks perfect even when he's damp and sweaty and dirty. I wiggle upward until I reach his lips. We kiss, heavily, until I can't handle it anymore.

"Let's go," I say. It comes out ragged.

Josh freezes.

And then he's lunging for his hoodie and backpack, tripping over himself to get moving. I grab my things, and he takes my hand as we sprint onto the narrow path. We're laughing, completely blissed out. We run down, down, down, and the farther we go, the more crowded the park gets. We race through an area that looks like a cave—perfect for making out, complete with a classical Spanish guitarist—but making out is no longer enough. We pass Gaudí sculptures, Gaudí buildings, Gaudí's famous lizard fountain, but they barely earn a glance as we whiz by. We only have eyes for each other.

We grab the first cab outside of the park. We're breathless. Josh hands the driver our hotel's address, and our tongues and limbs and hands are touching, searching, groping as the streets of Barcelona whiz past our windows. We pay our distressed cabbie way too much, mainly out of guilt, and tumble back out.

Josh kisses my neck as we check in. Our surroundings are a blur. The clerk, the stairs, the hallway. We slam our room door shut and toss our backpacks to the floor. We have the entire night, but we can't wait another minute.

We kiss fiercely. Urgently. I throw off my coat as Josh scrambles out of his hoodie. I remove his T-shirt as we collapse onto the bed. His chest drums against mine. I roll over, climb on top of him, and find that he's as ready as I am. He lifts my dress up and around my hips and then over my head. I pull back, breathless. "Do you have?"

"Backpack."

I bend over backward, stretching for his bag on the floor.

I reach it and yank it closer. I find them in the front pouch. I grab one, and he helps me sit back up. He stares openly at my matching pale pink underwear. Josh has seen all of me, but never all at once.

I unhook my bra. He takes it off.

He kisses my breasts, my stomach, the line above my underwear. And then the line below it as my last remaining clothing slides from my hips. I unbuckle his belt, unzip his jeans, and tug them down at the same time as his boxers. His breathing is shallow. Rapid. I lower myself onto him. We gasp. Our arms wrap around each other, and we move together, watching each other, checking in with each other with our eyes. *Is this okay? What about this? This?*

It builds. Faster.

I want him closer. I want him deeper. I want him, want him, want him. His eyes close and so do mine, and we finish as we started. Together.

chapter eighteen

Josh's stomach rumbles against my ear. The room is black. I unfurl from his body and lean toward the hotel's digital clock. It's nearly two in the morning. Josh feels me stir. *"Tapas,"* he mumbles. "We haven't had *tapas.*"

"I think we missed dinner."

"'s okay." He hugs me against his chest. "Too tired to get up anyway."

"We'll just have to come back."

"Tapas and *cerveza*. And then we'll make love on the altar of the Sagrada Família."

I pull away, he tugs me close, I pull away. "Be right back," I say. "Bathroom."

After I pee, I return for my toothbrush and toothpaste. He

follows me in, and we brush our teeth. We can't stop smiling at each other. I can't believe that adults get to do this every day. And I don't even mean sex, though it's wonderful, but things like *this*. Brushing our teeth at the same sink. Do adults realize how lucky they are? Or do they forget that these small moments are actually small miracles? I don't want to ever forget.

We climb back in bed and make sleepy, happy, minty-fresh love. He's careful to make sure that I'm taken care of first before he collapses against me. Moonlight shines in through the windows, and I trace the outline of his tattoo with an index finger.

"You've never told me about this," I say.

"You've never asked."

"I *love* it."

I didn't mean for that to slip out in such a gushy way. Josh laughs, but it's the tired laughter of relief. "Thank goodness."

"Tell me the story."

He shifts into a more comfortable position while carefully keeping me nestled against his body. "When I was sixteen, St. Clair convinced an artist in Pigalle that I was eighteen. Except he didn't *really* convince him. He was just so pushy and persuasive that the guy gave up. It was definitely illegal." I laugh as he continues. "St. Clair can persuade anyone to do anything. He's, like, drowning in charisma. It's so unfair to the rest of us."

"Eh," I say. "He's okay."

Josh pauses. And then I hear a smile in his voice. "This must be how you felt when I told you that you're hotter than your sisters."

I laugh louder this time. "I suppose it is."

"Anyway, it was just the two of us, and I was the only person who got one. It was a few days after my birthday—"

"Like now!"

"Like now. I'd decided on my birthday that I'd get a tattoo, so I designed this one for the incredibly inspired reason that . . . it seemed cool at the time."

"It *is* cool."

"I consider myself unbelievably lucky that I still like it."

"Oh, come on. You have taste. You'd never put something lame on your body." I pause, a new thought occurring to me. "Do you want any more tattoos?"

"I don't know. Maybe someday I'll get a big garden rose on my other arm."

"Ha-ha."

"I would." And he sounds hurt that I don't believe him. "I want a lot more of these nights with you, Isla. I want *all* of my nights with you."

When the sunlight streams in through the windows, it's the happiest morning of my life. We've shifted in the early hours, but our legs are still hooked together.

I stare at his adorable, sleep-rumpled hair and his long, lovely spine. I touch the skin of his back with the tip of one finger. He rolls over. He smiles at me languorously. With contentment. I scoot in closer for a kiss. "Mm," he says. "Is next weekend too soon to do this again? Switzerland. Let's go to Switzerland."

"You'll be in New York next weekend."

His smile falls.

"Next-next weekend," I say.

"Deal." He brushes my hair away from my shoulder, leaving it bare. "*So.* Tell me. Who's the better bedmate? Me or Kurt?"

"Kurt, obviously."

"I knew it." He kisses my nose and hops out of bed. "I'll be right back."

"Hand me my phone? I wanna double-check our departure time."

Josh digs it out from my bag, tosses it to me, and goes into the bathroom. The door shuts. I flip the volume switch from silent to on. The screen illuminates. My heart stops.

"No," I whisper.

Twenty-nine new messages. Kurt. Nate. Hattie. The school. My parents.

"Josh? Josh!"

The bathroom door bursts open. "What happened? Are you okay?" And then he sees the way I'm clutching my phone. The blood drains from his face.

"No," he whispers.

I start crying. He tears apart his own backpack, yanks out his phone, and swears at its screen. "Kurt. Nate. My mom, like, a hundred times. My *dad*."

I'm sobbing now.

He paces the room. He rakes his scalp with both hands. "It's okay. It'll be fine. I've messed up before. It'll be fine."

"How will it be fine? This'll go on my record!" My entire college future vanishes. I feel faint. My stomach churns, threatening upheaval.

"No. I'll take full credit for this. You won't get in trouble."

"How won't I get in trouble? I'm just as *here* as you are. In *Spain*." I scroll through the texts, trying to piece together a timeline of events, but I can't focus.

I listen to Kurt's voice mail, and he's completely freaked out. *Hattie was asking around for you, and Nate overheard, and then they noticed Josh was missing, too, and they came to me, and I had to tell them where you were. I'm sorry, Isla. I had to tell them.*

I'm an idiot.

I am *such* an idiot.

How could I have forgotten about Hattie? She's the one person that I can always count on to say or do the wrong thing. Of course she's behind this. And of course Kurt was the one who couldn't keep his mouth shut.

Josh sinks beside me onto the bed. He places one hand on each side of my face and touches his forehead to mine. "Breathe," he says. "Breathe. Breathe."

"I don't wanna breathe!"

"It's okay," he says. "I'll call the school. You call your parents."

Everyone is furious with us. Maman screams so loudly that I have to hold the phone away from my head. Josh gets an earful from Nate, and then I force him to call his mom. She won't pick up, so he leaves a message. He refuses to call his dad, but I insist, so he calls his dad's security aide instead.

And then he makes me text Kurt and Hattie.

They aren't furious—they just want to know that we're okay—but I'm not feeling so charitable toward them. I tell them we're fine, we're coming back, the end.

The train ride to Paris is the opposite of the one we took to Barcelona. The sky is sunny, but our car is dark. We hold hands, we don't let go, but our grasp still feels like that. Like *grasping.* Like we're trying to hold on to something that's slipping away. Neither of us speaks of the thing that we fear is about to happen. I cry, and Josh holds me. It was selfish to think about my problems first. What he's facing is much, much worse.

Our dread and terror grow. We're almost back to the dormitory when Josh can't take it any longer. He pulls me into someone's private garden. There's a pair of French students on lounge chairs, smoking clove cigarettes and soaking in the last warm rays of the year. They hardly even blink at us.

"I want you to know that I love you," Josh says. "And I want to be with you. No matter what happens."

My eyes fill back with tears. "Don't say that."

"It might happen."

"Don't say that!"

His shell is cracking. "I *love* you. Do you still love me?"

"How could you ask me that?" The change in Josh's demeanor is frightening. It's as if he could shatter at any moment. "Of course I love you. This hasn't changed anything."

"But it was my fault. This whole weekend was my idea." He's breathing too fast, and his eyes aren't focusing. He's having a panic attack.

"Hey. Hey." I wrap my arms around him and place my head against his chest. "I wanted to go. It was my decision, too."

But he can only cling to me. His fingers grip my shoulders so hard that it hurts.

"I love you," I say quietly. "I have *always* loved you."

His heart rate slows. And then again. "What do you mean? Always?"

I pull back to meet his gaze. I hold it, steady. "I mean that you never have to worry about me leaving you, because I've been in love with you since our freshman year."

My confession leaves him stunned.

"There's no story," I say. "I saw you one day, and I just knew."

Josh stares at me. He looks *inside* of me. And then he kisses me with more passion than he's ever kissed me with before. It gives us the strength to face our future. It gives us the strength to return to our dorm. And it gives us the strength to knock on Nate's door.

Unfortunately, Nate doesn't open it.

Mrs. Wasserstein does.

chapter nineteen

I had to catch a flight, and I *still* beat you here. Outstanding."
Mrs. Wasserstein throws up her hands in anger. Nate stands
behind her, tense, a prisoner of his own apartment.

Josh is in shock.

"Do you realize what an inconvenience this is?" she continues.
"Being called overseas *one week* before the election? Do you
even care?" Mrs. Wasserstein is petite, much shorter than
I'd realized, though you'd never dwell on it. Her presence is
huge. She looks as strong as she does on camera, but—in this
moment—far more frightening. She sizes me up with hazel eyes
that are startlingly familiar. "And you must be Isla."

My name sounds as unwelcome as I feel. My eyes drop to the
floor. "Hello."

Josh stands partially in front of me, shielding me. "I'm sorry. I'm so sorry, Mom."

"You will be."

Nate steps in. "I'm glad you guys made it home safely. Isla—"

"We have an appointment early tomorrow morning with the head of school," Mrs. Wasserstein says.

A catch in my throat. "All of us?"

"No." She frowns. "My *son* and I."

My face burns with the shame of being put in my place.

"Isla," Nate says, "your appointment is on Tuesday. Why don't—"

"Thank you for your help," Mrs. Wasserstein says to him. "I understand that my son has been making your job difficult. I'm sorry to have inconvenienced you like this."

I get the sense that *she's* been making his job difficult, but Nate only rubs his shaved head. "It's what I do. And it's okay, he's a good kid."

She clearly doesn't believe him. Maybe she would if she knew Mike and Dave. She gives him a brusque nod before turning back to Josh. "We're leaving."

His eyes widen. "Where are we going?"

"Your room. We have much to discuss, young man." She holds open the door and nods again, her farewell to me. "Isla."

My rib cage is compressing my heart into a tiny, painful stone. As he's led away, Josh squeezes my hand with the same unbearable force. Our hands let go only when they can no longer reach. There's a final exchange of anguished expressions, and he's gone. I'm rigid with silence. Nate sighs.

"We're in a lot of trouble, aren't we?" I finally manage.

"You'll be all right."

"Will Josh?"

Nate gives me a sad look.

Another horrible thought occurs to me. "Are *my* parents coming? Is that why my appointment isn't until Tuesday?"

"No. Your appointment is on Tuesday, because tomorrow is a holiday. Remember?"

Tomorrow is the first of November. All Saint's Day. It's a national holiday in France, which means that . . . the head of school is coming in on her day off to speak with Josh.

It's understood that Josh and I won't be seeing each other until after his appointment. But that doesn't stop me from checking my phone for texts every sixty seconds.

I hate my sister. Hate. Her.

If it wasn't for Hattie, I'd be in Josh's room right now—and his mother would not—and we'd be planning our Swiss rendezvous. My phone blips. I lunge for it, but the text is from Kurt: Train timetable says you should have arrived 3 hrs ago.

I reply: *We did.*

Are you ok?

NO.

A minute later, he knocks on my door. "Why don't you just push it open, like you always do?" I shout.

Kurt does. "You sound angry."

"I am."

"Are you angry with me?"

"Yes."

He wedges a textbook underneath my door. "I had to, Isla. They asked me."

"What did Hattie even want?"

"She wanted to borrow your hair dryer."

"My *hair dryer*?"

"Yeah. The . . . diffuser? Is that the thing you put on the end? She wanted to try to curl her hair."

"And she couldn't borrow one from somebody in her own stupid dorm?"

His left eye twitches. "I don't know."

A hair diffuser. I can't believe this entire situation was caused by a freaking *hair diffuser*. A pirate and a devil stroll past my open door, heading toward the lobby for Résidence Lambert's annual Halloween party. It's unfathomable to me that anyone would be in the mood for a celebration.

"Why—for once in your life—couldn't you just lie? That's *all* you had to do."

Kurt pulls up his hoodie. "They asked me a question. I gave them the answer."

"Yeah, well? Thanks to you? My boyfriend is about to be kicked out of school."

"That's not my fault. I didn't do that. He did that."

I don't care that he's speaking the truth. I don't care that it's our fault. It still wouldn't be happening if Kurt could've kept his mouth shut. He's supposed to be my best friend. I yank out the textbook and hold open the door even wider. "Go. Away."

He flaps his hands, upset. "Isla."

I close my eyes. "I can't deal with you right now. Just go."

He's still there. I sense the movement of his hands. I squeeze my eyes tighter, so tight that it hurts, until I feel him brush past me. The stairwell door *clangs* open.

"Boo!" a male voice says.

My eyes pop open. Someone in a *Scream* mask is two inches away from my nose. There's laughter down the hall as I slam my door shut in the jerk's face. I collapse into bed. I'm crying again. Maybe Mrs. Wasserstein is here to keep Josh from getting expelled. She's a powerful woman. I'll bet even the head of school is scared of her.

I'm scared of her.

She probably blames me for all of this. I wanted to make a good first impression on Josh's parents. I didn't know if they'd like me—if they'd think I was exceptional enough for their son—but now I don't stand a chance. I don't even know if they were aware of my existence before yesterday.

Josh still hasn't texted. I'm afraid his mom might be monitoring his phone, so I only text him once more. I keep it short and non-incriminating: *I love you.*

A few minutes later, there's a rapid-fire knocking. I spring from my bed and throw open the door. But it's Hattie. The sight of her fills me with a scarlet rage. She's wearing an oversize Hawaiian shirt that's been buttoned up wrong. Her hair is ratted out in every direction. She has dark under-eye circles, fake bruises, and a pencil-thin mustache.

"What are you supposed to be?" I ask, as calmly as possible. Which isn't calm at all.

She holds up a piece of cardboard. It's been painted white, and it has black lines labeled with inches and feet. "I'm a mug shot."

"Practicing for your future?"

"*Oui.*" She just stands there.

"What? What do you want, Hattie?"

"I wanna apologize, jeez."

I wait.

She waits.

"Was that it?" I ask. "That was your apology?"

"Yeah."

"Wow. I hope you feel better now. Because I sure do. I feel *so much better* knowing my boyfriend might be expelled because you were *that* impatient for a hair diffuser."

Her stone expression falters. "I didn't know I was gonna get you guys in trouble. I'm sorry. I'm really sorry."

"Me too." I slam my door shut.

It pops open. Hattie looks at me with a startled hope until she realizes it was an accident. We scowl at each other as I slam it back shut. I push against it, hard, until I feel the *click* beneath my palms.

The party carries on all night. Josh never texts. I don't remember falling asleep, but I startle awake around eight in the morning.

There's a swollen hush over the dormitory. Everyone is finally in bed. I was dreaming about the need to catch a train, but I couldn't stop putting on makeup. I was helpless as I applied layer after sluggish layer, watching the clock tick closer and closer and closer to my departure time.

Two knocks, low on my door.

I jolt into a sitting position. *That's* what woke me up. That's his second knock. The sound is heavy and foreboding. I lurch out of bed, but I'm terrified to open the door. I press my ear against the wood.

"*Josh?*" I whisper.

There's no reply.

I'm gripped by a new fear. He's already gone. I'm hearing sounds that never existed. I tear open the door, but he's there—of course he's there—and he's devastated. He falls toward the floor. I rush forward, and he collapses into my arms with a cry that's primal. Screw the rules. Screw this school. I shut the door and lead him to my bed. I cradle his body as he slams his fist against his own leg.

"It's okay." I have to be strong. One of us always has to be strong. "Everything will be okay." I grab his fist and hold it between my hands. I kiss the crown of his head.

"It's not okay."

"You had the meeting?"

"I'm gone. She finally kicked me out."

My bedroom spins. "And . . . when do you have to be gone by?"

"*This* is my last day. Today."

The world goes black. There's a loud buzzing in my ears. My

eyes focus, refocus, refocus like an automatic camera that can't get it right.

"One of the custodians took my mom to get shipping boxes. And then she's coming back, and then we're gonna pack up all of my stuff."

Refocus. Refocus. Refocus.

Josh pulls out his hand from mine to claw at me with all ten fingers. "But we'll see each other soon. Thanksgiving. You're still coming home for Thanksgiving, right?"

I nod robotically.

"And then there's winter break. We'll spend every day together, and on New Year's Eve, we'll meet at Kismet for a kiss. At midnight. Okay? And then we'll have spring break, and then it'll be summer again. It'll be over."

I swallow. "What will you do? Where will you finish high school?"

"My mom doesn't want to talk about it until the election is over. They're pissed. My parents are *so pissed.* I had to talk to my dad last night, and then my mom took away my phone. That's why I couldn't call or text you. I'm eighteen, and my *parents* took away my *phone.*"

"It's okay. It's okay." I can't stop saying it. "We'll be okay."

There's another knock, and Nate starts talking without preamble. "Josh, I let your mom into your room so that you and Isla could have a few minutes alone. But you need to go up there now."

Even Nate feels sorry for us.

My lie was more severe than I realized. Nothing—absolutely nothing—is okay.

chapter twenty

The head of school sits behind a desk as intimidating as it is large. Its mahogany is polished, and it carries the scent of musk and wealth. Two flags on indoor poles rest on each side—one American, one French. An overstuffed leather chair sits behind the desk, and two diminutive leather chairs sit before it. I am in one of the diminutive chairs.

"Your grades are slipping," the head says.

I stare at her.

"Not by much, mind you," she continues. "But there's enough of a difference in the quality of your work for more than one of your *professeurs* to have mentioned it to me. They're concerned. Can you guess when they noticed the change?"

I'm not actually here. I'm still in Josh's room. Yesterday.

We packed his life into cardboard boxes. His mom was angry

at him, angry at me, angry at every call. And she received a lot of calls. There was nothing I wanted more than to be away from that awful room, but I wasn't about to waste our final hours.

Josh took down the drawings from his walls. He laid them in a box—one on top of another, on top of another. He slipped the drawings of me from the Arènes de Lutèce into a separate, protective envelope. Compared with the number of drawings that he had of his friends, there weren't many of me yet. We've only been together for a month.

How has it only been a month?

"A month ago," the head says. "That's when you stopped giving your homework the time and attention that it takes to maintain your position at the top of your class."

She says this as if being school valedictorian is my singular ambition, when, really, it just happened. There are only twenty-four other seniors—twenty-*three*—and all of them have friends to hang out with and places to go and things to do. I've never had anything better to do than study. But for one month . . . I had something better to do.

Josh slipped the envelope inside his shoulder bag. It went on the plane with him.

Everything happened so fast. In one day, his room went from chaotic, bursting with art and food and life, to barren. We were only given five minutes to say goodbye. His mother left us in that empty space, and I cried again. Josh used his favorite pen to ink four letters onto the back of my fingers: *L-O-V-E.*

He held my face with both hands. "I love you," he said. "I love you. I love you."

I could hardly see him through my tears. "I love you," I said. "I love you. I love you."

"Isla," the head says. "You're going to meet many boys on this journey. You can't let them distract you from becoming the woman you are meant to become."

She's wrong. There's only one boy.

And who am I to become without him?

I stare at my fingers. The letters are fading, but the word still burns against my flesh.

Beside his mother's waiting car, the letters were sharp and dark. We kissed desperately. Mrs. Wasserstein opened the back door and called to him from the inside. "We're late. Let's go."

His hands gripped mine. "Thanksgiving."

I nodded.

He kissed me again, but this time, it was quick. And then he dropped my hands as if they stung, as if he physically *couldn't* hold them any longer, and he rushed into the car. The windows were tinted black. I couldn't see him, but I watched his window anyway until the car disappeared from view.

The head of school clears her throat. My gaze had drifted toward her window.

"For one month of reckless behavior? I'm giving you one month of weekday detention. I think you'll agree that it's a fair punishment. In addition, this gives you ample time to recommit to your classwork without any . . . distractions."

"Josh wasn't a distraction."

The head looks me over carefully. "No," she says, at last. "Perhaps, for you, that was the wrong word. Though I have my concerns about the other way around."

It's a cruel jab. How dare she suggest that I care more about Josh than he cares about me? What could she possibly know about our relationship?

I storm out of her office and into detention. For all of my time spent frequenting its threshold, I've never actually crossed it. But it looks like any other classroom. There's only one other student here, a sophomore. He doesn't look up from keying his desk. Professeur Fontaine—the computer-science teacher with the triangle-shaped head—is on detention duty. "Pick a seat, any seat," she says. She sounds like a street magician.

I wish I knew where Josh used to sit. I try to conjure his image. A figure with rounded shoulders and a furrowed brow materializes in the back corner. He's penciling his life into tidy panels. I step into this shadow, wanting to believe in its reality, and take the desk. The window beside us has a view of the school's courtyard, but everyone is gone for the day. Only the cobblestones and pigeons remain.

I never got to read those panels.

What if I'm the one who blew it? What if I can't get into Dartmouth anymore? Josh will still get into his college. All he needs is a GED. Perhaps he ruined *this* year, but I might have ruined our next four. If only I could hear his voice again. He made it back to New York this morning, where his mom granted him this single text: Miss you like crazy. Internet also confiscated. Don't know when we can talk next. I LOVE YOU.

After detention, I walk straight to the Treehouse. The night air is freezing, and my coat isn't warm enough. I remember Josh

placing his own coat around my shoulders—right here on our
first date—and cry for the hundredth time. I wrap myself in
the blanket and place my hand on his mural. I press my palm
against the house with the ivy window boxes and American flag.
I press my palm against it so hard that hurts.

Here, I think. *He is here.*

I try to be there, too.

"Turn that off." Kurt barges into my room and points at my
laptop. "You're supposed to be studying. You need a perfect
score on your physics test tomorrow."

"This poll is saying Josh's dad and Terry Robb are locked in
a dead heat. It's still too close to predict a winner."

"Stop reading that stuff. The election isn't for five more
days." And then he frowns. "Terry Robb. People shouldn't have
two first names."

I've finally put in a request to get my door fixed. I'm tired of
my privacy being violated. Our friendship is intact, technically,
but an unpleasant tension cloaks every interaction. Kurt is
unhappy that I'm unhappy. He wants our lives to go back to the
way they were, pre-Josh. And I'm unhappy with Kurt. I know
he didn't mean for any of this to happen, but it did happen. And
he could've stopped it.

As for Hattie, I haven't spoken to her since she was a mug
shot. She might as well *be* in prison, for all I care. I've been glued
to the news. I downloaded an app that tricks my laptop into
thinking I'm in the States, because international restrictions

were blocking too many important video feeds. Knowing what's happening in the election, minute by minute, is the only way that I feel close to Josh. His dad has to win. And not just for the obvious reasons, but selfishly, I hope it might relax his parents enough so that they'll give him back his phone.

"You," Kurt says. "Physics. Study."

"Don't be such an assjacket."

"Asswaffle," he replies.

"Asspickle."

"Asshopper."

He looks pleased with that last one. My mouth twitches, but I'm still annoyed. To cap off this perfect week, I feel my period coming on. I close my laptop. "Fine. You win. But I'm going to the bathroom first."

"Assroom," I hear him say as I go down the hall. When I return, our game is over. "You missed a call from a two-one-two area code."

"What?" I race to my phone. Someone from Manhattan has left me a voice mail. "Why didn't you answer it?"

"Because that's not my phone."

"What if that was Josh?"

"Then your screen would have said 'Josh' instead of 'unknown caller.'"

I barely muffle my scream of frustration. "His phone was taken away! If anyone calls when I'm not here, *answer it*. And if it's Josh, tell him to wait until I *can* get here."

Hey, Isla. My heart splits in two at the sound of his tired voice, which he's attempting to raise above a jumbled commotion of shouting and ringing and clanging. *It's, uh, Thursday. I guess it's already night in Paris? I'm calling from a volunteer's desk at election headquarters. This is the first time that I've been left alone near a phone. It's pretty bad here, but . . . I don't know. None of it even matters. I miss you. I'll try again as soon as I can.* A pause. *I hope you're all right. Okay, bye. I love you.*

I call back. After two rings, a woman with a nasal timbre answers. I hang up.

I listen to the voice mail again. And again. And again and again and again, and I don't know how many times I've listened to it before I realize that Kurt is gone.

A locksmith fixes my door. I never leave my phone.

I turn up the ringer as high as it goes before I shower, and then I keep the volume set there, even in class. My paranoia grows. I can't stop checking it—checking for messages, checking to make sure it's charged, checking to make sure that I haven't accidentally muted it. I want to speak with him so badly I might combust.

On Saturday before dawn, another 212 startles me awake. "Josh?"

"Ohthankgod," he whispers, exhausted and relieved. "I'm sorry it's so early, but I couldn't sleep. I'm calling you from the kitchen. If my parents catch me, I'm dead. But I had to hear your voice."

I grasp my phone harder. "I miss you so much."

"How is it possible that it hasn't even been a week?"

"It feels like a year."

"How are you? What happened with the head? Were you suspended?"

"No. She gave me detention, because it's my first offense. But it's for the entire month."

His voice grows heavier. "I'm sorry."

"The suckiest part? The moment that I have detention, you don't."

It gets a single glum laugh. "I'd take detention over this."

"I know." I soften. "How is it? How are your parents?"

"Pissed off. Busy. They're running me around everywhere with them, but they can hardly even look at me."

"They'll come around."

"Maybe."

One question is weighing on me, heavier than any other. I clutch my necklace for support. "Hey . . ."

"Yeah?"

"Never mind."

"Isla. Say it."

"I was just . . . did your parents know about me? I know you guys didn't talk often, but I was wondering if you ever mentioned me. Before all of this." My voice cracks. "I'd hate it if that was your mom's first impression of me."

His long pause gives me the answer before he does. "I was gonna tell them before Thanksgiving," he finally says. "I didn't want them asking about you."

I cry in silence. "Were you worried that they'd think I'm not good enough for you?"

"No. No. I just wanted to keep you for myself. We were in that perfect bubble, you know? Of course they'll like you."

"I highly doubt that."

"They will. They know this is my fault. And when the election is over, I'll tell them all about you. How smart you are, and how kind, and—"

"How ambitious? How I have no plans for my future?"

"Isla."

"Sorry."

"No, I'm sorry. I should've told them." There's another pause. "Did your parents know about me?"

"Of course."

Josh exhales.

"They were looking forward to meeting you."

"And now they aren't." He gives a sad little snort. "You worry about *my* parents, but I'm the one who was expelled." Suddenly, his voice grows lower. "Someone's moving around. I gotta go I love you bye."

I don't even get to say "I love you" back.

On Monday after detention, I find him in the background of some photographs taken over the weekend at a YMCA in Brooklyn, a last-chance campaigning effort. He's tall and handsome and smiling. He looks *almost* like my boyfriend. I can tell that his smile—no doubt convincing to others—is forced. There are no dimples.

"I didn't wake you up this time, did I?" he asks. The call arrives in the dead of night. There's a racket of people in the background, a general buzz of stress and excitement. Headquarters again. The election is only hours away.

"No." I hug my pillow, wishing it were him. "Getting sleepy, but I'm still reading."

"That's my girl. What's the subject tonight?"

"Orchid hunting. Did you know it was a surprisingly dangerous occupation?"

"Maybe *that's* your future career." A real smile creeps into his voice. "Orchid hunter. And I'll join you on the expeditions. We can wear those khaki hats with mosquito nets."

"How is it over there?" I ask.

"I'd rather be hunting orchids."

"I hope your dad wins."

"Me too. Otherwise he'll be intolerable for at least six months." The sort-of joke falls flat, and he sighs. "Speaking of. Guess who's sending a camera crew to my polling station? Guess who'll be on the morning news?"

"Guess who'll be glued to CNN's live stream, hoping to catch a glimpse?"

"Guess who'll be in class when it happens?"

"Oh." My heart sinks. "Right."

"Don't worry, it'll be uploaded to my dad's website. Aaaaaaand my mom's back."

"Iloveyou!" I say.

"I love you, too." Josh laughs in surprise. "Thanks for the enthusiasm."

"I didn't get to say it last time."

"Ah, well. From now on"—and I hear his smile grow into a dimple-bearing grin—"let's start with it."

chapter twenty-one

When school ends, I duck into a bathroom stall. I have ten minutes before I need to be in detention. I yank out my laptop from my bag. The race is still way too early for any of the poll numbers to be in, but I quickly scroll down the senator's website. *There.* The video.

Josh enters the polling station with his parents. He's cleaned up, as in . . . he looks *clean-cut*. He's wearing a suit that fits so well it must have been tailored just for him. He smiles and waves at the cameras. His parents exit their booths. "Who did you vote for?" somebody shouts, and Josh's dad says, "Was I supposed to vote in there? I thought I was placing a to-go order for breakfast!" Hardy-har.

It cuts back to Josh. He enters a booth while his parents

look on proudly. A female reporter with large teeth shoves a microphone at Josh upon his exit. "How does it feel to vote for your father for the first time?"

"Surreal." Josh flashes the camera a startling amount of charm. "It feels great."

He's not lying. And even though I understand that this *is* a genuinely remarkable moment in his life, it's . . . it's as if I were looking at a stranger. I rewatch the segment and pause it as he answers the reporter's question. I touch his image onscreen.

If we hadn't gone to Barcelona, he'd be back in Paris in twenty-four hours.

I push the thought down and away. Because if we hadn't gone to Barcelona, we also wouldn't have Parc Güell. Or a moonlit hotel room.

When detention ends, I run straight to my bedroom. I scour the internet, but the earliest poll numbers all read the same. The race is neck and neck.

Kurt shows up, and—to my surprise—he shuts the door behind him. "*Bœuf bourguignon suivi d'un clafoutis aux poires.* For you." He sets down a plastic cafeteria tray onto my desk. "I didn't know what to do, so I took the whole thing."

His embarrassment is touching, somehow. The still-warm dinner and pear dessert both smell intoxicating. "Thank you."

He pushes back his hoodie. "Nate said I could wait up with you so long as no one else ever finds out, under penalty of beheading. But I don't think he'd actually behead us."

My breath is bottling up inside my chest.

"I'm sorry I couldn't lie for you," he says. "And I'm sorry that Josh is gone."

I tackle him with a hug. It feels like the old days, even though we spend the night combing through the news instead of doing homework. Kurt crashes after midnight, but the race is too close for me to sleep. It's still early in the States. A live feed plays softly, volume turned down. Predicted winners from all across America are announced one after another. At two in the morning, I'm given six seconds of joy when it shows a clip from the Wasserstein headquarters.

Josh is standing beside his mother and father and a few hundred red, white, and blue balloons. The camera moves, and the balloons obscure his face. The feed switches to the gubernatorial race in Florida. An hour later, my eyes are barely open when I hear the newsman with the bad toupee say, "And in the closest race of the night, New York senator Joseph Wasserstein is still fighting to hold on to his seat."

I lean in toward the screen. As they watch the tallies, Mrs. Wasserstein still looks fresh and cheerful—ever the supportive wife—although I assume a makeup artist has given her a touch-up. The senator seems a bit haggard, but he's keeping a brave face.

Josh looks exhausted and annoyed. I hope his parents don't see this footage later.

Still . . . this is *my* Josh. Not the stranger from before. A tense-looking man, perhaps the campaign manager, whispers something into his ear, and Josh stands up straighter. The man must have told him that he's on TV. The camera cuts away.

The news drones on. My burst of adrenaline fades.

I wake up to my morning alarm. Kurt is gone, and the covers have been neatly tucked around me. There's a one-word note beside my pillow: *VICTORY.*

I have severely underestimated Josh's parents. In the wake of the senator's success, I imagined—at the very least—that they'd allow their son a celebratory phone call. No such luck. I wish I could tell Josh how happy I am for his family. I wish I could tell Josh *anything.* I've never before felt this helpless or cut off.

Two days later, the biggest morning news program in New York has an exclusive with Senator Wasserstein. I find the link on his website, of course. The interview is standard political fluff, but the background. Well. It's captivating.

It's Josh's house.

The camera follows his dad from the dining room into the living room. Everything is impeccably decorated, though perhaps too orderly. Delicate china plates hang in patterns on the walls. Extravagant vases are stuffed with seasonal grasses and pheasant feathers. It's hard to imagine anyone *living* here. Mrs. Wasserstein joins him on the sofa beneath a prominently displayed, seemingly out-of-place oil painting of the Saint-Michel *métro* station—an Art Nouveau beauty that's heaped in chained bicycles and dull graffiti. A teenaged boy languishes against one of the bike racks. It's St. Clair. Josh painted this portrait of his friend last year. I saw it drying inside our school's studio.

The interviewer, a beaky woman with shiny pale lips, knowingly asks about it, and Josh's parents gush about their son's promising future. It's a jarring response. I've always assumed that the rift between Josh and his parents was caused by his desire to pursue a career in the arts, but their praise and support seems genuine.

"He gets it from his mother," the senator says, beaming at his wife.

"His appreciation for art, yes," she says. "But the talent is all his own."

The interview flashes back to the polling station footage—Josh, so handsome, so charming—and when it returns, he's joined them. My heart picks up speed. It's that odd, clean-cut look again. An inexplicable pressure mounts inside of me.

The interviewer smiles, nosy and ominous. "We've heard that after that clip aired, young ladies flooded your father's office with inquiries about you. What do you think will happen now that they know not only are you easy on the eyes, but you're also an artistic genius?"

What?

Josh laughs politely. "I'm not sure."

"Tell us." She leans toward him. "New York is dying to know. Do you have a girlfriend?"

He pauses before giving another modest laugh. "Uh, no. Not at the moment."

My ears ring. I rewind, heart reeling.

Uh, no. Not at the moment.

A dark churning rumbles in my gut. I blink. And then again. Pinprick stars obliterate my vision as they replay a clip from election night. It's the one where Josh looks miserable, but now the interviewer says he looks *nervous* because he *cares so much* about his dad, and how it'll be a *lucky lady* who lands such a *compassionate young bachelor.* "You won't be single for long," she teases, and his parents chuckle.

Rewind. *Uh, no. Not at the moment.*

You won't be single for long.

Chuckle chuckle.

I reach for my phone and actually scream as I remember that I can't call him. I do it anyway. No answer. I send a text: CALL ME.

Kurt receives a second text: *911.*

"What's the matter? What happened?" he asks, two minutes later. He's out of breath.

I gesture frantically at my laptop. "Watch that. Tell me . . . what . . . just watch it!"

When it's over, his brow furrows. "When did you guys break up?"

"We didn't!"

"So why would he say that?"

"I don't know! You tell me."

His shrug is helpless. "You're asking the wrong person."

"No, there has to be a rational reason. Tell me! Tell me before I completely lose it!"

"Stop shouting." Kurt pulls up his hoodie. "Is it possible that he broke up with you, and you didn't realize it? People are confusing. They say one thing and mean the other."

"I would definitely be aware of Josh breaking up with me."

"Maybe . . . I don't know. Maybe his dad wants to work this as a new angle for popularity. But he's already won the election, so I doubt—"

"Of course!" I throw my arms around him. "Of course it's his father's idea."

But Kurt isn't convinced. I spend the next half hour talking him through it, building my case, but by the time he leaves in fatigued irritation, even I don't believe it. What if Josh panicked because this sudden influx of interest—*Why the hell didn't I know about this sudden influx of interest?*—has him curious about other girls? And who *are* these other girls, anyway?

I type his name into a search engine, click on the most recent results, and discover him in the comments of several different websites, including the home page of that infuriating morning news program. My spirit plummets even lower. They're the typical boy-crazy, stalker-y comments that one usually finds online, but this time they're different. This time they're talking about *my boyfriend.*

At one a.m., my phone finally rings. My hands shake with anxiety and anger.

"I love you," Josh says.

I'm thrown.

"Are you there? Isla?"

"Hi." I say it cautiously.

"I thought we were starting every call with 'I love you' now."

"I—I saw the interview."

"Yeah." He sighs. "I figured. My mom told me that you texted. She said I could call you to explain. I'm using her phone."

There's hope in my heart, but my voice cracks anyway. "Why did you say that?"

"I'm sorry." His voice turns anguished. "I wanted to warn you, but I couldn't. I said I was single, because I didn't want to drag you into all of this."

"I'm the girlfriend of a senator's son. No one gives a crap about me."

"You'd be surprised," he says darkly. "I didn't think anyone gave a crap about me, either."

"So . . . it's true? Girls are really calling for you?"

"Ugh. Yeah. Sort of. It's weird. I wish they'd stop."

Something glass, maybe a bottle, shatters on the pavement outside my window. A group of students drunkenly crack up. "So why wouldn't you want to say you're taken? It's not like you had to give them my name and social security number."

"I didn't mean to hurt you." He sounds pained. "That's the last thing I want. I was trying to protect you, I was trying to keep you in the *good* part of my life."

"But I want to be in all of it. Ugly parts included."

"You sure about that? Because I have a lot of ugly parts."

"Everyone does."

"What are yours?"

"I get jealous when I think about other girls liking my boyfriend."

"I get jealous when I think about Sébastien. And all of the guys at school who still get to see you every day."

I snort. "You can stop worrying. No one is interested in me."

"Nikhil likes you."

I'm startled. "What?"

"Nikhil Devi. I overheard him talking about you to one of his friends once."

Nikhil is the younger, nerdier brother of Rashmi and Sanjita. Not that I'm in any position to judge. He's a sophomore this year. "That's weird. What'd he say?"

Josh laughs once. "Oh, so you can leave me for him?"

"Yeah."

"Nikhil likes your caboose."

"I take it back. I didn't want to know that."

He laughs again.

"I've missed your laugh. I miss *you*." I want to reach through our phones and touch his hand on the other side. "Thirteen days until I'm home. How will we survive?"

Josh sucks in his breath, and there's a long and terrible pause. "That's . . . the other thing I got permission to call you about."

Oh, no. Please. No.

"My family has been invited to Thanksgiving dinner at the White House."

The . . . what now?

"Isla?"

"The White House," I say.

"Yeah."

"As in, where the president lives? That White House?"

"Yeah."

"Ha." I choke out. "Ha!"

"It's insane. I mean, a ton of families were invited, not just us. But still."

"My *boyfriend* was invited to the *White House.*"

"Your boyfriend—who was expelled from high school—was invited to the White House."

I begin laughing for real.

"My dad used to know the president, back in the day."

I laugh harder. And I'm crying.

"Oh, Isla." It sounds like his heart is breaking through the receiver. Whenever he says my name, he takes a part of my soul. I want him to say it again. "Please tell me that you know I'd give anything not to attend this dinner."

"I guess it's hard to say no to the White House."

"Impossible."

"What about winter break?"

"New York, I swear."

I pick at a loose thread on my map quilt, a green thread that belongs to Central Park. "You're sure you won't be invited back for Christmas?"

"We're Jewish."

Shit. "I'm sorry. I know that."

"I know you do."

"I'm just upset. I feel so far away from you."

"I know." And his voice disappears into the ether. "Me too."

chapter twenty-two

Y ou look sad to be home," Maman says with her light accent. She just made a fuss over Hattie's wild, self-trimmed hair, and she's gearing up for a second fuss over me.

The cab pulls away with Kurt still inside, headed the final two blocks to his house. Dad picks up my suitcase in one hand and Hattie's in the other, and we trundle upstairs to our landing. Our house smells like pumpkin bread. Maman has decorated everything in leaves and acorns and gourds. A garland of ribbons and red berries wraps around the bannister leading upstairs, and beeswax candles glow inside every room. Maman loves the holidays. And she loves having all three of her daughters at home.

"I'm not sad," I assure her, thinking about the airport. Josh departed a mere two hours before our arrival. The timing still feels freshly cruel.

"You are. And you're never the sad one."

"When does Gen get in?"

She tuts at my obvious evasion but cheers as she answers. "Late tonight. Just in time for Thanksgiving Day." Hattie shoots past us and slams her door shut, and Maman grows mournful again. "*Oh, mon bébés*. You will not ruin your beautiful hair, *non*?"

"No, Maman," I say.

She's the only family member without red hair—though, scientifically speaking, she must carry the gene somewhere—and this has made her overly protective of ours. Her own hair is the color of coffee beans. Maman and I do share the same height and the same upturned nose. Gen is tiny like us, while Hattie takes after our dad, tall and slim with sharp features. But Dad's the only one with a scruffy, burnt-orange beard.

"A package arrived for you this morning," he says. My father is generally mellow, so the way he announces this news is peculiar. It's hesitant. Maybe even a tad hostile. "I put it in your bedroom."

My brow furrows. "What kind of package?"

"It was delivered by courier. I think it's from Joshua."

Joshua. I'm getting the sense that he does not like this *Joshua*, but my entire being perks up. "Really? I wasn't expecting anything."

"The box is heavy."

I'm already bolting upstairs.

"He is still your boyfriend, *oui?*" Maman says, and I grind to a halt. "Because we saw him on television saying that he does not have a girlfriend. I do not like this, Isla."

I frown. "He was protecting me. Josh didn't want the press to hassle me."

She shrugs, slow and full-bodied. "It sounded like he was looking for tail."

"Tail? *Oh mon Dieu.*" I can't believe she's forcing me to defend this. I haven't even been home for five minutes.

"Why didn't he deliver the box himself?" Dad asks. "He's been in this city for three whole weeks, but he can't be bothered to introduce himself to your parents? It's the least he could do after what he's put us through."

"What he's put *you* through?" I throw my hands into the air. "No, forget it. I'm not going over this with you again. And he sent a courier because he had a plane to catch. To go to the *White House.* To have dinner with the *president.* Remember?"

"It'd still be the polite thing to do," Dad says.

"Why? So you can harass him about school?"

"We do want to know what his plans are for the future, yes."

"Do you even hear yourself?"

Maman cuts back in. "We just want to meet this boy who is so important to you."

"You'll meet him next month." And I storm the rest of the way upstairs.

"Will we?" Dad calls up. *"Will we?"*

In spite of everything, I'd been looking forward to coming

home. Now I'm not so sure. My energy levels are at an all-time low. It's taken everything I have to maintain my grades— *Dartmouth*—and, even though we're okay, things still aren't back to normal with Kurt. I'm in detention so much that we hardly see each other. Josh has sneaked in a few more calls, here and there, but it's harder now because his mom is less distracted now that the election is over.

And Dad harassing me about Josh's future is particularly stressful, because the last time we talked, Josh said his mom wants him to finish the year at a private school in DC. When I suggested he take the GED instead, he replied, "Why would I waste my time when they're just gonna put me in another stupid school anyway?"

I changed the subject after that.

My bedroom smells uninhabited and clean, that vacant scent it carries whenever I come home from abroad. A large box is in the center of my floor. I don't recognize the return address, and there's no name, but it's unquestionably Josh's exquisite handwriting. My pulse quickens. I slice through the tape with a pair of scissors, peel back the flaps, and cry out in a grateful sort of agony. *This* air smells like *him*.

On the top is a dark blue T-shirt, one of his favorites. He wore it on the first day of school this year. I press my nose against its cotton. *Citrus, ink, him.* My knees weaken. I hug it to my chest as I examine the contents below. The rest of my body weakens.

Boarding School Boy, bound in string.

There's a note slipped underneath the manuscript's binding.

I LOVE YOU. I love that he starts with this even in his letter. *I'M SORRY THAT I CAN'T BE WITH YOU IN PERSON, BUT I HOPE YOU'LL ACCEPT THIS PATHETIC SUBSTITUTE. I'VE SPENT ALL WEEK SCANNING AND PRINTING THE PAGES. I'VE NEVER SHOWN THE WHOLE THING TO ANYONE BEFORE. I'M NOT DONE, BUT HERE'S WHAT I HAVE SO FAR. I HOPE YOU STILL LIKE ME AFTER YOU'VE SEEN THE UGLY PARTS. YOURS, J.*

My eyes well with tears of happiness. I want to climb into bed with it this instant, but I have to wait. I want privacy. I don't want to be interrupted mid-read. I place Josh's shirt beside my pillow, but I push the box into my closet. My parents aren't the snooping type, but anything left out in the open is considered fair game.

I spend the rest of the day with them. When they inquire about the box, I give them a vague "Oh, you know. It was a care package. A letter, a shirt." But as soon as dinner is over, I claim jet lag and retire. I drag out the box to the side of my bed, switch on a lamp, and crawl beneath the covers. I'd wear the T-shirt, but I don't want to lose his scent. I snuggle with it instead. And then I untie the string and remove the first page.

The book is divided, as it was in his dorm room, into four sections beginning with FRESHMAN. Josh has drawn himself as skinny and naive, slack-jawed, as he takes in his new surroundings. He finds Paris equal parts intimidating and awe inspiring, but little time passes before he falls into homesickness. It's not that he misses his actual home—not the flights between cities, the endless campaigning, the neglectful parents. He misses the life that he glimpsed when he was younger. The cabin and the pine trees. A family in one place. He recognizes almost immediately that instead of trading in two lives for one, he now has three. And it's too late.

A single-panel page: Him in the corner, small and crouched, looking up at home, while the rest of the page—where home is supposed to be—is a blank space. He misses somewhere that doesn't exist. And he knows that Paris will not fill the void.

He tries to fill it by throwing himself into his art. He befriends St. Clair in their studio art class. St. Clair is a year older, but he's attracted to Josh's natural talent while Josh is attracted to St. Clair's natural charisma. At night, Josh lies awake in bed, rehashing things his new friend has said or done, hoping to learn from him. Emulate him. The pages are sad and sweet and full of humiliating truths.

St. Clair has a bushy-haired friend named Meredith, and Josh befriends her, too, and the three of them are uncannily reminiscent of Harry, Ron, and Hermione. St. Clair is the leader, Josh is the clown, and Meredith is the brainiac. But in this version, Hermione is clearly in love with Harry.

The scenes with his friends are fun. They feel like characters, not like the real people that I used to see around school. Though they do trigger that accompanying, always-underlying twinge of hurt. I'll never know this part of his life. But the scenes where Josh is alone, he becomes *Josh* again, and everything is heightened. I pore over these panels with an intensity that makes me feel uncomfortable, maybe guilty, but the harder the scenes are to read, the faster I turn the pages. Josh thinks about girls *constantly.* He sees a beautiful, too-tall French girl on the street, and I'm horrified to flip the page and find him masturbating back in his room to the thought of her. Over the summer, he gets his first kiss with an older girl who works at his favorite comics shop in Manhattan, but the next time he goes to see her, she brushes him off in embarrassment.

It took guts to draw these things.

It's a different kind of excruciating to read about them.

SOPHOMORE begins. St. Clair starts dating a girl named Ellie. She's two years older than Josh, and he struggles with feeling cool enough to hang out with them. He and Meredith swap unkind words about Ellie—each out of a different type of jealousy—but his eventual coming to terms with Ellie means getting to know *her* best friend.

Rashmi Devi.

She's pretty and smart and sarcastic. And I hate her. She flirts with Josh one day in their art class—*of course* she can draw, when I can't—and he becomes consumed by thoughts of her. Page after page of Rashmi shining like a gorgeous Hindu goddess. They go on forever. He woos her pathetically, desperately, until she agrees to go on a date with him. And then I'm forced to relive the painful moments of *my* past as they engage in on-the-page PDA.

It gets worse. Josh tells her that he loves her. She says it back. He touches her. She touches him back. And then they're losing their virginity on the floor of her bedroom beside her pet rabbit, Isis.

A rabbit.

Josh literally lost his virginity in front of a metaphor for sex.

There's another single-panel page, and this time Rashmi has been drawn naked like the ancient Egyptian goddess Isis, who—it turns out—is the goddess of *fertility,* and she's holding her pet rabbit, and she's surrounded by more rabbits, and *enough with the stupid rabbits and fertility and sex already.*

Ohmygod. I *hate* rabbits.

And I feel ill and furious, but there's no way I'm stopping now. It's masochism. There's a weird, out-of-place flashback to Josh getting his tattoo. It doesn't make sense. But it's probably because he was so eager to draw more naked pictures of his girlfriend that he figured the story of his own body modification could wait. Or whatever. I grab the next stack of pages from the box and realize, at some point, that I've pushed his T-shirt onto my floor. I don't pick it up.

Finally, Josh and Rashmi are fighting. And it's nasty. She's pissed because he's skipping school, and he lashes back at her in full force. I relish his anger. And I feel vindicated because *I* never yelled at him for skipping class to work on this book. Though maybe I would've if I'd known what was in here. But then the school year ends, and he flies out to join her family at their vacation home in Delhi.

He once told me that he'd spent "some time" with her family one summer, but . . . an entire month? In India? No wonder he knew so much about Sanjita. Somehow, the idea of Josh spending an entire month with the Devi family hurts almost as much as the rabbit.

JUNIOR begins without any mention of Josh's time in New York. His parents were everywhere in the beginning, but they've almost entirely disappeared. It's a strange omission.

School kicks off, and St. Clair moons over Ellie's absence, even though she's attending a college nearby. Anna shows up. I remember watching her in the cafeteria that first week of school, seething with jealousy because she made the leap to their table so effortlessly. I wanted her luck. I wanted her confidence.

And then, suddenly, Josh is alone.

St. Clair gets a crush on Anna. He's torn between her and Ellie, and he spends so much time running between them that he hardly has time left for Josh. And the more time that Josh spends alone, the more he realizes how alone he actually is. All of his friends will be gone the next year. Josh grows increasingly antagonistic toward school, which makes Rashmi increasingly antagonistic toward him, which makes him increasingly antagonistic toward her. And she's upset because Ellie dropped her as a friend, and Meredith is upset because now St. Clair likes *two* girls who aren't her, and Anna is upset because St. Clair is leading her on, and *then* St. Clair's mom gets *cancer*.

It's a freaking soap opera.

As the drama between his friends grows, Josh pulls away and into himself. His illustrations become darker. The slack-jawed freshman is long gone, the oversexed sophomore has disappeared, and now he's a sullen junior. His parents briefly, randomly, appear to hassle him about the election. He wants to break up with Rashmi, but he's too depressed to find the energy.

He stops drawing and skips class to sleep. The head of school—having called him into her office for the hundredth time—tells him, "I think you're passively trying to get me to kick you out. So I'm not going to."

I've never thought about their actual interactions. I'm shocked as the head pulls out his records and informs him that he had the highest pre-acceptance test scores that she'd seen in years. He's the brightest student in our class.

Josh is the brightest student. Not me.

I'm ashamed to admit that this hurts. It definitely hurts. And yet . . . I've always known it to be true. I've always known that he's been putting on an act. That he can see through the bullshit, and he's not willing to participate in it. It's one of the reasons I was attracted to him in the first place.

"For a certain type of person, high school will always be brutal," the head says. "The best advice that I can give you is to figure out what comes next, and work toward that."

The following scene shows him in detention. My skin flushes when I see him hunched over in the back corner of the classroom beside the window overlooking the courtyard with the pigeons.

I *have* been sitting at his desk. I knew it. Somehow, I knew it.

Josh throws himself back into his work. He wants to lose himself in it . . . and maybe find himself in return. But when St. Clair breaks up with Ellie, St. Clair's newfound joy with Anna only further cements Josh in solitary misery. And by the time Josh and Rashmi break up, they both know it's coming, and they're both ready. They're exhausted. Too tired to keep fighting. He begins traveling to other countries every weekend—in secret and alone—separating himself from his friends before they can do it to him.

And then it's summer. *Our* summer.

My heart is hammering as I grab the last stack from the box. On the first page, he's alone inside Kismet. And then I'm on the second, shouting his name and startling him out of a waking slumber. There's a dreamlike tone here. It mirrors both how I acted and how he reacted. I cringe at everything I say, but the way he draws me is like a beacon of light.

There's a flashback to our freshman year, and his brushstrokes becomes softer. He sees me reading Joann Sfar. He tries to talk to me, but he's a bumbling idiot. And then *I'm* the one who gives him a crazy look.

The story returns to Kismet. Josh realizes that I'm flirting with him, which he finds puzzling and hilarious. But also pleasing. He walks me to my door and then hurries home to draw me again—the garden-rose-halo illustration—before falling asleep. The next night, he returns to the café and discovers me with Kurt. He curses, drags himself home, and then he's back in DC, where he spends a miserable summer dreading his senior year.

The last few pages are loose, rough sketches of his first day of school. Hard to follow. His interactions with me are flattering, but the messy panels make it feel less concrete. Like the ideas inside of them are still subject to change.

And then . . . I'm out of pages. The box is empty.

chapter twenty-three

I'm filled with too many strong emotions at once. Jealousy. Sadness. Anger. There's certainly an acknowledgment, though it's unreasonably begrudging, of the fearlessness it took for him to create this, but the negative thoughts keep shoving their way to the top. They sour the positive. I thought I knew my boyfriend, but it turns out that I had only an out-of-focus snapshot. Now I have the full picture.

Josh had . . . this entire *life* before me.

How can something so obvious be so shocking?

And Rashmi. I knew she'd be in there, but how could I know *all* of her would be in there? I didn't want to see her. With Josh. Like that. It's not fair that I've seen it, because I'll never be able to un-see it.

I kick at my sheets. I'm thinking about rabbits. I'm thinking about too-tall French girls. I'm thinking about Josh thumbing his nose at an education that I've chosen to take seriously. It's never bothered me before. Why is it bothering me now? I toss and turn for hours until I'm jolted awake—out of a restless sleep I didn't even know I'd succumbed to—by a flying leap. An oddly fuzzy sister is bouncing up and down on my bed.

"Wake up!" Gen bounces the bed harder. "Hattie and I are already dressed and coffee'd. The balloons aren't gonna make fun of themselves."

Great. Because this is exactly what today needs. A parade.

Our house is on the wrong side of Broadway to see or hear the Macy's Thanksgiving Day Parade, but it only takes a few minutes to walk someplace where we can witness the grotesque spectacle firsthand. My sisters and I have a tradition of poking around the parade's outskirts in the early hours of daylight.

My head is throbbing from crying all night long. "I don't feel well."

"You have to get up so Maman will stop bugging me about my hair."

Her orange-red fuzz is about two inches long. It sticks out in a thick sphere around her head. "You look like a corgi," I say. "Are you growing it back out?" But Gen is rifling through the papers on my bed. I lunge between her and the manuscript.

"Did Josh draw this?"

I snatch at the paper that's still in her hands. "Give it!"

"Jeez, calm down. I just wanna see." She extends her arm,

holding it as far away from me as she can. "Wow. What *is* all of this?"

"Please." I'm on the verge of tears.

Gen looks at me, startled. She hands it back slowly. "Sorry."

"It's just . . . it's private. Don't tell Hattie, okay?"

"Okay."

"Seriously. You know how she is."

"Yes, darling. I *seriously* won't tell her about your *seriously* weird reaction to something I *seriously* don't understand."

I clutch my pillow against my chest. She stares at me for a long time. Finally, she stands and heads for my door. "Five minutes."

"I'm not going. I don't feel good."

"It's not optional."

When Gen wants something, it's impossible to stop her. I know better than to try. I place the manuscript back into the box. I'm careful not to crease the pages—any more than they're already creased—but I don't bother putting them in order. I shove the box back into my closet, throw on some clothes, and meet my sisters at the door.

Hattie frowns. "What's up with you?"

"Leave her alone," Gen says.

"Your hat clashes with your gloves," Hattie says to me. "And they look even worse with that coat. Won't you, like, *die* or something if you don't look perfect?"

I pull down the woolen hat farther over my eyes. Gen links her arm through mine and marches me outside before I can change my mind. Or my outfit. Hattie trudges behind us.

The feeling in New York in the autumn is what you'd

expect elsewhere in the spring. Renewal. Locals are happy to be outside again. The subways have cooled, the humid stench of summer has passed. Celebrations and festivals are everywhere. The air is crisp, and its accompanying scarves and boots are a comforting return. I try to appreciate my surroundings. I search for yellow or orange or golden leaves, my own favorite aspect of the season, but the branches are already bare. I'm too late. Everything is dead.

Gen chatters away about her life in Massachusetts while Hattie interjects with colorful commentary. I don't really pay attention. We cross Columbus, and the streets grow crowded with families and dancers and cheerleaders and police officers. Several marching bands are warming up—there's a hum of brass, staccato drills on snare drums, and airy scales on woodwinds. The enormous Horton the Elephant balloon peeks out from behind a building, a street ahead, and its trunk is holding a bright pink flower.

"Cheer up," Gen says to me. "I've signed you up to walk the route with them this year." She points at a group of dancers in blue cowboy chaps and goofy fringed vests.

At least a dozen horrifying clowns in tattered rainbow jumpsuits pop into the drugstore beside us. "Over there," I say. "They're looking for you, Gen. They need you."

"Have you seen those tap-dancing Christmas trees? They asked if you'd swing back around and have a second go with them. You won't be too tired, right? I mean, I already paid for your tinsel pants."

"I'm glad you guys didn't sign me up for anything," Hattie

says. "Because it's really awesome doing nothing."

I shoot her an annoyed look. When Gen sees that I'm still not willing to fulfill my usual role as peacekeeper, she steps in. I sink back into myself. Back into the manuscript. I can't erase this image from my mind: Rashmi, covered in rabbits. The Kermit balloon floats out from behind another building, and I think about rabbits. We get cold and walk home, and I think about rabbits. Maman calls us into the kitchen, and I help her make crescent rolls. Rabbits. I help her set the table. Rabbits. The turkey is carved, the drinks are poured, the toast is made. Rabbits, rabbits, rabbits. The plates are cleared, the mashed potato and gravy remains are scraped into the trash can. My boyfriend loses his virginity, and, oh, who's that looking on?

It's a rabbit.

My family parks around the television for a feel-good movie. I'm still thinking about rabbits an hour later, when I hear the faint sound of my phone ringing inside my bedroom. My heart catapults into my throat. I sprint upstairs and barely catch it in time.

"I love you," Josh says. "Hold on." There's laughter and loud voices, and then the sucking sound of a sliding door being shut. "Okay, I'm on a patio. Or a private balcony. Or something. Actually, I don't know where the hell I am."

"But you're at the White House?"

"Yeah."

Rabbit.

"I know," he says, when I don't say anything. "It's weird. I'm sorry."

"No, it's not that." *Rabbit rabbit.* "I'm just tired. It's been a long day."

"My mom said I could call you. I'm using her phone again."

"So, um. How is it?"

"Did you get my package?" he asks over my question. I can practically hear his sweat dripping into the receiver.

"I did. I read it last night. It was great."

There's a long, dead pause. "Wow." His voice is as dull as my delivery. "That didn't sound convincing even to you, did it?"

"No. I just——" And then I burst into tears, hating myself.

"What's the matter?" He turns panicked. "What is it? Which part?"

"No. It's good." I can't stop crying.

"Please," he begs. "Don't. Listen, I know I was a dick to Rashmi, especially when we fought, but I swear that won't happen with us. It's so different with you. I would never be like that with you." It's the fastest I've ever heard him speak. "I was younger, and I was so much stupider——"

"It wasn't the fighting. It was . . ." My tears explode into gut-wrenching sobs. "*The rabbits.*"

"Rabbits?" But his confusion is only momentary. "Oh. *Oh.*"

"Why would you draw those things? Why would you show them to me?"

"I——I didn't think it would be that big of a deal——"

"You didn't think it would be a big deal for me to see your ex-girlfriend *naked*? To learn the explicit details of you guys losing your virginity together?"

"I don't know." He's reached a full panic now. "I wrote

about it because it happened. And I shared it with you, because I wanted to be honest with you. I wanted to show you everything. *The ugly parts, too,* remember?"

"Well. Maybe not everything belongs in a book."

"I'm sorry. Ohmygod. I'm so sorry, Isla."

I don't say anything. It's unfair, but I'm hurt. I want him to hurt, too.

"Please don't hang up. What about the end, the part with you? How was that?"

"Yeah, those eight whole pages were fine." I regret the words the moment they leave my mouth. I've never said anything more selfish in my life. It's not like he's even had time to draw us yet. It takes forever to do the kind of work he does. He shared something personal with me, and I threw it in his face.

His silence is terrible.

"I shouldn't have said that. I'm sorry." Tears and snot are rolling down my face. "Your book is great, really."

Josh snorts, but now he's crying. My guilt quadruples.

"It *is.* It just caught me off guard. I *know* what you draw. I should've known what would be in there. We shouldn't even be talking about this, I should be telling you about all of the parts that I loved—"

"And now you're apologizing to me, and that's insane."

"It's not!" I clutch my phone harder. "I'm sorry. I'm so sorry."

There's no reply.

"Hello? Josh? *Hello?*"

"My mom is calling me. Shit. They're about to serve dessert or something."

"No!"

"Do you still love me?" His panic rises again. "You didn't say it when you answered."

I pull out a handful of tissues from a box. "Of course I do!"

"I can't believe I have to hang up right now."

"Don't go. I love you."

"I'll call you back as soon as I can." And the line goes dead.

Like the sucker I am, I stay beside my phone all night hoping that *soon* means "soon." It doesn't. How could I have lashed out at him like that? He trusted me. He bared his soul, and I held it against him. I hate this. I hate that I hurt him. And I hate that I'm still upset about his work, and I *really* hate that I'm gonna have to pretend like I'm not.

I keep the box in my closet, hoping for an out-of-sight, out-of-mind experience, but it's impossible. It's the *only* thing on my mind. By Saturday night, I still haven't heard from him. Fear of my wrongdoing reaches a critical peak. I have to do something. I add a small peace offering to the box and carry it to the Wasserstein residence, using the return address already on the package. The weight of the box is heavy, burdensome. But it still doesn't take me long to get there.

Their brownstone looks similar to the others on the street—beautiful, old, and well kept. They have miniature evergreens and ivy in the window boxes, an American flag hanging from the second story, an autumn wreath on the door, and a silver filigree mezuzah affixed to the doorframe. The curtains are drawn.

I knock, hoping for an answer from the Secret Service or whatever organization it is that watches over this nation's more famous senators. No one answers. I knock again, and a stocky man with broad shoulders, stylish gray hair, and a security earpiece opens the door. "May I help you?" His voice is as solid and sturdy as his appearance.

"Isla Martin." My own voice trembles. "I'm Josh's girlfriend. From France? I know he won't be home until tomorrow, but that's when I'm leaving, so I was hoping you could pass this along to him."

"I know who you are."

"You *do*?"

The tough guy act is dropped for a moment. He smiles, and it's surprisingly warm. "I'm paid to know that."

"Oh." My cheeks turn pink. "Well, would you please give this to him?"

He takes the package from me. "Sure. But I'll have to scan it for explosives first. As long as it passes, he can have it upon his return."

I laugh.

"That was a serious statement. All parcels are checked."

My cheeks deepen into red. "Of course. Thank you, sir." And I scuttle away.

The next night, when I check my phone in Paris, I have a text from an unknown Manhattan number. He doesn't mention the return of the manuscript—nor the fact that I left its pages wildly out of order—but he does say this: I can't believe how much I missed your scent. Merci for the scarf, my sweet rose.

chapter twenty-four

The pallor of winter further overcasts the already gray city. Olympic rings, bright and colorful, provide the only visual relief. They're plastered on every advertising surface, including the sides of entire buildings. This February, the Winter Olympics will be in the Rhône-Alpes region of southeastern France, though, by the adverts, you'd never know they weren't in Paris proper. The French athletes are the stars of the posters, naturally, but a few of the biggest names from other countries have also made the cut.

Kurt and I exit the Denfert-Rochereau *métro* station and pass a larger-than-life poster of a fierce-looking American figure skater named Calliope Bell.

"Who do you root for?" I ask. "The Americans or the French?"

The Olympics have always been a source of mixed feelings

for me. I know I'm supposed to feel a sense of national pride, but which nation? I feel loyalty toward both.

Kurt glances at the poster. "I root for the best athlete in each event. They don't have to be American or French."

"So . . . you root for the winner. Isn't that sort of cheating?"

"No. I root for the person who appears to be working the hardest."

It's a strange answer, but it's still a good one. It gives me something to think about. We enter a small, nondescript, dark-green building. It's empty of tourists today. We pay a guard, pass by another guard, and tromp down a spiral staircase until we reach a long, low tunnel. Water drips overhead. We splash through shallow puddles. It's cool down here in the catacombs, but not cold, because there's no wind.

Kurt points toward a tunnel that's been gated off from the public. "Have I told you there are over a hundred and eighty miles of abandoned tunnels in Paris?"

Yes. He *has* told me. He's been talking about the tunnels nonstop since our return to school. In the last month, he's gone from intrigued to full-blown obsessed. While I sat in detention, he read everything about them—the *métro* tunnels, limestone quarries, utility lines, sewer systems, and crypts—which together make one of the most extensive underground networks in the world.

He wants to map it, of course.

It's odd how the two most important people in my life are both interested in maps. Kurt in the most literal sense. But Josh, too. By chronicling the major events in his life, Josh is also drawing a map. I wonder how long I'll be a part of it. Where and when does my story fall away from his?

"Maps of the tunnels exist," Kurt continues, "but none of them are complete. And they're often purposefully misleading to keep people away."

Exploring them is illegal, and as a bona fide rule-follower, this is Kurt's greatest frustration. But that hasn't stopped others from doing it. The tunnels attract all types, known collectively as cataphiles—historians, graffiti artists, ravers, spelunkers, musicians, treasure hunters. Some have gone into the tunnels to restore priceless art. One group ran an underground cinema. The French resistance hid down here during the Nazi occupation, and then the Nazis used the exact same tunnels to flee.

It won't be long before Kurt's obsession overpowers his need to follow the rules. But, for now, he's been visiting and revisiting the legal part—les Catacombes. More than six million bodies were carted down here in the late 1700s, and the endless walls of their stacked bones are available for viewing at a small fee. Some of the bones are arranged into simple shapes like crosses or hearts. Some are arranged by size or type. But most of them were thrown in at random for practicality's sake.

As a child, I found the catacombs frightening. As I got older, they grew fascinating. Now they're almost tranquil. But maybe all of these skulls are just reminding me of a certain someone's tattoo. I sit on a folding chair that's meant for a guard while Kurt surreptitiously pokes around.

It feels fitting to be here. Quiet yet undeniably gloomy,

much like my state of mind. Since Thanksgiving, I've finished detention, toiled over homework assignments, and crammed for exams. I haven't been reading for fun. Schoolwork is better at distracting me from the enforced silence between Josh and myself.

How did my parents live before texting? Before the internet? I'm used to *knowing* things and all of this *unknowing* is driving me mad. We send each other handwritten letters, but it takes so long for the mail to arrive that he's often in the wrong city by the time my correspondence reaches him. His family has been traveling nonstop between New York and DC.

I *think* he's in DC right now. At least, that's where I mailed his Atheist Hanukkah present, a box of his favorite pre-packaged French foods. If only I could talk to him, I know I'd feel better. I carry his letters in my purse, I use his stein as my everyday drinking glass, and I've hung up his drawings beside my bed— the one of my necklace from the first week of school as well as the Sagrada Família's dove-covered tree, which he gave me after he was expelled. But he still feels so far away.

And the more time we spend apart, the more I can't shake the ending of *Boarding School Boy*. Our time together was only eight rough pages. The head of school thinks I was a distraction for Josh, which means she thinks that I take our relationship more seriously than he does. But that's not true. He did take it seriously.

Does he still?

He hasn't given me any reason to doubt him, but the more

time we spend apart, the more clearly I see that our relationship was founded on unstable ground. His loneliness. How long will it take before he realizes that having me as a girlfriend was easier than being alone? I was convenient. I *was* a distraction.

Josh is a romantic. He likes being in love, and he craves love to fill the void left by his absentee parents. Maybe our relationship didn't happen quickly because we're perfect for each other, but because we each got swept away by it—him because of this insatiable *need,* me because of my preexisting crush. Did those three years of longing cloud my perception of reality? How well do I really know him? Since I've last seen him in person, I've been faced with several incarnations that I didn't even know existed.

And he still hasn't made a decision about finishing high school. What if Dartmouth accepts me, and I move to New England, and he's not there? What am I supposed to do without him? I still don't have a plan for myself, nothing that doesn't involve him. But his plans are no longer concrete. They're as fragile as a wall of bones.

I get through midterms on the hope that I'm only plagued by these doubts because I've been away from him for so long. Seeing him again will fix this. The night before my last day of class, I'm surprised by a call from Mrs. Wasserstein's phone.

I answer, praying that it's actually Josh. It is. But a follow-up worry kicks in, and I'm instantly on the verge of hysteria. "You're staying in DC for winter break."

Josh laughs. "No, I'm calling with happy news. For once. It's an invitation to a Christmas party at the Met. Black tie. Movers and shakers. It'll probably be atrocious, but my parents invited you, so that's a good sign."

It *is* a good sign.

"And you'll get to wear a fancy dress, and I'll get to show you off. As my *girlfriend*," he says pointedly. "So long as you still want this world to know you exist?"

"Yes! Yes, please."

He laughs again. "Then it's a date."

When his mother reclaims her phone, I leave my room for a stretch down the hall. My heart is lighter than it's been in weeks. Josh was laughing. We're going on a public date. His parents want to spend time with me.

I stop in my tracks. *His parents want to spend time with me.*

No. Stay positive. This is a good sign, really. I check my mailbox. There are two envelopes stuffed into the back, one fat and one skinny. I pull them out, giddy with renewed cheer, until I realize that neither envelope is from Josh.

One is from la Sorbonne, and the other is from Columbia.

One is an acceptance letter, and the other is a rejection.

chapter twenty-five

I can't decide which is better, your hair or your dress." Maman sighs. "They are *perfect* together."

My wavy locks have been swept to one side and fixed, cascading over my shoulder, and my dress—which we spent all of yesterday frantically shopping for—is a dark shade of emerald green. For once, my pale skin is glowing thanks to a healthy dusting of shimmery powder and my natural flush at being reunited with my boyfriend. He flew in from DC only three hours ago. We haven't seen each other yet.

Gen grins at us from my doorway. "It looks like prom night in here."

"*Prom Night,* the slasher film," Hattie says.

Much to the dismay of girls like Sanjita and Emily, the

School of America in Paris doesn't have any formal dances. I've never minded, but—now that I'm dressed up—I'm *almost* on their side. I twirl in a complete circle. "I feel like Cinderella."

"Cinderella was blond," Hattie says. "Redheads are never the princess."

"Bullshit," Gen says, and Maman tut-tuts her. "Amy Adams. *Enchanted.*"

"Hello, Ariel?" I say. "She was a princess, too."

"She was a fish," Hattie says.

"Isla!" Dad's voice booms from downstairs. "Your date is here!"

Is it possible to be both clammy *and* feverish? I don't know what's more nerve-wracking: seeing Josh for the first time in two months, introducing him to my parents, or hanging out with *his* parents. Except, no. It's definitely the last one. The thought of speaking to his mother again has kept me from being able to eat all day. At least my parents are glad—and relieved—to finally be meeting Josh. They're also impressed that he's taking me to such a prestigious party.

Maman acknowledges my worried expression with an encouraging smile. "Prince Charming awaits."

"I wonder if he's as skinny and weird as I remember," Gen says.

"Hey," I say.

I wait for Hattie to cattily agree with Gen, but she's silent. She hasn't spoken a single word on the subject of Josh since Halloween. Maman shoos them both downstairs. My stomach is in knots. I can't decide which of his parents scares me more.

"There's nothing to be afraid of," Maman says, reading my

mind. "His father will love you. His mother will learn to love you. You're intelligent, charming, and kind."

"Of course *you* think that."

"I would never describe your younger sister as charming."

That gets me to crack a smile.

"Come on. Don't you want to see what your boyfriend looks like in a tux?" Maman nudges me before whisking away. She calls out from the top of the stairs, "Joshua, *mon cher.* Lovely to finally meet you."

"Great to meet you, too." There's a smile—that professional, political smile—in his voice. "It's hard for me to believe, but your home looks even better than your windows at Bergdorf Goodman. I saw them last week. They're extraordinary."

She laughs. "Don't *you* know exactly what to say."

My legs turn gelatinous. Until this moment, I honestly don't know if I believed that I'd see him tonight. Excitement overtakes my nerves. I grab the jeweled clutch borrowed from Maman, dash from my room, and promptly freeze at the top of the stairs. Josh looks *immaculate.* His tuxedo is not a rental. He's saying something to my dad and wearing his trustworthy, son-of-a-senator face. And then he follows my father's upturned gaze, and absolutely everything about him changes as he stops talking mid-sentence.

Josh *weakens.*

There's a lump in my throat. It looks as if he's so grateful to see me that he's in physical pain. The feeling is reciprocated. The house vanishes, the voices disappear, and the air holds its own breath. Our eyes remain locked as I descend. Closer. Closer. Our hands outstretch, our fingers are about to touch—

"Green and red." My dad gestures from my dress to my hair. "You look just like Mrs. Claus!"

The needle scratches across the record. Everyone turns and stares.

He blushes. "I meant Christmas. She looks like Christmas."

"You can't tell a girl that she looks like a *holiday*," Gen says.

"He was right the first time," Hattie says. She's standing on the periphery, as far away from Josh as possible. "You look like an old lady."

"Isla." Josh's voice catches on my name. "You look beautiful."

Because I see it in his eyes, I feel it in my heart. He takes my hand. His skin touches mine, and he's *real* again. And then we lose restraint, and he sweeps me into an embrace and kisses my cheek. And then again. I hug him. He squeezes me too hard in return, but it's wonderful and perfect and sublime.

Dad examines Josh with a renewed distrust. "When will you be home?" he asks me.

"I don't know," I say honestly.

"The gala is usually over by midnight, so she'll be home no later than that," Josh says. "Would you like to speak with Brian? He's our driver-slash-security tonight."

My dad brightens at the mention of security. He peeks through our curtains and then waves at someone down on the street. Brian, I assume. "That's okay." He scratches his thick beard, worries somewhat assuaged. "Midnight it is."

I make a move for the front door. "Don't want to be late."

"Wait!" Gen holds up her phone. "Just one picture."

"Two," Maman says, reaching for her own.

I groan with embarrassment, but Gen cuts me off. "Oh, come on. It's not every day that my little sis gets all dolled up."

"What do you mean? Isla wears a stupid dress every stupid day," Hattie says.

"Manhattan. Darling. Shut your mouth," Maman says.

A dozen pictures later, Josh and I are out the door and in the hall. As soon as we turn the corner—away from the gaze of the keyhole—I throw my arms around his neck. He leans into me but quickly pulls back. "Your lipstick."

"I don't care."

Josh pushes me against the wall. We kiss with everything we have, tasting each other, aching for each other. His lips are cracked with winter. He's brushed his teeth recently, and his mouth is sharp and clean. His hands slide across my back and down my hips. Our kissing grows more intense, frenzied from longing. A tremor runs through my body into his, and he bursts apart from me, gasping for breath.

"Your parents," he says. "They'll be watching from the window. Waiting for us to appear."

We stumble downstairs, laughing and hurrying. He wipes off the lipstick from his mouth, I wipe it off the skin *around* my mouth, and then we stroll out of the building as if we've been deep in conversation. I'm sure we look guilty as hell. I glance up to the window, between the bare limbs of the climbing rose, and Maman and Gen wave down happily. Dad gives a brisk nod. Hattie isn't there.

A solid-looking man with stylish gray hair and a security earpiece opens the backseat door of a black town car. It's the same man who took the package from me at Josh's house over Thanksgiving. "Good evening, *mademoiselle*."

"Oh! *You're* Brian."

He gives me a wide grin. "It's nice to see you again. You look enchanting. Easy to see why our boy here talks of little else."

I glance at Josh, pleased, and he shrugs in a "what did you expect?" way.

We climb into the car, but as Brian moves toward the driver's side, Josh's smile drops. "This isn't my usual mode of transportation, you know."

"I *don't* know," I tease. "Seems like the two of you spend a lot of time together."

"Well, yeah, but usually at home. Or my dad's office. I don't want you to think that I'm always . . . chauffeured around like this. I take the subway."

I soften. "It's okay. I wasn't judging you."

"I know, I just—"

The driver's side door opens, and Brian slides in with a surprising amount of elegance and pizzazz. He turns out to be a great storyteller, which is helpful, because it keeps me from wishing that this posh car were even more posh—say, a limousine with a partition for privacy—because all I want to do is re-jump my boyfriend. Instead, I touch up my makeup. I don't want to arrive looking like a disheveled floozy. Even though that's probably what his mother thinks about me anyway.

Brian wasn't lying. He knows enough about me to ask if I've heard back from Dartmouth. He winks at Josh in the rearview mirror, but Josh doesn't notice. His eyes are only on me. I tell Brian the truth—I'm waiting to hear back from them. I still haven't told Josh that I've heard from the other two schools. I still haven't told him that, so far, the only school that wants me is in France.

The Metropolitan Museum of Art is one of the most European-looking structures in Manhattan. As Josh leads me toward the entrance, it feels as if we've time-traveled back to October. Back to Paris. The white facade, the gargantuan columns, the long steps. If only we were headed toward a date at the Musée d'Orsay and not this meet-the-parents extravaganza. If Josh's mom is that intimidating, what will his *dad* be like?

Josh catches my expression and squeezes my arm. "You'll do great."

"Your parents hate me," I say.

"They don't hate you. They hate me."

"Let's go back to my place and make out in the hallway."

He grins down at me. "This place has *a lot* of hallways."

I've been here many times before, but the museum's Great Hall is still impressive. The domes and arches of its grand entryway—so reminiscent of the Panthéon near our dorm—

are decked with gold ribbons, swags of evergreens, and giant ornaments and baubles. The echoing hall is filled with a buzzing stream of men and women in black tie. I'm glad Maman helped me dress for the occasion. At least I have confidence *there*.

Josh hands our tickets to an elderly woman in pearls and a black spangled top, and then we follow the crowd toward the party in the Medieval Sculpture Hall. He leads me in a gentlemanly manner, adultlike and formal. The surrounding couples move in a similar fashion. They look as if this stilted sort of behavior is routine, but it's a first for us. I want to walk against him, wrapped *into* him, arms and hands entangled in one mess of limbs. This careful entrance only heightens my self-consciousness.

He guides me like this toward the distant sound of a string quartet—aside the main staircase, through a narrow room of Byzantine artifacts, through another room with a masterfully marble-carved altar canopy, and straight into the bustling Sculpture Hall. The room is larger and taller, though still not as big as I'd remembered. Banners of heraldry in mixed patterns of red, blue, yellow, and white hang down on each side. Below them, the walls are covered in tapestries of stags and ladies in medieval garb. And in the center of the room—the clear star of the collection—is a massive iron gate. From previous visits, I know it's a choir screen from a cathedral in Spain.

Centered before the screen is an equally massive blue spruce surrounded by hundreds of crèche figures from the eighteenth century. The tree itself is covered in angels and cherubs and lights that look like candles. It's dramatic, to be sure, but it's also . . . stiff.

"Merry Agnostic Christmas," Josh says. "Welcome to the most Jewish Christmas party in America."

I smile.

"There." He smiles back. "More of that."

We scan between the alabaster sculptures for his parents. Best to get this over with. We find them along the edge of the room beside a rough-looking statue of a clown. When we get closer, I realize that the statue's pointy red hat is a *pope* hat. It doesn't matter that I didn't say any of this out loud. I still feel stupid.

Josh's parents have their backs to us. They're holding glasses of white wine and conversing with a short man in perfectly round spectacles. *"Judge Lederman,"* Josh whispers in my ear. *"New York Supreme Court."*

Yeah. Sure. No big deal.

"Joshua." The judge smiles and waves us over.

I try to act like it's normal for a state supreme court judge to know my boyfriend on a first-name basis. Josh's parents turn around. Their initial reaction is happiness, but it's quickly masked by a demeanor better described as *professionally pleased.* With a layer of curiosity. And perhaps another layer of mistrust.

Josh guides me forward by the small of my back. I imagine that I look like a mouse, weak and easy to discard from the premises. "Judge Lederman," Josh says. "It's good to see you." How bizarre to hear his interview voice being spoken live from his actual mouth. "This is my girlfriend, Isla Martin."

The judge shakes my hand. "A pretty little thing you are."

Gross. I smile. "It's nice to meet you, sir."

"Mom, you remember Isla," Josh continues as if our last encounter wasn't a shame-filled agonyfest. "Dad, I'd like to introduce you to my girlfriend. Isla, this is my father."

"It's nice to meet you, Senator."

Wait. Was I supposed to call him Senator? Mr. Wasserstein? Senator Wasserstein? I should have said "sir." Why didn't I say "sir"? Oh no! I called the judge "sir." Was I supposed to call him "your honor," or is that only in court? But Josh's dad smiles and reveals a comforting pair of familiar dimples. He pumps my hand. "Great to meet you. I've heard so many stories that I feel like I already know you."

I'm taken aback. He sounds sincere, but . . . is he? It must be that practiced politico charm. I hadn't realized how lucky it is that our first meeting is in public. Josh's father has to pretend like everything is cool, even if it's not.

"Sam," he says to Judge Lederman. "Isla studies abroad."

"Ah, that's right," the judge says to Josh. "I forgot you lived overseas. England?"

"France. Though I'm finishing my schooling here in America." Josh's reply is smooth. Anticipated. His parents smile with ease, and it occurs to me that everyone playing this game is a pro. Everyone but me.

"Isla is the top student in her class," the senator says.

My face pinkens as a surreal conversation occurs in which I am the subject, and Josh's parents are bragging about my accomplishments. It's uncomfortable to hear them praise me when they can't possibly mean what they're saying. There's no reason for them to like me. I'm a nobody. A nobody who took their son to Spain for sex and then got him expelled from high school. This situation is so unexpected that I can't even answer their questions, and Josh is forced to pick up my end of the dialogue. Before I know it, the whole thing is over, and Josh is pulling me away.

"We're off to find something to eat," he tells his parents. "It was good seeing you again," he tells the judge, shaking his outstretched hand while steering me in the opposite direction.

"Nice to meet you," I call out. Which is the only thing I've said to any of them this entire time. Josh's parents probably think that he's been lying about my intelligence, too.

"That went well," Josh says.

"Did it?"

He glances at me. "We'll talk to them again later—just the four of us—after they've had a few more glasses of wine."

That's not an answer.

Josh swiftly pushes us through a cluster of uptight partygoers. He heads straight toward the canapés, grabs an uncharacteristically small sampling, and parades us past his parents again. He lifts his plate to them in a toast. His mother raises her glass in return. And then he's ducking and weaving us into the thickest crush in the room. His plate vanishes somewhere in the mix.

"Excuse me, pardon me," he says.

I'm scrambling to keep up. "These heels. They weren't built for this."

Josh throws me a mischievous smile, and I recognize a plan behind it. He continues threading us through a neighboring gallery—past stained-glass windows and a Pietà, glazed jugs and earthenware—until we come to an abrupt halt before a closed door.

A closed door *and* a museum guard.

But the middle-aged guard in the navy suit loses all rigidity the moment he recognizes Josh. He breaks into an unexpected grin. Josh jerks up his chin in the universal guy-nod. The guard returns the nod, whisks open the door, and lets us pass.

The door shuts behind us.

The sound of the party instantly dims. We're in a very large, very dark, and very empty room. It's a vast indoor sculpture garden. We're in the American wing, but it feels as if we're back in Paris thanks to a gorgeous pair of flickering turn-of-the-century electric streetlamps. I wonder if the guard left them on for us.

"What," I whisper, "was that?"

"We," Josh says at normal volume, "are taking a break from the soirée."

My heartbeat accelerates. "We are?"

He takes my hand—the way he did at school, comfortable and relaxed and himself—and strolls me past the streetlamps.

My heels click and echo. "Who was that guard? How do you know him?"

"Chuck Nadelhorn. We've taken a lot of art classes together over the years." He sees my furrowed brow and grins. "Don't be ageist."

I laugh, caught.

"*I* was the odd one out. I was the youngest in each class, by far. Chuck was one of the few people who treated me with respect."

"Then I like him even more than I already did."

Josh plants a singular kiss on my lips. "This way."

He moves forward, and I follow. "I assume you set this up—whatever it is—with Chuck in advance?"

"There were a few people involved. I've had some time to prepare," he says slyly. "But we'd better hurry, we only have twenty minutes. Nineteen now."

"As long as I'm not about to be arrested for trespassing. Or for stealing a nondescript, though no doubt priceless, artifact."

"Only if we're caught."

I stop.

He tugs me forward by our clasped hands. "Come on, come on!"

We race through the room into a corridor gift shop, and we're no longer in Paris, we're in Barcelona—two crazy kids running away to discover our own private world. Exploring. Taking risks. A sharp right, and we enter an even darker and even more vast room, but this one couldn't be mistaken for anything else. Anyone who has visited this museum would know it.

"The Temple of Dendur." Josh says it with a finality that tells me we've reached our destination—the ancient Egyptian sandstone temple.

I'm intrigued. But baffled. "Any particular reason?"

Josh shrugs in a way that's almost bashful. "I like the temple's reflecting pool. I kind of just wanted to sit beside it and make out with you."

It's actually the best answer he could have given me.

This time he leads me quietly, delicately, to the ledge beside the pool. The reflecting pool is beautiful in its dignified silence. An entire wall of this room is a window, and the lights of the city twinkle inside the still water. We sit down. The air is cold, the granite ledge even colder. He takes off his tuxedo jacket and swings it up and around my shoulders. And then he uses his own lapels to pull me into him. His mouth is warm. We slip into each other as if no time had passed between now and Spain. If there wasn't a thousand museum cameras on us, we'd lie down and make love. But touching him is enough. Smelling him is enough. Tasting him is enough.

Being here with him is enough.

And then . . . we're lying down anyway. His body is on top of mine. We press against each other, our hands and mouths traveling everywhere. We do everything except the one thing we *can't* do right now. After what feels simultaneously like no time at all and eternity, Josh unwraps his limbs from mine, and we readjust our clothing.

"Before we go." He picks up his jacket from the floor and reaches into an inside pocket. He removes a small tube. I can't believe I didn't feel it earlier. *"Joyeux Noël."*

My heart is in my throat. It has to be a drawing. I pop open the cap, and sure enough, there's a thick scroll inside. I slide out the paper. I unroll it slowly, because I know that, whatever it is, it's more valuable than anything inside this museum.

It's a tiny island. But instead of the stereotypical single palm, he's drawn a prickly Joshua tree in its center. Underneath it are two entwined figures. It's impossible to tell where one ends and the other begins. They've become a single naked body. The entire illustration is done in rich black ink . . . with the exception of the girl's bold red hair.

He's nervous. "Do you like it?"

"Let's move to this island tonight. Right this second." I can't hide the genuine longing from my voice. Nor the fear and dread of our upcoming re-separation.

Josh tucks a loose strand of my hair back into place. "We'll move there next autumn, maybe even this summer. And then we'll never be apart ever again."

chapter twenty-six

Back at Chuck's door, Josh returns the tube to his jacket pocket. My fancy jeweled clutch is too fancy to be of any actual use. Josh knocks—a normal knock, not his special knock—and the door opens. Chuck nods his approval. "With thirty seconds to spare."

"Anything you need, you let me know," Josh says as we steal back inside.

Chuck's smile widens into a grin. "Oh, I'll let you know."

"Thank you so much," I say.

Chuck gestures toward the right strap of my dress, which has loosened and keeps falling off my shoulder. I shove it back up. My boyfriend's ensuing blush matches my own. Chuck laughs. "You kids have a good night now, you hear?"

As soon as we're out of earshot, Josh says, "Nothing like an adult to remind you that you aren't one."

I laugh, but as we place our drink order at the bar, our matching ginger ales make the sort-of joke feel all too real. It's always uncomfortable to come home from school only to be faced with even fewer freedoms. The last time we were at a party, we drank champagne. We stayed out as late as we wanted. And zero family members were involved. "Should we find your parents again?" *Please say no.*

He sighs. "Yeah."

"Ohmygod. Is that the *mayor?*"

A snappily dressed, elderly photographer is taking pictures of an equally elderly man with tipsy-red cheeks and a sober-looking, much younger partner.

"Yep," Josh says, unenthused.

As we pass them, I follow Josh's blasé lead, and I don't turn my head to stare. Even though I want to. This evening will never stop being weird.

We wander, searching for his parents, but it's a slow-moving process. Everybody seems to know Josh, and they all want to congratulate him on the reelection. Political lifers. Josh remembers the names of children and locations of vacation homes, and he introduces me to everyone. I munch on bland canapés. This is the type of conversation that he despises, but his distaste never shows. It strikes me that if he had the desire . . . he could be one of them, too. He's a good actor.

It's a little unsettling.

But not nearly so unsettling as the other type of partygoer who keeps pulling Josh aside. Society girls. The female version of him—always someone's daughter—but with a drive that's both alarming and intimidating. They laugh. They flirt. I eat more canapés. They tower over me. Even the ones who aren't tall *still* manage to tower over me through their confidence alone. A brunette with an unwinterlike tan does a particularly swell job of pretending that I don't exist. Her hand touches the sleeve of Josh's jacket twice.

After the third sleeve-touch, Josh makes our excuses and steers us away. But even that doesn't stop her from following him with her eyes as we move throughout the room.

Over an hour later, after emoting my most sociable holiday cheer during countless conversations in which I am invisible, we locate his parents beside a large copper . . . vat? I read the sign. BAPTISMAL FONT. Unexpectedly, I'm relieved to see them. At least I know they won't ignore me.

As Josh predicted, they've partaken in a few more glasses of wine. They're relaxed and happy. Mrs. Wasserstein even compliments my shoes. But soon another stranger interrupts us, some famous journalist, and then the pushy brunette re-approaches Josh from behind. She stands in a way that forces him to turn his head away from us to hear what she's saying, which means that *I* can't hear what she's saying.

The journalist envelops Josh's parents in a conversation about tax incentives. They glance at me occasionally, including me in the discussion with their eyes, but I contribute nothing, feeling dumb and unimportant. The brunette laughs. Josh turns his head to shoot me an apologetic look.

I smile as if everything were fine.

We've only been here for two hours, but I'm ready to leave.

A tapestry of a medieval lady snags my gaze. She's giving me a distinctly incredulous "oh, no, this is *not* happening" face, and I'm grateful that *someone* sees what's going on here. Even if she is woven.

Josh finally cuts off the brunette, and his father sweeps him back into their conversation. "I'm sorry," Josh says, "but Isla and I are heading out."

What now? I perk up.

The senator looks disappointed. "Come by the house for dinner this week," he tells me. "I'd like to have a real chance to get to know you."

I'm touched. And panicked to think about an evening with them unprotected by a public safety net. "Thank you. I'd like that."

"Marvelous seeing you again." Mrs. Wasserstein gives me a limp, one-armed hug. The words sound friendly enough, but the warmth in her action is debatable.

"It was nice seeing you, too. Thank you for inviting me."

"Are you going straight home?" she asks Josh.

"Nah, we're gonna get some real food first. But I'll probably still beat you back."

"Is Brian taking you?"

"I just texted him." Josh holds up her phone and grins.

She snatches it back, but she's smiling as she hugs him goodbye. "Pickpocket."

"Warden."

It's the first Josh-like exchange that I've heard in a while. His mom is placated enough by his answers, so he puts an arm around my waist and guides me toward the exit. "It's strange," I say, the moment we're alone. "The way you've been steering me around like this tonight."

He yanks away his arm as if it'd been caught in a compromising position. "Sorry, I didn't mean—"

"No, I know. It was the environment. It just feels . . . weird."

"That whole *scene* is weird, right?" He gestures toward the fading laughter and string quartet.

"You seem comfortable in it, though. If I didn't know any better, I'd never guess that you hate it."

"Well, I do." He sounds defensive.

"I know. I'm only saying that you're a good actor."

Josh shoves his hands into his pockets, and the museum's dim light catches the sheen of the tuxedo stripe on his pants. "I don't think that was a compliment," he says at last.

"That's not what I meant."

But . . . it was. And Josh knows it. For some reason, now that I've started, I can't hold back. "The whole thing reminded me of Televised Josh. You, looking so polished. Speaking in that voice. Standing so straight."

Josh opens the museum door for me. His teeth are gritted.

"Knowing all of these people and things that I don't." *Shut. Up.*

"Yeah, because they've been a part of my life for, like, ever. I'm not gonna be a dick in front of the people who keep my dad in office."

"I know! And I know you're a part of this life, so you *have* to act like that—"

"I don't *have* to do anything. I *choose* to be a decent person."

It's a sword through the chest. I've gone too far. I've gone way, way too far. "I'm sorry. I don't . . . I don't know why . . ."

"Forget it." But his head is turned away from mine. He's scanning the line of cars for Brian, but, really, it's an excuse not to look at me. I can't blame him. Why couldn't I keep my stupid insecurities to myself?

It's freezing, and I wish I'd brought my winter coat. For the first time ever, either Josh doesn't notice that I'm shivering or he chooses not to offer me his jacket. Not that he should *have* to give it to me. It's my own fault for leaving my coat behind during the excitement of his arrival at my house.

"I'm sorry," I say again.

He shrugs.

"Do you still wanna get something to eat?"

"Of course." Josh sounds surprised. He pulls his hands from his pockets and crosses his arms. After a minute of uneasy silence, he uncrosses them and rubs the back of his neck. "I'm sorry, too. For bringing you. Not that I didn't want you here," he adds quickly, "but because I knew it would suck. These things always do. Not that *all* of that sucked," he adds again. "Twenty minutes of it were fantastic."

"You don't have to apologize." I stare at the pavement. "You have this big life that I'm not a part of. And I wanted to see it."

Josh's frown deepens.

I open my mouth to try again when a black town car pulls up to the curb and flashes its lights. The wind turns abrasive as we hurry toward it. The locks pop, Josh opens the back door, and we slide inside.

"Sorry I'm late," Brian says. "I wasn't expecting you for at least another hour."

Josh shakes his head. "No problem. You know how these events are."

"Do I ever." Brian grins at us in the rearview mirror. "You've got ninety minutes before curfew. Can I take you somewhere else?"

Josh leans forward in his seat. "You know that café on Amsterdam? Kismet?"

Brian snorts. It tells me that he already knows the story. "I think I can find the place."

"Thanks." Josh sits back. And then he turns to me with a sudden alarm. "Is that okay? Sorry, I'm still in stupid party mode. I didn't even ask. I know we're going there for New Year's, but I thought an early visit would be nice. For nostalgia's sake."

"No, it's perfect." I force a smile. "Thanks, Brian."

"That's what I'm here for," he says.

But the feeling inside the car is not *perfection*. There's no hand holding. We're quiet and ill at ease. As Brian merges into traffic, he tries to lighten the mood. "So, Isla. Did you get to see any of the museum?"

It's a leading question. Clearly, Josh tells him a lot of things. "I did."

"Aaaaand?"

I force another cheerful smile. "It was a beautiful gift."

He pumps his fist. "Nice."

"Went off without a hitch," Josh says. "Thank you, Chuck."

"Thank you, Chuck!" Brian repeats.

They discuss the plan, some last-minute part of the arrangement with Chuck that Brian hadn't heard yet, and I squirm in my seat. How many people knew about this? Has Josh done this sort of thing before? The less private it gets, the more uncomfortable I feel.

There's something I shouldn't say, but for some terrible and unknown reason, I have to say anyway. I should save it for a more appropriate, less emotionally stressed day. I should save it for when we're alone. I shouldn't *ever* say it. *Don't say it.*

"Rashmi likes ancient Egypt, doesn't she?" I ask.

Shit.

"What?" Josh's response is sharp as his attention snaps from Brian to me.

"I—I mean, in your book. Her rabbit, Isis. And then she goes to Brown to study Egyptology."

"Yeah, she goes to Brown because she *goes* there. Those things are true."

"And there's that drawing of her as an Egyptian goddess." I can't believe I'm saying this out loud. *And* I'm saying it in front of *Brian*. I don't know what's happening, but something inside of me has short-circuited. I'm freaking out. The Egyptian thing is a coincidence, I know this, but I can't stop. "Was that how you knew about the temple?"

His brow furrows in angry confusion. "Huh?"

"The Temple of Dendur. Did you ever take her there?"

Josh gathers himself. "First of all, I *like* the reflecting pool. I wanted some time alone with you tonight, so I chose—what I thought was—the museum's nicest room. Second of all, *no*. I did *not* take you someplace where I previously made out with my ex-girlfriend. Or whatever else it is you think we might have done in there."

"Well, I know *that* much. If you'd done anything more, I would have read about it. Very graphically! In your graphic memoir."

Time stops.

And that's when I know that I've just said the worst thing that I'll ever say in my entire life. And I've said it to the person whom I love the most.

Josh's voice is deadly quiet. "Anything else you'd like to share with me right now? Any additional criticisms of me or my work?"

I want to speak. I want to apologize. This isn't about his ex or his work. I have no idea why I just said those things. I'm confused. I'm not sure why I feel this upset, why I'm picking fights about things that don't even matter.

Brian glances at me in the rearview mirror, and his expression is unbearably strained, as if he'd jump through the car window if he could fit through the hole.

"No. Really," Josh continues. "As long as you're finally opening up to me, why don't you go on? Tell me what else is wrong with my book."

I've backed myself into the farthest corner possible. "Nothing is wrong with it."

"But there are things you'd change?"

"No! I mean, yeah, but . . . small things. You know?" *Stop talking.* "It's not a big deal. All books require a little bit of editing."

The streetlights cast Josh in shadow. I can't see his expression, but it doesn't *feel* nice. He remains silent. Waiting.

"Okay." I gulp. "Well. There was this one flashback that was in a weird place. When you get your tattoo? That scene . . . it just didn't flow with what came before and after it."

"All right." It comes out like ice.

"And your parents. They were, like, this big deal in the beginning, but by the end, it was like you didn't even *have* parents. They completely dropped out."

"Because they live in another *country.*"

"Yeah, but that doesn't mean they weren't in your life anymore. Even if it's their *absence* that matters, it's still something that should be acknowledged."

His jaw is clenched. "Anything else?"

"Um." My voice lowers to a near whisper. "There were a lot of drawings of Rashmi. In the middle."

"*Shocker.*"

"No," I say quickly. "I mean, there were a ton of one-page panels that were just . . . *there.* Completely unnecessary. They didn't contribute anything to the story." I can't believe that I'm saying this—*all of this*—aloud. A good girlfriend would keep her mouth shut. "And then sections of your junior year were really crowded. You needed more variation between the panels. More space."

"More space."

"Um, yeah. Spaces. Breaks. For the reader to contemplate things. To figure out what's important, on their own."

"Spaces," he says. "To figure out what's important."

"I'm sorry." I'm drowning in a river of my own making. "I didn't say anything earlier, because I didn't want to hurt your feelings. It's *great,* I promise."

He won't look at me anymore. "You've used that word to describe it in the past. And yet, I still don't believe you."

"I'm sorry." I say it again, my voice desperate.

"Are you sure you aren't just pissed off? Maybe because it isn't about you?"

"No!" The shame is overwhelming. "I wasn't even in your life until this year. I know that. I know I'm not an important part of your story."

For the first time in several minutes, Josh is thrown. He turns back to me. "What do you mean, you're not important to my story?"

"I haven't been around that long. And you had this whole life before me, and you'll have this whole life after me—"

"*After* you?" His voice gets an octave higher. "What do you mean *after?*"

"Vermont. Your school. Your future."

Josh is baffled. "But . . . you're coming with me."

"Am I?"

"When Dartmouth accepts you—"

"I wouldn't be so sure," I say.

He punches his fist against the seat. "Stop saying that. Why are you always putting yourself down? You're gonna get in. There's no way that you're not getting in."

"Tell that to Columbia."

And now he's thrown again. "What?"

"I didn't get in."

"*What?* When? Why didn't you tell me?"

I can't look at him. My failure is humiliating. "A few days ago."

"I'm so sorry. God, I wish you'd told me. I had no idea."

"I got a letter from la Sorbonne, too. Accepted."

Josh deflates with visible relief. "That's great. You deserve it." But there's sadness, too, as his posture sinks farther. Because if I attend la Sorbonne, there will still be an ocean between us. "So what if Dartmouth does accept you? Where will you go?"

"I don't know." And I realize I'm crying. "I haven't decided."

"But . . . I thought . . . I thought we had a plan."

"No, you had a plan. You *have* plans."

Josh shakes his head in disbelief. "What are you talking about?"

"You know exactly who you are." Tears stream down my cheeks. "You know how to be yourself, but you also know how

264

to be a different kind of yourself on television and in society. And you've *always* had a passion for art, and you've *always* known where you're attending college. You already even know what kind of apartment you'll rent when you move there! Not to mention what kind of car you'll drive, what kind of cat you'll adopt, and how you'll spend your weekends in the wilderness. I don't know any of that. I've never cared about *anything* like you've cared about your work. I don't even belong to a single country. I'm nobody. I'm nothing."

"Isla . . ." My words have stunned him again. He has no idea what to say.

"And you're right, maybe I *am* upset about your book for selfish reasons. I know you haven't had the time, I know it takes months for you to draw them, but . . . eight pages. I was only *eight pages*." My voice cracks, hollow and desperate. "I thought maybe I'd finally learn something if I could see myself through your eyes. But I wasn't even there."

Josh strains against his seat belt. He reaches for a hand, but I pull them both into my lap. "You'll be in it," he says. "Of course you'll be in it."

"I used to think so." My chest is splitting in two. "Don't you see? Don't you get it? I'm a placeholder."

"What do you mean?"

He's trying desperately to get me to look at him, but I can't. I'm in agony. "Your friends left school, and I was there, but I wasn't enough to *keep* you there. You had to keep breaking rules. And then you left me."

"It wasn't like that. You know it wasn't like that!"

"No," I say. "It was. You tried *really* hard for a *really* long time to get expelled, because you couldn't admit to your parents that you didn't want to be there. Your plan just succeeded at the wrong time. And now that you're gone—now that you're here, and I'm not—sooner or later, you're gonna realize that I was only a distraction. Something to keep your mind off your misery. Something to keep you going until the next phase of your very carefully planned-out life could begin. But I no longer believe that you'll actually want me there. And"—I swallow loudly—"I don't want to be around when you discover it."

Josh is reeling. "Wh—what are you saying?"

"I'm saying that I don't see myself in your future."

"Isla." His voice shakes. "Are you . . . are you breaking up with me?"

And there it is. The question that, once spoken aloud, is always inevitably its own undoing.

"You don't love me like you think you love me," I whisper.

Now he's crying, too. "Why are you doing this?"

My entire world is crumbling, but I have to finish the destruction. I have to destroy what's left of my heart before he can do it for me. "Because if it hurts us this much now," I say, "I can't imagine how much it'll hurt when you come to this realization yourself."

I'm as shocked by my words as he is.

I don't understand how this could happen in one car ride, but as a deathly somber Brian pulls over in front of Kismet, I already know that I'm getting out. And Josh isn't.

chapter twenty-seven

Isla? Are you okay?" Kurt's dad is watching me on the camera installed outside their building. I ran all three blocks from Kismet.

"Let me in. Please let me in!"

The door buzzes open and then slams shut behind me. I race up the two flights of stairs to their apartment, and Scott and Sabine are already in the hall. Kurt's parents refuse to let me call them Mr. and Mrs. Bacon, because they refuse to believe that they're old. "What happened? Are you okay? Are you hurt?" Their questions all come at once.

"Is Kurt here?" I ask.

"Of course he is here," Sabine says in a French accent. She ushers me inside with a slender, gentle arm. "He went to bed an hour ago, but he is probably awake. What happened? Why are you dressed up like this?"

I blurt it out. "I've broken up with my boyfriend, and I don't want to go home."

Their bodies tense.

"Did he hurt you?" Scott undergoes a Hulk-like transformation, which looks peculiar on his strung-out ex-rocker body.

"Yes!"

Scott's body completes the Hulk transformation.

"No." I sob hysterically. *"Emotionally."*

Scott shrinks back into his natural form. Sabine exchanges a look with him. "Of course you can stay," she says.

"Will you call my parents? I don't want to have to explain. Not tonight."

She leads me to Kurt's bedroom. "I'll call your *maman* right now." She hugs me, and the comforting familiarity of her violet perfume keeps me in her arms, crying.

Kurt opens his door. "What's going—oh. What happened?"

Sabine releases me into his care. I flop onto his unmade bed, and he closes the door behind me. "It's . . . it's over!" I say.

Kurt places a solid hand on my back as I emit huge, gut-wrenching sobs. "Josh broke up with you?"

"No. *I* broke up with *him*."

He's quiet for nearly a minute. "I don't get it," he finally says.

I tell him the story to the best of my current ability, and when I'm done, he scratches his head. "So you broke up with Josh before he could break up with you."

"No." My head is swimming. "It wasn't like that. Or . . . it was *more* than that. I don't know."

"You've never been able to believe that he could like you as much as you like him. You were afraid he'd dump you. So you picked those fights to get a conversation going in which you could dump him first."

"No," I say again. But something awful and truth-y stings inside of me.

Still. That doesn't mean it was wrong to break up with him. I *do* believe that Josh would have left me, most likely before college even began. But maybe he wouldn't have until *after* we were already in New England, already living together. Which would've been even worse. My heart couldn't take it—moving someplace new and strange and then losing the person who'd brought me there. Because eventually, no matter what the circumstances, he *would* see the real me. Josh is a beautiful, messy, passionate work of art, and I'm . . . a blank canvas.

There's nothing here to love.

"You told him that you're a placeholder in his life," Kurt says. "So does that make me or Josh the placeholder in yours?"

My attention jerks back to him. "Huh?"

"Now that Josh is gone, you came straight to me. In his place."

The word *gone* is a sucker punch, but what he's suggesting is even worse. "That's not the same thing. Not at all. You guys don't . . . share the same space. You don't"—I struggle to put it in terms he'd understand—"perform the same function in my life."

"Because you and I aren't romantically involved?"

"Exactly."

"Josh and I don't perform the same function," Kurt agrees, "but we do take up the same amount of your time. And you gave him the time that you used to give to me."

The guilt. I can't deal with it on top of everything else. A shrill ring from inside the jeweled clutch saves me from having to reply. We sit up, alert. My phone rings again. Kurt pulls it out and examines the screen. "It's a Manhattan number. Do you want me to answer it?"

I shake my head.

"It's probably Josh."

"I know."

"He's probably using Brian's phone."

"I know."

"You told me that I should always answer it if I think it might be Josh."

"That's not valid anymore."

"Okay."

The phone stops ringing. A minute later, it blips with a voice mail. I turn off the volume, but I see the Manhattan number call me again. And then again. Kurt throws my phone underneath his bed to curb my temptation to answer it.

"I'm tired," he says. "Go brush your teeth."

I brush them with his toothpaste and an index finger, and I wash off my makeup with his liquid hand-soap. My face is a blotchy mess. I ditch my dress and replace it with one of the worn T-shirts from the pile on his bathroom floor. When I return to his room, he's asleep. I tuck myself up against him, and—all night long—I lie awake and watch the green light of my phone flashing out from underneath his bed.

Forty-two missed calls. Three voice mails.

Merry Christmas Eve.

I listen to the voice mails on my walk home. Josh is angry and sad. He begs me to call him back. He begs me to reconsider. He says he doesn't understand what happened. It was all a mistake, a misunderstanding. Something we can fix.

He says it over and over and over again.

This is Brian's phone. I'll have access to it for the rest of the night. Please call me. Don't do this to us. I think you're afraid. I don't know why—I don't know what I could've said or done to make you distrust me—but for once in your life, Isla, take a risk. Take a fucking risk. If you keep playing it safe, you'll never know who you are. I know who you are, and I love who you are. Why don't you trust me?

His voice fills my heart with pain. His words rip it apart.

I believe Josh—that he thinks he loves me. But I also still believe he's missing the point. Between his expulsion from school and the pressures from his family, he's too distracted to see that he's repeating the same mistake with me that he made with Rashmi. He stayed with her for so long because he liked the *idea* of being in love. He has an empty well in his heart that needs to be filled by someone. Anyone. But that's not enough for me, and it won't be enough for him either once he finally realizes the truth.

Brian must have taken pity on him, because a few hours later—after what I estimate to be three hours of sleep on Josh's behalf—the calls begin again. I don't know what to do, so I don't do anything. My fear is paralyzing. I turn my phone on silent and hide it in my sock drawer. I hate myself for this.

Josh refuses to be silent. He comes to our house in the evening, and my parents turn him away. A minute later, there's a knock on my door. It's Maman. She hands me a small tube. "He wanted you to have this."

I stare at it.

"What's inside?" she asks.

"My Christmas present."

"Was it a nice one?"

"Yeah."

She sits beside me on my bed. "I'm sorry."

I cry. She stays with me until I can't cry any longer.

Christmas Day. Mainly I hang out beside the tree and attempt to read one of my presents. It's a book about a man-eating tiger, but I can't muster up any of my usual enthusiasm. My parents don't ask me to help them in the kitchen, and Gen picks up the extra slack. Even Hattie silently takes over my portion of the dirty dishes.

That's when I know things are really bad.

I peek at my phone before bed and discover only two missed

calls. No messages. Either he's getting the picture, or he's respecting my Christmas Tree Agnosticism.

Even *thinking* that phrase hurts.

"May I come in?" But Gen is inside before I can answer. I drop the phone back between my socks and slam the drawer shut. "I used a desk drawer," she says. "When my girlfriend broke up with me."

"Sarah broke up with you?" Now I feel awful about that, too.

"Yeah. Right after Thanksgiving, actually."

"Did she call you a lot afterward?"

"No." Gen gives me a sad smile. "I hid my phone for the opposite reason."

"Oh. I'm sorry."

She shrugs. "Doesn't matter. It sucks either way, right?"

I sit on my bed, and she sits beside me and places her head on my shoulder. We're the same height. Strangers have often mistaken us for twins. "Do you still miss her?" I ask.

"A little. It's better every day, though."

"Why'd you break up?"

She sort of laughs. "Apparently, I'm domineering."

"I'm replaceable."

Gen lifts her head, hackles raised. "He *said* that?"

"No, but it's true. He fell for me because I was there. I could've been anyone."

"Don't say that. Why do you say things like that?"

"Because that's what happened."

She stares at me in disbelief. "You've always been so hard on yourself."

I stare at my hands. I *am* hard on myself. But isn't it better to be honest about these things before someone else can use them against you? Before someone else can break your heart? Isn't it better to break it yourself? I thought honesty made people strong.

"Hey." Gen nudges me. "Show me what's in the tube." My head shoots up, and she shrugs. "I saw him drop it off yesterday."

I can't stop myself. "How'd he look?"

"Like you'd torn out his heart and stomped on it with your tallest stilettos."

I'm a bad person. I've hurt him. I never wanted to hurt him, and somehow it happened anyway.

"Do you really think breaking up with him was the right thing to do?" Gen asks.

"I don't know." But I shake my head. "That's not true. It was right. It *was*."

"But you still love him."

I swallow. "Yeah."

"A lot."

"Yeah."

She pauses. "Would it make it better or worse if you showed me what's in the tube?"

"Ohmygod. You're relentless."

"The word was 'domineering.' Get it right."

"Ugh. Fine."

Gen opens my sock drawer. "I had a feeling I'd find you in here," she tells the tube. She pops off the top and gently taps out the paper. She unrolls it. "Whoa, nelly."

Shit. I'd forgotten he drew us naked.

"So. You guys were serious."

"Please, Gen. Don't."

"Is that a Joshua tree? On an island?"

"Yeah."

"Well . . . fuck. That's a *really* romantic gift."

"I know."

"He's good. The art," she clarifies. "I mean, he was good when he was a freshman, but this doesn't look like it was drawn by someone in high school. Not even a *talented* someone in high school. This is, like, the real deal."

"Will you please stop complimenting my ex-boyfriend?"

Ex-boyfriend. The word tastes sick on my tongue. I hadn't even let myself think it until now. Every single part of me wants to take the word back.

"I'm just saying he's talented."

"Why don't you tell me more about Sarah?"

Gen rolls up the drawing and slides it back into the tube. "You win."

But she's wrong. I've lost everything.

One miserable week and no phone calls later. No messages. New Year's Eve. There's shouting and singing and general drunken revelry down on the street. Our neighbors have been blasting dubstep for the last three hours. I've been watching television in my bedroom alone. Just like Josh and I talked about on our first date.

Ten minutes until midnight.

Josh and I were planning to meet at Kismet. We were going to ring in the new year with a kiss. I've never had a New Year's kiss.

Nothing about this decision has gotten any easier. That awful word torments me. *Ex-boyfriend.* I can't accept it as the truth. I don't think . . . I don't . . . I don't know why I'm doing this anymore. I think I freaked out that night in the car. I *know* I freaked out. And I have a very deep, very ugly gut feeling that I've made a mistake.

Josh told me that I'll never know what kind of person I am if I don't take any risks. Apologizing would be a risk, groveling would be a risk, begging for his forgiveness on my knees would be a risk.

What have I done? I love him.

Of course he's worth the risk.

Suddenly, I'm ripping off my pajamas and throwing on a dress and coat and boots. I'm racing past my sleepy parents in the living room, and I'm shouting that I'll be right back. I'm ignoring their cries of concern. I'm running downstairs, onto the pavement, across the street. The air is frosty and sharp, and the wind is strong.

Josh, I'm coming. I know you're there. Please don't leave.

I tear around the corner, and there it is. My beacon of hope. I race toward its glowing front window, dodging taxis and bumping into a guy being shouldered home by a friend. There's a loud cry of anger, but I keep running until I burst through Kismet's shining glass door. The café is still open. But it's empty.

Two employees are sitting at a table. They look up at my entrance, surprised.

"Excuse me, but is there a guy here?" I'm panting, but I have to raise my voice over the loud rock music blasting from the speakers. "*Was* there a guy here? About my age?"

A woman with a chest covered in electric-bright tattoos shakes her head. "Sorry, honey. We've been dead for nearly two hours."

In the distance, there's an eruption of explosions and cheering. Cars honk, people shout from their windows.

It's midnight.

I run back outside, frantically looking up and down the street, but he's nowhere to be found. Two college-aged girls run past the café hollering at the top of their lungs.

No, he's coming. He'll feel me here, like he felt me the last time.

"Are you okay? You don't look so well." The tattooed woman is standing beside me, and her forehead is wrinkled in concern.

"My boyfrie—my Josh. Josh. He's coming. He should be here any second."

The other employee, a wiry guy whom I belatedly recognize as pierced Abe Lincoln, pops his head out the door. "You forgot my kiss, Maggie."

"I forgot nothing," she says.

"He's coming," I say again.

Maggie side-eyes me. "How old are you? Do your parents know you're out?"

I shoot her a nettled glance. "I'm petite. Not a child."

She shrugs. "O-kay. But I'm still gonna wait out here with you."

"You don't have to do that." The cold wind howls, carrying

with it the continued sounds of celebration. I hug my coat around myself tighter.

"Jesus." Abe shivers. "At least wait inside."

They coax me back into the café, and I sit at the table in the window. The one I sat at more than half a year ago. They turn up their music even louder. My ears hurt. I glance at my phone, watching the minutes tick past. Ten. Fifteen. Twenty. Josh hasn't called me since Christmas Day. Before I can talk myself out of it, I call Brian's number. It goes straight to the voice mail of a scary-sounding protective service agency. His employer. I leave a message explaining where I am, pleading for Josh to meet me, and then I run outside again as if that should be enough to make him appear.

He's not there.

I sit back down, wait until two minutes have passed, and then bolt outside again. I repeat this pattern for an hour. I call again. I leave another message. I look outside, but nothing has changed. Josh isn't coming.

He's not coming.

I crumple in the doorway, vaguely aware of Maggie and Abe rushing toward me. It's the deathblow. It's over.

chapter twenty-eight

It's been a month. Josh never called me back. This gaping, bloody, open wound—the wound that *I* created—still rubs me raw. I have to keep convincing myself that I was right in the first place, that I was right to break up with him, because it's clear that he's finally realized the truth of what I've always feared. That what he felt for me wasn't love, after all, but convenience.

He's moving on.

I wish that I could move on. I'm clinging with every last fiber of my being.

At night, I lie awake in bed, pretending that his body is pressed against mine. I close my eyes and imagine the weight of his arms draped across mine. Holding me tight. In class, I day-dream about placing a love lock on le Pont de l'Archevêché, a bridge near Notre-Dame. Couples write their initials on padlocks and snap them onto the gates as a public declaration of their love. I ache for this sort of unbreakable, permanent connection.

After New Year's, my father and I took a train to Dartmouth. I didn't want to go, because how can I possibly say yes to them, even if I *am* accepted? But Dad wanted me to see the school in person. He's excited that I've applied somewhere unexpected.

Everything was covered in a thick layer of pristine white snow. Dad had scheduled an interview for me, and the encouraging woman behind the desk showed me pamphlets of the campus in the spring and autumn. It looked even more beautiful. She was impressed with my transcripts, and she assured me that a lot of students don't know what they want to study when they arrive. I left the interview feeling hopeful and buoyant and alive.

I died again somewhere on the train ride home. Dartmouth is a future that I might've had, but I lost. It's no longer mine. Furthermore, my ugly secret wish has been granted: A college rejected me, and my choice was made for me. I'll stay here in Paris and attend la Sorbonne. Maybe I'll meet someone someday, and he'll make me forget about Josh. Maybe we'll get married. Maybe I'll live in France forever.

But some things *have* changed.

Kurt's placeholder comment has returned to haunt me. *I've been replaced.* While I spent a month in detention, he started talking to these two sophomores, Nikhil Devi—I cannot escape that family—and Nikhil's best friend, Michael. Kurt had overheard them talking about the tunnels, and he discovered that they're obsessed with them, too. He mentioned their names a few times last semester, but I was so preoccupied by my own problems that I didn't realize they were actually *hanging out*. They kept in touch over the winter break, and now their friendship has reached the next natural level.

Nikhil and Michael are sitting at our cafeteria table.

This must be how Kurt felt when Josh ate with us. And it's not that Nikhil and Michael are ignoring me—they don't, just like Josh never ignored Kurt—but they're not exactly sitting at our table because they like me. Though, okay, maybe Nikhil does seem to *like* like me, which is yet another awkward situation.

It's weird knowing that Nikhil has spent a significant amount of time with Josh, through Rashmi. I wish that I could ask him about them. What were they like as a couple? And how did Josh and I compare? But that would be mean.

Not that I'm a good person anymore.

I can't help but think that Kurt is pulling away from me on purpose. And not just because he got tired of sitting in my backseat, but also because Josh did this same thing when he was a junior, when his friends were close to graduation. He pulled away from them. And Kurt will always be my best friend, of course he will, but things have changed. For the first time ever, Kurt wasn't the most important person in my life. That's hard for me to deal with. It must have been hard for Kurt, too.

And yet . . . he's thriving. Which has only made it that much more clear that I'm the reason why we haven't had any other friends. Not Kurt. *I've* held us back. When I disappeared, he found new people to hang out with, but I still don't have anyone else. How do people even make friends? How does that happen?

I can't stop thinking about risk. I took one risk in going to Kismet and another in calling Brian's phone. Neither worked out. It takes the entire month of January for me to build up the courage to attempt another. Even though Josh is no longer an option, I still want to tackle these other problems—my lack of friends and lack of everyday courage.

It happens one evening in the cafeteria. There's a rare conversational break between Kurt and his friends, and I pounce before I lose my nerve. "Angoulême is this weekend. You guys wanna go with me?"

Angoulême is the name of a town about three hours southwest of Paris by train, but it's also shorthand for the largest comics festival in Europe. Its black-and-white wildcat mascot has been crunched in every advertising space not already occupied by the Olympics. It feels like a symbol of everything that I've lost. If Josh were still here—and if we were still together—we'd take the day-trip without a second thought. I need to prove to myself that I can do it without him. And I've seen Nikhil and Michael reading comics, so surely this is not an unattractive offer?

"I thought you were done with leaving this city without permission," Kurt says.

"It's one afternoon," I say. "The school will never know."

Nikhil sits up eagerly. He's tiny and excitable, a kittenish ball of energy, and he always speaks in an enthusiastic babble. "That sounds fun. Yeah, guys, let's do it! We should totally do it."

Michael grins at him with a full mouth of braces. "I wonder why *you* want to go."

"It's because he wants to bone Isla," Kurt says.

"Kurt." I'm mortified.

"Yeah." Michael rolls his eyes. "I know."

"Oh." Kurt sinks. They may be friends, but they don't have each other's rhythms down yet. And then he immediately perks back up, because he still has the upper hand on information. "It won't happen. She's still hung up on Josh."

"Kurt, I'm sitting right here." I try to give Nikhil an apologetic wince, but he stares determinedly at his food tray. His dark brown skin has taken on a pinky-red undertone.

Crushes are so awful. I wonder if they suck worse for the crush-er or the crush-ee. I consider my three years of watching Josh from afar. Yeah, definitely the crush-er.

Poor Nikhil.

Poor me.

"It doesn't matter anyway," Michael says. He speaks with a shrewd authority that's belied by his ungroomed, sticky-uppy hair. "Saturday is the only day Arnaud can take us underground."

"Who's Arnaud?" I ask.

Kurt stabs a roasted potato with his fork. "Our first connection. Michael found him. He works at the sewer system museum."

"There's a sewer system museum?" On the upside, at least this means there are still things for me to learn about Paris.

Since I'll be here for a while. If Kurt stays interested in this stuff, I suppose someday I'll be crawling around underground, too. It doesn't sound so bad. Cramped and dirty, yes. But it'd be an adventure. I suppose.

"Yes, of course," Kurt says. As if all cities have sewer museums. "Why don't you come with us this weekend instead?"

I imagine drainage and mud and darkness. And then I imagine a train and the open countryside and a sleepy town filled with comic books.

Yeah. I'll make friends another day.

That night, there's a letter waiting for me. I stare into my mailbox, afraid to pick it up. I want it to be from him. I want it to be from him so badly.

My arm trembles as I reach inside and pull it out.

It's not from him.

The blow to my chest is as strong as ever. I'm still not any closer to being over Josh. Not even a centimeter closer, not even a millimeter. People say that the only thing that heals heartbreak is time. But how much time will it take?

The return address comes into focus, and I'm hit with a second shock wave. I shred open the envelope, right there in the hall, and rip out the letter. My head reels. I read the first sentence again, but the words haven't changed. It's a different kind of heartbreak. *On behalf of the faculty and staff, it is with great pleasure that I inform you of your admission to Dartmouth College.*

The streets of Angoulême overflow with red balloons and swarms of happy readers. But their excitement can't stop the rain. Why does it rain every time I travel? This time, I don't wait to buy an umbrella. I haven't seen the last one since Barcelona. Josh must have it. Or maybe we left it in the park. Umbrellas are so small and sad and easy to forget.

I wander through the town, the venues, the comics museum. Festivals like this aren't as crazed as their American counterparts—and there are far fewer people in costume—but the Europeans in attendance are still showing less restraint than usual. I try to get caught up in their enthusiasm, and occasionally it works. Like when I discover a new-to-me author-illustrator who writes about a split life between China and the United States. It's only after I purchase two volumes that I realize how much Josh would like her work, too. And the fact that I can't share it with him makes my heart hurt all over again.

It gets worse when I find myself faced with a large display featuring only titles by Joann Sfar. And then even worse when I discover one of Josh's favorite artists in the flesh, and I have to talk myself out of getting a book signed for him. It feels selfish, so I talk myself back into it, thinking I'll just have something signed. No personalization. If I ever see him again, he can have it. But the moment the cartoonist asks, I blurt, "'To Josh,' please." And before I can correct my mistake, my ex-boyfriend's name—at least I can say *that word* now—has been inked onto the front page beside an illustration of a rose.

Of all things. A rose.

I can't win.

Back in Paris, the posters for the Olympics make me wonder if I should buy a ticket to Chambéry next month. But the thought of another crowded train, another crowded town, all of those crowded hotels . . . ugh. No.

That's how I'm feeling about everything these days: ugh. No.

The city remains as cold as ever. A few days after Angoulême, I pop into one of the Latin Quarter's identical gyro joints, seeking warmth in the form of hot *frites*. Or French fries, which should really be called Belgian fries, if America wants to get correct about it.

Ohmygod. No wonder I don't have any friends.

The restaurant is empty. I sit in the back with the second volume of the Chinese-American split-life autobiography. I haven't been able to put it down. Much of it is depressingly, satisfyingly familiar.

The door *dings,* and another customer enters the restaurant.

Sanjita looks as startled to see me as I am to see her. She waves, uncertain. I return the gesture. She also purchases a sleeve of *frites,* and I'm thankful that she's the one who has to make the decision: leave or join me. The restaurant is too small, and we have too much of a history, for her to sit alone.

She's hesitant. Fearful. She joins me anyway.

"It's freezing out there," she says.

I'm surprised by how grateful I am for her company. "I know. I wish it'd hurry up and snow already."

"Me too. It feels wrong for it to be this cold without it."

There's an uncomfortable pause. It's the kind that follows any general statement about the weather, the kind that's filled with everything we *aren't* saying. I'm trying to come up with another neutral topic when she asks, "How's Josh doing?"

The blood drains from my face.

Sanjita doesn't notice. She pokes at her fries. "I felt so bad for you guys when he had to leave."

This unexpected moment of compassion tugs on my heart. "I . . . don't know how he's doing. I think he's okay. We broke up last month."

"You *did*?" She raises her head in surprise. "But you were perfect for each other."

The floor dips. "You thought so?"

"Of course. And you'd been in love with him for, like, ever. That must have been crazy when you actually started dating him."

The relief I feel at being understood—really and truly understood—is profound. The emptiness inside of me transforms into an instant flood of emotion. "It *was* crazy. It was amazing. It was . . . the best thing that's ever happened to me."

Sanjita scoots forward, and her dangly gold earrings sway.

"So what went wrong?"

"I liked him—I *loved* him—but I don't think he loved me the same way in return."

Her shoulders fall. "He broke up with you."

"No. I broke up with him."

She winces. "Oh. *Ouch.*"

"I know."

But her frown only grows. "I don't get it. You guys were glued to each other. I *saw* the way he looked at you. He never looked at Rashmi like that."

My heart stops. I could never ask Nikhil, but . . . Sanjita.

"Wh—what were they like as couple? Your sister and Josh?"

She shrugs, and her long earrings sway again. "I don't know. They bickered constantly. I think they were more similar, more stubborn and determined, than they realized. It was why they sort of worked together, but why it never could've lasted. There was no balance."

Josh and I had balance. Didn't we?

"Not like she ever told *me* anything." Sanjita scowls. "But, from the outside, it seemed like they'd both be better off with partners who were softer. Like you."

I'm not sure I like that word. *Softer.*

She sees my expression and shakes her head. "Not, like, *weak* soft. I meant . . . someone who'd give them the space they need to flourish. Who wouldn't try to change them. Who'd support them—even when they were being dumbasses—but who'd be ready to guide them back when they needed it."

"And . . . you think that's me?"

"Are you kidding? You're the most patient and forgiving person I know."

A strange thing is happening. Something deep inside of me recognizes her words as true. I *am* patient and forgiving.

Just not with myself.

She looks away from me again, re-hiding her face, and I know she's thinking about Kurt. About how she tested me for months. About how I wanted to be friends with them both, but how she forced me to choose anyway. I can see her shame. She clears her throat, pushing herself back into the present. "So why don't you think Josh loved you?"

"I felt like I was . . . a nice distraction. He was so unhappy here, you know?"

"Phones are distracting. The internet is distracting. The way he looked at you? He wasn't distracted. He was *consumed*."

I get the sense that she's being extra nice to me to make up for the past without having to say she's sorry. It feels cowardly. But it also appears as if she believes what she's saying. It's simultaneously my greatest fear *and* my greatest hope. Is it possible, after all of this second-guessing, that Josh really did love me as much as I loved him? Is it possible that he saw something in me that I have trouble seeing in myself?

Is it possible that I'm worthy of being loved by someone whom I love?

My heart pounds at double its usual speed. "Either way," I say. It sounds defensive. Like I'm making an excuse, which I suppose I am. "He needs to get his act together. The last time we talked, he still hadn't figured out what he was going to do about school. He's a semester away from graduation, and he's just *sitting* on it. And he can't go to New England without a degree. So, basically, he's not going anywhere."

Sanjita looks confused. "New England?"

I tell her about his school and everything else spills out, too. "And I thought I was getting used to the idea of la Sorbonne, but I don't know. Back when we were dating, it sounded exciting to go someplace new. I did all this research, and Dartmouth seemed really cool, you know? Different. And when I went up there a few weeks ago, it was even better than I'd imagined. But when we broke up, it became *his* place again—"

"I thought you said he wasn't going anywhere."

"Well, I don't know that for sure—"

"Who cares? Go to Dartmouth."

"Yeah, but what if he thinks I want to move there for him?"

"Do you?"

"No, but—"

"So go to Dartmouth."

I frown, and she stares at me like I'm dense. "I'm not sure what's so difficult about this," she says. "You got into the school that you wanted to get into. *So go to it.*"

Holy shit. She's right. Is it really that simple?

Sanjita crosses her arms, smug. She knows she's won her argument.

"You used to want to be a lawyer," I say. "Do you still want that? Because you're good at arguing your case."

She grins. "What else do you need me to fix?"

"I don't know. My sister? Can you fix her?"

"Hattie, I assume?"

"She's relentless." I grind *une frite* into its paper sleeve. "She showed up in my room the other day—unasked, of course—and immediately started rifling through all of my belongings. I told her to cut it out, but that only made her push this huge stack of books off my desk."

"Maybe she's just curious about you. Maybe she didn't mean anything by it."

I shake my head. "Hattie never does anything without purpose. She was doing it to get under my skin, and it worked. Like it always does."

Sanjita arches an eyebrow. "I don't know. It sounds like you're treating her like a child so she's responding like one."

I can't contain the surprise from my expression. Or the outrage.

She holds up her hands in defense. "I have three older sisters. They might as well be three mothers. I've been making a conscious effort not to do it to Nikhil this year."

One of my hands clutches my necklace. "Like . . . how?"

"Have you ever *invited* her to your room? Or anywhere else, for that matter?"

There's a long and empty silence. Sanjita correctly interprets it. "What about Gen? Do you guys ever hang out, just the two of you?"

"She lives on the other side of the Atlantic." It comes out pricklier than intended.

"But you do, don't you? Over the holidays."

I think about Gen in my bedroom over Thanksgiving. And then again over Christmas. The truth washes over me in a tidal wave. It's true. Hattie has been trying to tell me for years. I treat Gen like a friend, and I treat her like a child.

I mother her.

Hattie hasn't been my baby sister in ages. I've been condescending, and I've never seen nor treated her like an equal. She needs me to be a confidante. A friend. And then the unexpected flip side illuminates inside of me: I need her to be mine even more.

"You should consider a double major," I say. "Law *and* psychology."

Sanjita smiles as if she's pleased to be seen. Just like me.

chapter twenty-nine

Sanjita and I talk more about college and the future. But we don't talk about Kurt. And we don't talk about Emily. And as January rolls into February, I realize that we probably never will. We've grown too far apart, and our past hurts were too big. Real friendship is no longer an option. But I don't feel melancholy about it—I feel relieved. There's a measure of respect and well wishes between us. And that's not nothing.

Our conversation also made me realize how much I've missed having a female friendship in my life. Sanjita and I may never hang out again, but there's someone else here that I've been ignoring for far too long: Hattie.

It's time to let go of this stupid grudge. I know she didn't mean to get Josh and me in trouble. And she *didn't* get us in trouble. She *didn't* get Josh expelled. We got ourselves in trouble, and Josh got himself expelled.

The pain of losing him is as visceral as ever. The only way I'll ever move past it is to make sure that the loss wasn't in vain. That I've learned something. At the very least, being proactive will feel better than sitting around and feeling sorry for myself. It takes me a while to figure out the right way to simultaneously apologize *and* make a gesture of friendship, but it takes me even longer to work up the nerve to talk to her.

She's my sister, but she's still intimidating as hell.

I find the courage on an empty Sunday afternoon when Kurt is out spelunking with his friends. Or . . . maybe it's not so much that I find the courage. Maybe it's more that I'm forced into it, because every time my world comes to a standstill, all I can think about is the Josh-size hole in my heart. It's too sad for me to be alone.

Hattie is skeptical at my text, but she agrees to meet me more willingly than I would've guessed. I wait outside her dorm. "Why did you want me to dress warmly?" she asks. "Are you taking me to a Siberian prison?"

I smile and cross the street without her. "Nope."

She hesitates. And then she catches up and walks beside me. "Abandoned research station in Antarctica?"

"Nope."

"You're taking me to practice for our two-person skeleton race at the Olympics."

"Yes."

"Do you think it's finally gonna snow?"

I'm thrown by her question, which sounds like a real one.

She's staring at the sky. "I doubt it," I say. "We haven't been lucky so far. Why would that change now?"

"You used to be the positive sister," Hattie grumbles. We walk together silently to the other side of the Seine, and she's only further exasperated when we reach our destination. "Tante Juliette's. Is this an intervention? Did you find out about my sex addiction? So I like old men in baby diapers, what's the big deal?"

"I didn't bring you to Tante Juliette's."

She snarls. "I've been here, like, a million times, remember?"

"Just shut up and follow me."

For some reason, Hattie does. She follows me up the stairs. Around the third floor, I look back over my shoulder and say, "Diapers, huh?"

"And those adult-size cribs. That's hot."

I laugh.

There's the quickest hint of a smile before she drops back into deadpan. "And unibrows. I like a geezer with a giant, coarse unibrow."

I laugh again. "Oh god, Hattie."

We pass by the purple door with the leopard-print mat. "Yeah, see, that's definitely Tante Juliette's door," she says.

I lead her to mine. "And this?"

"Her stupid roof. Gen once threw my teddy bear over the edge, and a moped ran over him. Sludge was never the same."

"She did? For real?" I'm startled. I don't remember this.

"Yeah, for real."

I unlock the door and head up the rickety steps. "Well.

Sludge is safe. I promise I'm not leading you up here to reenact a traumatic moment from your childhood."

"I know you wouldn't." I almost don't hear her say it, it's so quiet.

I pop open the trapdoor, and she squints into the sunlight. I reach for her hand and help her onto the roof. Her eyes widen. My unmovable, unshakable sister looks surprised by her surroundings. "Who did this?" she asks. "It's yours, isn't it? This looks like you."

I'm not sure if that's good or bad. "It's on loan. I've been using it for a few years."

Hattie whips around and narrows her eyes at me. "So Gen gave it to you? This is your place? The two of you?"

"Gen? No, Tante Juliette gave it to me sophomore year. It was a place where Kurt and I could escape from . . . everyone else. Gen doesn't know about it."

"She doesn't?" There's a heartbreaking note of hope in her voice. And I know that everything Sanjita said is true.

I smile gently. "Nope. It's a secret. She doesn't know."

"It's pretty," Hattie finally says.

"Thanks. I'm glad you like it. Because it's yours now."

For the second time in a single minute, Hattie looks surprised. I hold out the key. She takes it slowly. "Don't you want to give this to Kurt? Isn't it his, too?"

"Kurt has new places to explore. And . . . he's not you. He's not my sister."

She almost appears to be shaken. Almost.

"And, you know, you don't have to keep any of this stuff, it's just junk we've picked up over the years——"

"No! No, I like it." She glances around, and her eyes catch on the mural, which I've been trying my best to ignore. "You brought Josh up here, too."

I tuck my hands inside my coat pockets. "Yeah."

"So was this some sort of gross sexual playground? Did you do it on top of this carousel-horse head?"

"Hattie!"

She laughs at my reddened cheeks, and after a moment, I can't help but join in. "No," I say. "But *maybe* you should wash the blanket in that trunk."

My sister squeals with genuine horror, which only makes us both laugh harder. When we finally stop, she pulls her gaze away from mine again. She focuses on the river. "It's cool of you to give this to me. So . . . thanks."

"I'm sorry." I take a deep breath. "For being so awful to you this year. And for blaming you for something that wasn't your fault."

Hattie nods. She doesn't take her eyes off the Seine. But I know we're okay.

I take another deep breath, and . . . *there it is.* A new and distinct smell in the air. Hattie turns her head and smiles at me as the first snowflakes of the year swirl down upon Paris. The city is cold and hushed and beautiful.

"Will you miss this next year?" she asks, and when I look at her in surprise, she adds, "Maman told me they mailed the first check to Dartmouth."

I hesitate, and then I tell her the truth. "I *will* miss Paris.

And I'll miss New York. I'm excited and scared, but . . . I think I'm more excited than scared. I think," I say again.

"You think?"

"I think." I slide down the wall until I'm sitting. She sits beside me. We cross our arms, shivering. "When Josh and I were in Spain, we went to this park. This really, really beautiful park. And it started these ideas in my head about how maybe I wasn't the person that I thought I was. Maybe I'm *not* a city girl. Maybe I was only thinking about Paris versus New York, because nothing else seemed real, somehow. Like, everywhere else just seemed like something—"

"You'd read about in a book."

"*Exactly.* But being in this beautiful park with this beautiful boy talking about this alternate future in which I'm someone who learns how to camp and climb rocks and build fires and sleep below the stars . . . in that moment, it seemed possible."

"So what? You're gonna be a park ranger?"

I laugh. "I just want to try those things. They sound fun."

"What about Josh?"

My eyes catch on his mural. On the brownstone with ivy window boxes and the American flag. "What about him?"

"He's not a part of your plans anymore?"

"Well . . . no. We broke up. And I don't need him to do those things."

"Yeah, duh," Hattie says. "But that's not what I meant. I meant don't you still *want* to do those things with him?"

"Yes," I whisper. "I still want to do everything with him."

"Isla . . . why do you think that Josh didn't love you?"

My voice grows even smaller. "Because I thought no one could love me."

"And why did you think *that*?"

"Because I didn't think I was worth loving."

Hattie takes this in. And then she hits me in the stomach. I yowl in surprise, and she hits me again. "Don't be stupid."

"*Ow.*"

"Everyone is worthy of love. Even a dumb sister like you."

I snort. "Yeah, thanks. I got that. I'm okay now."

"Are you? Because you don't act like a person who is okay. You mope around school, and you hardly ever leave your room, and you always look unhappy."

"Says the sister with the permanent scowl."

"You need to talk to him."

I sigh and stare at my lap. "I know."

"So why haven't you?"

"Because now I *do* believe that he loved me. And I'm afraid that after all this time, after everything I've put him through . . . he doesn't anymore."

"Ugh. So take a risk and find out. The sooner you ask him, the sooner you can get on with your life. Either way," she adds.

Thanks to Josh, I *am* taking risks. I've learned that if I never leave those areas of my life that feel comfortable, I'll never have a chance at a greater happiness. Accepting Dartmouth was a risk. Asking my sister to hang out with me was a risk. But the biggest risk of all is still Josh himself. I don't yet have the courage to give him the opportunity to say no. It's impossible, the not-knowing, but it's better than getting the wrong answer.

There's a muffled ring from inside my coat pocket. I pull out my phone to silence it, and then it drops from my hands and bounces against the concrete.

Josh.

It's his *actual name*. I haven't seen it on the screen of my phone since before Barcelona. My heart wrenches. "Is that him? How can that be him?"

"Whoa. He heard us."

I pick up my phone. "What do I do?"

"One more ring until voice mail." Hattie peers over my shoulder. "Tick-tock."

I scramble to answer. "He—hello?"

There's a strange hiccup of silence. And then he speaks, and his voice—*It's him, it's him, it's him*—is awash with strangled relief. "I didn't know if you'd answer."

"You got your phone back."

"Yeah. Last week."

I feel a stab of sadness that he didn't call me immediately. And then a second stab, this one of guilt. I broke up with him. Of course he shouldn't call me.

"It's Sunday night," he continues. "You aren't at Pizza Pellino."

"No, I'm at the Treehouse with Hattie." And then I'm so dizzy that my vision goes black. "How . . . how did you know that I'm not there?"

But I've already anticipated his answer.

"Because *I'm* here."

chapter thirty

I'm trembling. Hattie's ear is pressed against my head, listening in. Silver-white flakes catch in our tangle of red hair.

"Isla?" Josh says. "Isla, are you still there?"

"I'm here."

"I was hoping you'd be *here*. At Pellino's. My friends and I are on our way to the Olympics, so we stopped by for old time's sake. I wanted to introduce you. I mean, I know you already know them. But I wanted you to *know* them."

My head swims. "You want me to know your friends?"

"Is that too weird?"

"I don't know."

"I'd like to see you again. We could talk?" His question is tentative.

He's caught me off guard. I'm not ready for this. I have to

prepare for this. "How long will you be in town?"

"Just tonight. We're catching the train to Chambéry in the morning."

Hattie is nodding her head like a madwoman.

"Um," I say. "Sure. I guess I could be there in . . . twenty minutes?"

"Great!" Josh says. "Okay, bye."

I stare down at my phone's screen. "He hung up."

"He was afraid you'd take it back," Hattie says.

I put my head between my legs. "I feel ill."

"That was the strangest timing. *The strangest.* It's like fate, if I believed in fate. I don't know. Maybe I believe in fate now."

The tone of her voice makes me lift my head. She grins.

"Hattie." My heart seizes. "What did you do?"

"Jeez, nothing."

"Tell me what you did!"

"Ow." She covers her ears at my shouting. "Maybe I mailed your stupid book to his dad's stupid office in DC, I don't know."

I frown. "Huh? What book?"

"The one you brought home from Angoulême, thanks for not inviting me, that I stole from your room to read and discovered you'd had it personalized? I thought it was so sad and pathetic that I mailed it to him. And maybe I attached a note saying how you were totally still in love with him, and he should try calling you again."

It's the only thing that could shock me more than Josh's call. Finding out that I have *Hattie* to thank for it. I'm speechless.

"You're welcome," she says.

"Thank you? I think? I'll let you know when this is all over."

"You'd better." She pulls me to my feet, leads me through the trapdoor and down the stairs, locks the door, and slides the key into her pocket.

The pressure inside my chest is growing at a paralyzing rate. "I don't know about this."

"Shut up. You're being annoying again." Hattie leads me, stumbling, into the closest *métro* station. I feel like I'm moving both too fast and too slow. She shoves me through the turnstile and says, "Don't be a chickenshit. Tell him how you feel."

"What if he doesn't love me?"

"He does."

"What if he doesn't?"

"Ugh, then who cares? You won't lose anything you haven't already lost." She flicks a snowflake from the tip of my nose. "For once in your life, listen to your younger sister. She's taller, and she knows better than you."

The flakes are scattered, here and there, as they float down to earth. I glance at the gray-white sky. If only a blizzard would burst from above and bury me alive. That would be better than what I'm about to do. The temperature is below freezing, but I'm sweaty and feverish and short of breath. My feet touch Pellino's threshold, but my body won't go any farther. *One step at a time.* I place my hand on the door.

Pushing it open has never felt so impossible.

A chain of brass bells signals my entrance. The maître d'
brightens at the sight of me. *"Où est Monsieur Bacon?"*

"Kurt has other plans tonight," I reply in French as my gaze
darts around the room.

"Oh. Are we sad?"

"No, it's fine. I'm actually meeting—"

"Isla!"

It comes from the corner table. St. Clair is waving me
down as Josh turns around in his chair. Everything transitions
into slow motion. The maître d', the noisy chatter, the smoky
fragrance of the wood-fired pizza—they vanish as I wait for his
eyes to find mine.

We lock.

The entire contents of my heart reflect back at me in his
expression. *Joy, pain, strength, wonder, sadness, beauty, hope.*

He is everything.

"Ah," the maître d' says. "Of course."

He guides me toward the table as my heartbeat thumps in
my throat. The room closes in. My soul aches with attraction.
There are four empty seats, and the maître d' pulls out the
chair beside Josh. I'm shaking as I place my coat onto the back
of it. I'm shaking as I sit down. I'm shaking as Josh glances at
the maître d' with a look of unmistakable gratitude. Does that
glance mean what I want it to mean?

"Where's Kurt?" Josh asks.

"He's out with some new friends. Underground. It's a long
story."

Josh lifts his eyebrows in surprise as the rest of the table beams at me—St. Clair, Anna, and Meredith. "Wow," I say. "The gang's all here."

"Everyone but Rashmi," St. Clair says.

Anna gives him a swift kick below the table, but I catch it. "It's okay," I say awkwardly. At least it's answered a question. They know about my history with Josh. I glance at the three empty seats. "Is she coming?"

"One of those was for Kurt," Josh says, and I'm touched.

"The others are for our friends who got us into the Olympics," Anna says. "We split up today, and they're still out sight-seeing. They should be here any minute."

"Friends from California?" I grab the opportunity to show them that I'm not completely in the dark. Just mostly.

She nods. "Yeah, Lola and Cricket. Étienne and I—"

"*Étienne,*" Josh says, and Meredith cracks up.

"They're teasing me because I'm the only person who calls him that," Anna explains.

"You're the only person *allowed* to call him that," Josh says. "You and his mom."

St. Clair smiles. "The only two ladies I need."

"That's sick," Meredith says, but she's still laughing. She has a wonderful, friendly laugh. A tiny nose ring catches the light and twinkles. Everything about her is cheerful.

It's unreal to be surrounded here, in person, by his friends. Those faces from his artwork.

Anna is one of those naturally beautiful girls who has no idea that she's beautiful. She dresses in jeans and T-shirts, and she has this gap-toothed smile and a bleached stripe in her long brown hair. She's comfortable in her own skin. Her boyfriend is also beautiful, but he's aware of it. Not that St. Clair acts like a jerk. He's just loaded with confidence. He's short, but it's never gotten in his way. Nearly every girl at school was in love with him, not to mention most of the guys and half the *professeurs.*

But I was never in love with him. Not when Josh was around.

Anna clears her throat. "Anyway. *Étienne* and I—"

Josh and Meredith snicker.

Anna grins. "—work with Lola at a movie theater. Cricket is her boyfriend, and Cricket's twin sister is Calliope Bell. The figure skater?"

My eyebrows shoot up. "I've seen her face on about a billion advertisements."

"That's the one. She's going for the gold."

"And you're all here to cheer her on?" I glance at Josh. He appears to be calm, but it's superficial. A frenetic energy is pulsating from his core. Vibrating against me. I rub my arms, hair on end, but the others don't notice.

"Sort of." St. Clair shrugs. It's slow and full-bodied, very French. Maman has the same one. "Mainly we're using it as an excuse to visit."

I turn to Meredith. "Did you come in from Rome? That's where you're attending university, right?"

"Yeah." She puts an arm around Josh and her curly head on his shoulder, but they're clearly gestures of friendship. "When I heard everyone was coming, I couldn't resist."

"And you?" I don't look at Josh. He knows the question is for him.

He can't meet my eyes either. "Same for me, I guess. Couldn't resist."

St. Clair waggles his eyebrows at Josh, but the moment he sees that I've caught him, his expression changes to a flirtatious grin. "Aw, mate," he says to Josh. "Admit it. You couldn't resist *me*."

Josh relaxes into a smile. "You're like a gorgeous little bonbon."

"Delicious in every way," St. Clair says.

Anna rolls her eyes. "Wait until you try his creamy center."

St. Clair bursts into laughter as Meredith squeals. The chemistry between the four of them is as if they hadn't spent a day apart. My heart squeezes, but it's not from jealousy. It's out of happiness for Josh's sake. He leans across the table to jostle St. Clair, but he knocks against my arm instead.

"Sorry," Josh says quickly. His voice turns strained. He sits, and the jovial mood crashes down with him, but his touch shudders through me in waves.

Longing. As fierce and powerful as ever.

I look away, not wanting him to see how badly I wish he would touch me again. And then I discover a strange apparition outside the restaurant's window. I blink. It's still there. In the winter, the streets of Paris are gray and the coats that walk them are black.

So this . . . this is like . . .

"The circus," Josh says, finishing my thought out loud. "It's like the circus has come to town."

"Brilliant," St. Clair says. "That must be Lola and Cricket."

A boy and a girl enter the restaurant. The boy is ridiculously tall and skinny—far more extreme than Josh—and it's only emphasized by the tightness of his pinstriped pants. He could almost be wearing stilts. He's wearing a bright blue military jacket, and his wrists are covered in rainbow-colored bracelets and rubber bands. The girl is wearing a gigantic, poufy skirt with pink and yellow and turquoise crinolines peeking out from underneath. She also has a military jacket, Vietnam-era army green, but hers has been decorated with pink glitter. And she has matching pink hair.

"Hi!" Lola plops down beside me, and her skirt *fwoomps* up and onto my lap. "Yikes. Sorry about that." She smiles as she jams it underneath the table.

"How did you manage to fit all of that into a suitcase?" I'm impressed.

Her smile grows from ear to ear. "I'm a championship-level packer."

St. Clair snorts. "She also brought three times the amount of luggage as the rest of us."

"But she *is* a good packer," Cricket says. "You'd be amazed at how much she managed to squish into those extra suitcases."

He pulls out the chair beside her, and she reaches up with both arms to hold him as he sits down. Not because he needs steadying, but because they're clearly in the earliest stages of love. She simply *needs* to touch him. They double-hold-hands below the table. I feel a sharp pang as I remember doing the same with Josh. Lola gives Cricket a kiss, square on the lips, and he looks as if he might explode from happiness.

"Hey," Lola says, suddenly seeing Josh. "I think I saw you on TV a few months ago."

"It's possible," Josh says.

"You must be Isla and Josh," Cricket says.

I almost correct him—*Oh, no, we aren't a couple*—when I realize he means Isla and Josh. Not Isla-and-Josh. I shake his extended hand, feeling sad. "And Meredith," he says, leaning over me to shake hers.

"I like your hair," she says.

"Thanks," he says. It stands on end, further adding to his manic height.

"So none of you have to ask," Lola says. "Six four. Without the hair."

"Étienne is five four," Anna says. "*With* his boots."

"Without," St. Clair protests. But his grin tells another story.

"You're shorter than I thought." I say it without thinking. "Sorry." I wince. "I only meant you don't seem that small." I wince again.

"*Confidence,* darling." He leans across the table and touches a finger to my cheek. "You could learn something from me, you know."

My face turns pink. But I laugh, pleased to be included in their good-natured ribbing. Josh looks at me, worried, and I turn in my seat to face him full on. I smile. He exhales with relief, and I lean in closer.

"We're okay," I whisper. "Aren't we?"

"It's all I want," he says.

Our server appears. We startle apart, and my heart races. Does that mean he wants to be friends again? Or am *I* what he wants? With all that *wanting* connotes?

We place an order for a ton of pizzas. Normally I'd be thrilled about the variety, but all I want to do is return to the previous conversation. But our window of privacy is gone. The table pulls us into discussion about the Olympics. Apparently, Cricket's twin would be a shoo-in for the gold medal, but she's convinced that she has a second-place curse. Everyone says they're sure she'll be fine, but Cricket is weird and jittery. I get the sense that he believes in the curse, too. Talk turns to everyone's schools. I wait for Josh to chime in, but he never does. I wonder if that means he still hasn't enrolled anywhere. But maybe he's waiting for me to speak first.

The silence in our corner grows.

The pizza arrives. With each bite, I beg myself to ask if he's finishing high school. I beg myself to ask if he's still moving to Vermont. But, the truth is, I'm afraid of his answer. It's been less than two months, and I left him brokenhearted. How could he have already found the energy to attend—or care about—a new school?

My guilt and fear push us further apart.

"Are you okay?" Josh asks. "You've hardly eaten anything."

I look at his plate. "Neither have you."

He opens his mouth to reply, when St. Clair stands. "We're

off," he says, meaning him and Anna and no one else. She looks as surprised as the rest of us.

"We haven't even had dessert," Meredith says.

"I'm taking my lady friend somewhere special for dessert."

"You are?" Anna says.

"I am."

Anna looks happy enough. "Okay." She gathers her things and looks bewilderedly at the rest of us. "Guess I'll see you guys tomorrow?" Her eyes fall on me. "Oh, no! I wanted to catch up. Well, hopefully, we'll be seeing each other again. Soon. Good luck."

I pounce on her words. *Soon. Good luck.* They're general statements, but they feel specific. They feel promising. Anna and St. Clair hug everybody goodbye, even me. The hug between Josh and St. Clair lasts the longest. It's a real hug, not a lame guy-hug. My heart breaks a little more. Anna and St. Clair leave the restaurant. Meredith, Lola, and I sit down, but Josh and Cricket exchange a meaningful look.

Josh flags down the server. *"L'addition, s'il vous plaît."* Check, please.

"We're leaving?" I can't hide the disappointment from my voice. A proper French dinner should keep us here for at least another hour.

Josh pauses, mid-reach for his wallet. He looks at me, searching, and I find hope in his eyes. It makes me feel hopeful, too. He smiles. "Something better is about to happen."

"Hurry, hurry, hurry." Cricket is bouncing on the balls of his feet.

"Do *you* know what's happening?" Lola asks me.

I shake my head as Meredith looks between Josh and Cricket. "Didn't you two *just* meet?" she asks. "How can you already have secrets?"

Josh grins so wide that his dimples appear. My heart stutters at the well-missed sight. He and Cricket toss down some euros, and then Josh is yanking out a bulging shoulder bag from behind the table. "Come on." He's still smiling at me as he throws on his coat. It's his going-on-a-date coat, of course.

That coat. It hurts how much I love it.

The five of us race through the snowy white streets toward the River Seine. The sun has gone down, and most of the Latin Quarter appears to be staying inside tonight. Josh glances at my feet. I'm wearing heeled boots, but I'm keeping in stride with everyone else. He shoots me an impressed eyebrow-raise as we burst out of the neighborhood, directly across from Notre-Dame.

"Where?" Cricket asks Josh.

"In the square, near the main entrance." Josh points across the bridge. We run across it toward Notre-Dame's courtyard.

"*Oh,*" Meredith says, understanding. "Seriously?"

Lola looks at me, and we explode into helpless laughter. Neither of us has any idea what's happening. We're panting, out of shape and out of breath.

"Stop!" Josh says.

We tumble to a halt behind him. We're on the edge of the square facing the massive cathedral. "I assume we didn't run all of the way here to see a structure that hasn't left this spot in hundreds of years?" Lola readjusts her pink hair, and I realize it's a wig. "What am I looking at?"

But then I see them.

Several yards away—closer to the cathedral's legendary carved doorways—Anna and St. Clair are standing on top of Point Zéro. It's been hand-brushed clear of its dusting of snow. Point Zéro is the bronze marker, a star, which designates the official center of France. There are at least two superstitions about it. One is that anyone who stands on the star will return to France. The other is that you can use it to make a wish.

"Wait for it," Josh says.

Lola stands straighter, excited. "No!"

"Yes," Cricket says.

I'm the last one in the dark, until—suddenly—it happens. St. Clair removes something from his pocket. And then he gets down on one knee.

Anna's entire body lights with shock and joy and love. She nods a vigorous yes. St. Clair places the ring on her finger. He stands, she throws her arms around him, and they kiss. He spins her in a circle. They kiss again. Deep, hungry, long. And then he turns to us and waves—with the biggest smile I've ever seen—clearly aware that we've been standing here the whole time.

chapter thirty-one

I've never witnessed a moment like this. I didn't even know that I was *old enough* for a moment like this. Friends—are they friends? They feel like they might be friends to have included me here tonight—getting engaged to be married. At nineteen!

Anna shows off her ring. It's small and simple and lovely. Her eyes suddenly shine, and she wheels around to face St. Clair. "So *this* is why you got a job."

He grins. "I wasn't about to buy you a ring with my father's money."

Josh bear hugs St. Clair. "I'm only sorry you're off the market."

"Don't tell Anna, but I bought one for you, too," St. Clair says.

Lola throws her arms around Cricket. "I can't believe you didn't tell me this was gonna happen."

"I wanted to," he says. "But sometimes you think about things . . . out loud."

"I do not!"

"You do," Anna and St. Clair say together.

Lola grumbles, but she's smiling.

"Attention, attention," St. Clair says. "My fiancée and I——"

Everyone laughs at how strange and foreign the word sounds. It's like discovering a new language or being a part of a new culture. The culture of adults. And we don't yet know how it works, but it feels good so far.

St. Clair clears his throat. "My *fiancée* and I are headed out for a celebratory dessert. I'd ask you all to join us, but I don't want you there."

We laugh. Everybody hugs one another goodbye again, and this time, Anna and Meredith have the longest hug. Meredith whispers something to her, and Anna looks moved. She hugs Meredith again. And then Anna and St. Clair are bouncing off into the distance, weaving a path through the accumulating snow. He loudly hums a happy tune.

Lola glances at the full moon. "You know . . . it's not *that* late."

Cricket extends his arm. "Shall we stroll?"

She slips her arm through it and hugs him closer against her body. "I can't believe we're in *Paris. Together.*"

"It was nice meeting you," Cricket says to me, and I feel sad that everyone is leaving. "See you in the morning?" he asks Josh.

Josh nods.

Lola and Cricket wander away, a splash of brilliant color in a white night. And now there are three. Josh's expression turns solemn. He places an arm around Meredith, and the gesture makes me recall that, once upon a time, she was in love with St. Clair.

"You okay, Mer?" he asks.

"I am," she says. "But thank you for asking."

Another hug, a long one filled with memories. She pulls away first. "Sorry," she says. "You'll have to forgive me. My day started early, and I'm beat. I'm gonna head back to the hostel." But Meredith is definitely not *beat*. She's bowing out to let us talk. She's choosing to be alone—on a night that might be bittersweet for her—to give us a chance at . . . I'm not sure what.

"It was nice seeing you again," I say. And I mean it. I'm grateful for this sacrifice.

"Don't get too sad. I'm sure we'll see each other again someday." And she winks before leaving. "See you tomorrow, Josh," she shouts.

Josh's hands are in his pockets, and his shoulders are up to his ears. "She's not my most subtle friend. Which is saying something. Sorry about that."

"It's okay. She's really nice."

"She is."

"All of your friends are nice."

He looks at me. "I'm glad you think so."

We're quiet. The snow falls softly against his dark hair.

"So," I say.

"So." He glances at his feet. "Can I walk you home?"

My body flushes. "Yes. Please. Thank you." I look away, embarrassed.

Without needing to say it aloud, we choose a route toward the dorm that will have fewer people. We walk in silence. The flakes are getting fatter. The hush should feel peaceful, but the nervousness inside of me only grows.

He looks so beautiful in the lamplight. I think I was wrong about him. I *hope* I was wrong about him. I know I was wrong about myself. We don't say a word until we reach the dormitory. The first time we walked here together, it was ours. Now it's only mine. He's brave for coming back here again, and I can be brave, too.

"Would you . . . , " I say.

Josh watches me. He waits for me to finish the question. He wants me to say it.

"Do you wanna come inside?" I ask. "And talk?"

It looks as if what he's about to say might kill him. "I wish that I could, but I don't think I'd be welcome in there."

Please don't reject me. "Since when do you care about the rules?"

"I don't want you to get in trouble."

"I don't care," I say.

"I do."

My heart twists harder, heavier. "Will you at least be around for breakfast? When does your train leave?"

"I'm not sure," he says.

I close my eyes. How could he not know the answer to that question? What kind of excuse is that?

"I want you to have this," he says.

I open my eyes again. He's struggling to remove a manuscript from his bag, and now I can see that it's the reason why it'd been so bulky. The papers take up the entire thing.

My heart breaks. *This* is why he wanted to meet me tonight.

Against my better judgment, I hold down the bottom of his bag so that he can pull it out. He clutches the manuscript against his chest before presenting it to me with shaking hands. I don't know if they shake from nervousness or from the weather.

I take it. There's a new title. *Spaces.*

"You were right," he says. "About . . . a lot of stuff. I've been working really hard on it, and I'd love your opinion. On the changes."

Please don't make me read this again. "Um, okay."

He turns hopeful. "Yeah?"

"Yeah. Sure." The weight of his work grows heavier in my arms. "Uh, when would you like this back?"

"Oh, no. That's yours. To keep."

Silence.

"Okay," I finally say.

He tucks his hands back inside his coat. "Will you call me as soon as you're done?"

I'm startled. "You want me to read it now?"

"Yeah. I mean, no. You don't have to. But I'm leaving tomorrow—"

"No, it's okay. I can read it now."

"Yeah?" he asks.

"Yeah."

"All right. So. You have my number."

This now ranks as the most awkward conversation that we've ever had. It's way worse than anything before we dated.

I nod. "Yep."

Josh leans in for a hug. He hesitates, just as I'm leaning in. So he leans in again. The manuscript sits cold and heavy between our bodies. And as he awkwardly pats me on the back, I realize that this is the last time that we will ever touch.

chapter thirty-two

I set the manuscript down on my bed. I'm exhausted.

I remove my wet shoes, my coat, my leggings.

I wash my face.

I brush my teeth.

The manuscript's paper eyes bore into the back of my head. I stare at it in the mirror's reflection above my sink. It seems both tragically dead and frighteningly alive. And I have no choice but to climb into bed with it. I fiddle with a stubborn wave of hair. I poke at the pores on my nose. I take a long time turning on my lamp.

I slip into bed. I'm listening for the snow, which is coming down harder, but I can't hear it. I can only see it streaming through the streetlight outside.

I pull the manuscript into my lap. I read.

It has a new beginning. It no longer starts with his first day as a wide-eyed, slack-jawed freshman. It starts with an older, wiser, and more embittered Josh. It's the summer before his senior year. He's sitting alone, drawing in a café.

And then . . . I'm there.

I appear like a dream, and Josh is whisked into a surreal, blissful night that makes him forget his troubles. It makes him feel hope for the first time in years. There's the page that I've seen before of him racing home to draw me, but then there's a new full-page illustration of me with the garden-rose halo. I glow on the page like something sacred. Josh is on his knees at the bottom of the illustration, looking up at me, weeping, his hands clasped. The word *Salvation* pours from his lips.

My own hands are trembling so hard that I can barely get to the next page.

FRESHMAN, it says. And the story I'm familiar with begins. Most of this section is the same. It's funny, it's sad, it's sweet. It's innocent. But there are some differences. He's added subtle brushstrokes to draw attention toward areas of the story that I know will have greater meaning later on. Things that he couldn't have known would be so important when he drew them years ago.

And then there's me. Again. He's chronologically added the panels of the first time we spoke, when he saw me reading the

Sfar book in the cafeteria. He's even added a tiny heart above his head while he speaks. And then a broken one when he thinks that I don't like him.

I touch the broken heart with the tip of my finger.

The story turns familiar again, but this time the panels with Rashmi are less painful. The sadness I feel comes from remembering how much they hurt me the first time. He's trimmed down her scenes and the excessive one-page panels. She's still a large part of the story, as she should be, but the focus remains squarely on him. Also as it should be.

Last summer. Kismet. A callback panel signals a return to the beginning of the story, and then it cuts back to him discovering me with Kurt the following night.

New pages appear. Josh with his parents. There's an increasing distance between them—now self-created, out of spite—as he simultaneously yearns to be closer. He wants them to fight for his attention. He returns to school for his senior year. When I read this in November, these pages were rough sketches. Now they've been lovingly inked in. It gives everything a new sense of permanence.

And then I'm reading about his crush on me, and I'm reading about him longing for me at Oktoberfest, and I'm reading about our first date. I'm reading about him falling in love with me. I'm reading about the Treehouse and the college applications and his birthday, and we're going to Spain, and we're making love. He draws us beautifully. The emotions on the page are so much bigger than anything he's drawn before.

And then it's a two-page spread: a single panel being ripped in half. I'm on one side, and he's on the other. Our hands grasp at the space between. *Almost* touching.

My cheeks are wet. I'm not sure how long I've been crying.

The pages turn angry and wild, swirled around the election and parents, who are always present yet always absent. He grieves for our loss. He blames himself. He's depressed, and he doesn't know how to tell me that we won't be seeing each other for Thanksgiving. I want to tell Josh-on-the-page that it's okay, but I can't. It won't be okay.

He fights with his parents. They want him to finish at a private school. He wants to take his GED. Neither happens. He sinks deeper into depression, and he won't leave his room, and he draws me again and again and again. And then he draws my Christmas present. I don't know if I can handle reading about Christmas, but it's coming anyway.

I pick a fight. I am cruel. I annihilate him.

He thought we'd be together forever. Images of New England, a wedding, children, old age crumble into the background of a dark panel in which he's curled on the ground in the fetal position. He tries to call me. I won't answer. His devastation turns into fury. New Year's Eve arrives, and he sits alone in his bedroom watching television. He thinks about our first date, just like I did. Brian calls his house shortly after midnight with the urgent message that I'm waiting for him at Kismet. There's still time to make it.

I turn the page, fearing what I'll find next.

Josh chooses not to go. He wants me to suffer in the way that I've made him suffer. It's awful to read, though it's no less than I deserved. But as the days pass, Josh realizes that he's made a mistake. And as they continue to pass, it gets harder to call me. He's afraid that now I will have given up on him for good.

And then . . . his naked figure tumbles into space.

A completely black two-page spread. On the following page, no illustration, only my own words written in Josh's beautiful handwriting: *"SPACES . . . BREAKS . . . TO CONTEMPLATE THINGS . . . TO FIGURE OUT WHAT'S IMPORTANT . . ."*

A series of near-identical panels are next, showing an excruciating passage of time. A certain truth is settling in. That one of the most hurtful things I said to him—that he passively campaigned for his own expulsion, because he couldn't admit to his parents that he'd made a mistake in moving to France—only hurts so much because it's true. And that the head of school and his ex-girlfriend had been telling him that for years, but it didn't matter until he heard the words from the person who mattered the most. Me.

But he's also still angry with me for invalidating his own feelings. He loves me, and I won't let him. He decides that he has to prove it. He confesses to his parents that leaving home for Paris was a mistake, but that he's ready for Vermont. He won't mess it up this time. They say they'd like to believe him, but they're concerned with his ability to see things through. An offer is put on the table. They'll send him to Vermont if he can finish the project that means the most to him, the project that will also serve as his official portfolio for admission: this graphic memoir.

They understand that he's been writing about his private life—and that some of it includes *them*. They give him their support anyway.

His parents are understanding and supportive about . . . *a lot* of things.

I'm reading faster now, flipping the pages more and more quickly, as Josh throws himself back into his work. He locks himself away in his room in order to reconnect with the world. Day and night, he makes the changes and pushes ahead. Pushes through. His resolve is admirable as he forces his way through the monotonous long hours and the renewed shooting pains in his right hand to bring his vision onto the page.

He signs up to take the GED and nails it in a weekend. He talks to St. Clair, learns of the engagement ring and the upcoming trip, and he marks the date on his calendar. But he marks it with the word *Isla*.

His mother sees it. She nods.

My heart is racing. The pages are no longer inked, they're penciled sketches. A month of hard work in January turns into two weeks of agonizing work in February. Doubt creeps back in. He considers canceling his flight, but that's when Hattie's package arrives, and he's overwhelmed and overjoyed, and it gives him the courage to press forward. He flies across the Atlantic. He meets his friends, and he takes them to Pizza Pellino for dinner, where he knows he'll find Kurt and me. Because it's Sunday.

I have now exited Josh's real past and entered into what he *hopes* is his future.

The sketches get rougher. Kurt and I are at the restaurant, and Josh and his friends—St. Clair, Anna, and Meredith—join us for dinner. Our table's conversation is similar to what occurred earlier tonight, except that Josh is more vocal. He tells me it was important for me to meet his friends, because they're the people that he chooses to have in his life. Not like the people at the Christmas party whom he deals with for his family's sake. He wants me to be friends with his friends, too.

He asks me about Dartmouth, and I tell him that I was accepted. "I knew you would be," he whispers. We watch the proposal, glancing at each other with hope and nervousness. We split apart from the others, he walks me home, and he hands me a copy of this manuscript. He tells me to call his phone when I'm done reading it.

I'm holding my breath. I can hardly turn the page . . .

There I am. I'm reading this book by lamplight. I finish it, call him, and he tells me that he's on the corner outside of my window. His hands are tucked into his pockets, and he's shivering in the freezing February night.

Isla-on-the-page runs outside. Josh embraces her.

"I'm in love with you," he says. "I'll do anything to be with you."

"I'm in love with you," Isla-on-the-page says. "I'll wait for you."

I tell him that I'll wait for him to finish his book and earn his passage to college. I tell him that we'll meet again this summer. And then, he tells me, we'll never be apart again.

It's after two in the morning when I set down the manuscript. My heart is drumming so loudly that I can't hear myself think, and I can hardly see through my tears. I climb out of bed, pull aside the curtain, and peek out my window.

He's there.

I drop the curtain, and it swings back into place. I pick it up and look outside again. He's still there. He's on the corner with his head ducked underneath his coat, shivering. The snow is falling like crazy. It covers him as if he were a mere fireplug or bicycle or tree. He doesn't see me. I yank on my boots, grab my key, and race down the hall. I throw open the door, and he must hear me running, because he turns the corner just as I reach it.

"You forgot to call," he says.

I throw open my arms. He pulls me into him, and we kiss, and his lips are cold, and I think he's crying, and I'm definitely crying, and I pull back to say, "I am so in love with you, Joshua Wasserstein. Of course I'll wait for you."

chapter thirty-three

His voice is a whisper. "I don't want to get you in trouble."

I shut my door with precision silence. "I'm not on a final warning, and you've already been expelled. What's the worst that could happen?"

"I don't know." Josh is genuinely worried. "Maybe it could go on your permanent record and keep Dartmouth from accepting you?"

I smile. "My parents have already sent them the first tuition check."

His knees weaken. And then the rest of his body follows. I guide him onto the edge of my bed. "Do you mean?" he says. "Are you. . . ?"

"I'm going to Dartmouth."

Josh's head drops into his hands. His whole body shakes. I sit beside him and press my head against his shoulder. Because I *can* again. He lifts his head, and his eyes shine with tears. "I'm sorry. I'm just . . . really overwhelmed right now."

"Me too."

"I love you. I've *always* loved you, Isla."

"I know." I take his freezing hands and rub them between mine, trying to warm them. "I'm sorry I didn't believe you. I doubted myself, and that made me doubt you. But you weren't the problem. You were *never* the problem. I should have trusted you, but I didn't, because I couldn't trust myself."

"But you do now? Trust yourself?"

"I'm . . . getting there. I'm beginning to think that maybe it's okay to be a blank canvas. Maybe it's okay that my future is unknown. And maybe," I say with another smile, "it's okay to be inspired by the people who *do* know their future."

"It goes both ways, you know."

I link his icicle fingers through mine. "What does?"

"Artists are inspired by blank canvases."

My smile grows wider.

"A blank canvas," Josh continues, "has unlimited possibilities."

I close my eyes, lean over, and kiss his cold lips. "Thank you."

His shivering grows more severe.

I jump to my feet. *"Oh, mon petit chou."* I pull out his arms from his snow-soaked coat. "I can't believe you were waiting out there this whole time."

His teeth chatter. "I—I would have waited all night."

I hang up his coat inside my shower and return for his shirt. "This, too." I tug it off, over his head. His skin is pale. Almost lavender-colored. "And these." I remove his shoes and socks, but his pants prove to be a challenge. They're practically frozen to his legs. When they finally release, I topple over backward.

He smiles through his shivers. "Not . . . quite . . . how I imagined . . . undressing with you again."

I hang up his shirt and pants beside his coat to dry. Over my head, his socks and boxers go flying onto the shower floor. I laugh. He's wrapped himself up inside my quilt, and only his face is peeking out.

"This doesn't mean you can take advantage of me," he says.

I laugh again.

Josh sweeps out a hand across the surface of my bed as a gesture for me to sit beside him, but the quilt catches on his manuscript. It knocks over on to the floor in a loud, crashing, never-ending nightmare. We freeze in horror.

We listen for Nate. Nothing.

We smile at the miracle that has been granted to us.

I sit beside him. He scoots in toward me, but I pull back my head. "Don't you want to know what I thought about your book first?" I ask.

"I don't know." He laughs nervously. "Do I?"

"You know it's good. You know it's really, *really* good."

His face disappears as his entire body slumps into the mound of blankets. "You can't even begin to imagine how relieved I am to hear you say that."

"I've always known you're brilliant. And you've just proved it to the world."

A hand pokes out from underneath the quilt. I squeeze it. "For what it's worth?" he says. "You'd make a great editor someday. Everything you yelled at me was true."

I look away from him in shame. "I'm so sorry."

"Don't be."

"No. I am. I'm sorry about so many things. And I'm especially sorry for . . . using your ex-girlfriend to fuel my own stupid insecurities. I want you to know that I don't love this"—I gesture toward his manuscript, scattered across my hardwood—"because there's less of her in it. Or more of me. I want you to know that I love it because it has *you* in it—the good parts *and* the ugly parts. I love you. I love *all* of you."

He grips my hand harder. "Thank you."

"The praise is a long time coming." I rub my thumb against his index finger. "And I have so much more of it to give."

"Tomorrow. Right now, I only want you."

But my heart grows heavy again. "You mean *today*. Did you find out when your train leaves?"

"Isla." He looks surprised. Like I should already know this. "I never bought a ticket."

My breath catches. "What?"

"I'm not going to the Olympics. I came here for you."

"Does . . . does that mean you're staying?"

He scoots in closer. "Two weeks. Through the end of the games, if you'll have me. But then I'm stuck in DC until June."

"Yes. Yes, I'll have you!"

Josh smiles impishly. "Oh, you will?"

I shove him through the blankets. He topples over onto his side, laughing, pulling me down with him. He stares into my eyes. His smile fades. "I've missed you so much."

I rub my arms against the chill. "I've missed *you*."

"You're cold." He holds open the quilt. "Come here."

I scoot forward into the blankets and sheets and pillows. Into him. The quilt falls against my back, enveloping me against his body. I press my cheek against his bare chest. He tightens his grip around me. We lie very, very still. The world is silent except for the steady beat of our hearts.

I look up at him.

Josh stares back. His heartbeat quickens.

I slide upward until our noses are pressed against each other. I kiss the corner of his mouth, and I feel him smile as he kisses the corner of mine. His fingers trail down my back as he unzips my dress. He pulls it all the way down, past my ankles, and lets it drop to the floor. He removes my bra and then my underwear.

He removes my compass necklace last.

Our kisses are soft. Teasing. Restrained. Our skin is clammy, and then warm, and then hot. Our kisses grow longer. Our breathing gets faster. I fumble for a condom. He presses against me, and it feels so good, so intense that I cry out. He meets my gaze to make sure that everything is all right, everything is *more* than all right, and my hips arch against him in response.

His eyes close in rapture, and he's guiding my body, and we're finding our rhythm, and we're together again, at last.

We can't say the words enough.

I love you.

They're a chant through the night as we move together slowly. Then quickly. Slowly. Then quickly. We don't fall asleep until the break of dawn. Josh's body curls around mine. Our hands clasp together over my heart. We're still in this position when my alarm rattles us awake an hour later. I roll over and turn it off, groaning with deep annoyance, and then roll back into him. I resettle against his chest. I sigh happily.

He moves my tentacle arms away from his body. "Mm, no you don't," he mumbles.

I give a tiny whimper.

"School," he says.

"But you're here. That's not fair."

He hugs me, despite himself. "I have to pick up my suitcase. It's still in Meredith's room at the hostel. And I wanna say goodbye to everyone before they leave."

"Can't I do that with you?"

Josh nuzzles his nose against my cheek. "I'll be here when you return."

"I fixed my door. You'll need a key."

"I'll take good care of it."

"What if I won't give it to you?"

"Then I'll break the door again."

"This dormitory makes me feel so safe."

He smiles and pushes me from the bed. "Goooooooooo."

I force him to get ready with me. The building is loud and active now, so we can move around without tiptoeing. We shower and brush our teeth and dry our hair, and everything seems twice the miracle that it did in Barcelona. Because this time we know it can't be taken away from us. This *will* be our future.

His clothes are still wet, so I dry his pants with my hair dryer and give him back the T-shirt that he gave me over Thanksgiving. It's tucked inside one of my pillows. When he sees it, he looks sad and happy and amazed. "I thought you probably threw this away. I still sleep with the scarf you gave me."

"I want that back, you know."

"The scarf?"

I smile. "That shirt."

Josh returns my smile as he pulls the shirt over his head. "I'll give it back with extra me-scent."

I hug him, tucking my head against his chest. "Do I really have to go to school today?"

"I'm *not* getting you in trouble again."

I look pointedly at my closed door. And then back at him.

"Okay." He grins. "Maybe I'm willing to throw you under the bus for that one."

When Kurt hears that Josh is in my bedroom, he insists on sneaking back to the dorm with me for lunch. I'm proud of him for breaking another rule, but I'm worried about what will happen. There's not the slightest hesitation when they see each other. Josh greets Kurt with the same genuine and enthusiastic embrace that he gave St. Clair.

"I hope those are tears of happiness," Kurt says, when he looks at me.

"They are," I say.

"I'm glad you're back together," Kurt tells Josh. "And I'm glad you're here."

"Me too," Josh says.

"I like Isla better when you're dating. I didn't think that would be true—I thought I liked her more *without* you—but that wasn't the case at all."

Josh laughs. "I'm glad to hear it."

"She's been miserable company," Kurt says.

Josh laughs harder, delighted for this news, as I whack Kurt's arm. But I'm grinning, too.

"Will you be staying here?" Kurt asks Josh.

Josh and I immediately tense. I'm sure he's reliving the same memory—Kurt, unable to lie. Barcelona.

"I am," Josh says. "I don't want to get Isla in trouble, but I'm good at keeping quiet."

"I won't say anything to anyone," Kurt says quickly. "And if Nate corners me, I'll tell him you've been staying at a hostel. Not here."

I can tell that Josh is as surprised as I am. "I appreciate that," he says. "But I won't let you lie for me. If we're caught, we'll deal with the consequences ourselves."

Kurt ponders this for a moment. "You've changed."

Josh smiles. "So have you."

"Oh," Kurt says. "You guys should tell Hattie this time, though."

"Definitely," Josh and I say together.

We stay together happily and quietly. Josh doesn't let me skip any more school lunches or break any additional rules. Only the big, obvious, boy-in-my-room one.

It's wonderful sharing a space with him.

While I do my homework, he draws. We each have our own space inside of this shared space. I imagine that our apartment next fall might feel like this. The thought fills me with more joy than I thought possible. I borrow Hattie's television, and from the opening ceremonies onward, the games are never turned off. The spirit of the events—of being in the host country—is thrilling. Even better, the sound of the television is *incredibly* handy when it comes to muffling untoward noises.

As always, the women's figure skating isn't until the end of the games. The short program is first, and we're excited when Cricket's twin, Calliope, bursts into first place with an acrobatically powerful performance. In the stands, the camera shows Cricket and Lola exploding from their seats with joy, but the announcers focus on Calliope's curse instead. Predictions are made that she'll be too scared to pull off her second event.

"Why can't they let her enjoy this moment?" I say.

"Don't worry," Josh says. "Assholes always eat their own words."

Two nights later, it happens. It's the free skate. Her gaze is sharp, and her black costume is shimmering and transcendent. Her music is from the 1968 film *Romeo and Juliet,* and she *becomes* Juliet—in love, in death—before the entire world. She wins the gold medal by a landslide. Cricket and Lola clutch each other and cry. I even see Anna and St. Clair jumping up and down behind them. But Calliope is all triumphant grin.

"Told you," Josh says, as if he can predict the future. But maybe he can. He's always known what he's wanted, and he's getting everything that he asked for. I haven't always known. But now I have what I want, too. The rest of it, the unknown . . . it'll come.

And I'm looking forward to it.

The medal program ends, we turn off the television, and— as we wrap ourselves around each other—we're faced with the truth that our time together is coming to an end, too. Josh holds me tighter, but it's not enough to stop the clock. The next evening, the Olympic flame is extinguished. The games are over. And he's gone.

chapter thirty-four

It's midnight. It's sweltering.

It's the top of June.

I cross Amsterdam Avenue underneath a clear sky. I'm nervous, but it's a good nervous. An anticipatory nervous. In the past few months, the last traces of shyness and doubt have been removed from my step. I've found the Right Way.

And I'm walking straight toward it.

The golden light of Kismet winks at me. *There.* In the window. Everything about this moment is exactly how I pictured it. His shoulders are rounded down, and his head is cocked to the right. His nose is nearly touching the tip of his pen. He arrived earlier this evening on a flight from DC.

I stop directly in front of the window. The light changes on the surface of his paper, and he looks up. We smile softly.

I touch my hand to the glass. *Hi,* I mouth.

Josh touches the other side. *Hi.*

He nods toward the door for me to come in. I open it, and I'm greeted by the warm fragrance of strong coffee. He stands. I walk straight into his embrace. We kiss, and we kiss, and we kiss. He tastes like Josh. He smells like Josh. He feels like Josh.

"You're so *real*," I say.

He touches my cheek. "I was thinking the same thing. I love the real you. I've *missed* the real you." His finger is splotched with fresh ink, and I feel the tiniest wet drop press against my skin. He tries to wipe it away, but I stop him.

"Please," I say. "Leave it. I've missed the real you, too."

Josh squeezes both of my hands with both of his.

"What are you working on?" I ask.

"The last page." He gestures toward the table, where a penciled sketch is being turned into inked brushstrokes. It's a drawing of us, in this café, in this moment.

I smile up at him. "It's beautiful. But what comes next?"

"The best part." And he pulls me back into his arms. "The happily ever after."

acknowledgments

This book—and myself—were rescued from the brink on three separate occasions: (1) in November 2011 by Carolyn Mackler and Sara Zarr, (2) in July 2012 by Holly Black, and (3) in daily phone calls with Myra McEntire. I will forever be grateful for their concern, caring, and counsel. Thank you, you astounding women, you.

Myra, you deserve your own paragraph. Because . . . TWYLA.

Thank you, Kate Schafer Testerman, for being my rock. My cheerful, encouraging, tough-as-an-Olympic-gymnast rock.

Thank you, Julie Strauss-Gabel, for your unrivaled patience and intuition. For recognizing my three girls as individuals and for helping me craft their worlds. Further thanks to everyone at the Penguin Young Reader's Group for providing me with support and enthusiasm in equal measure. Exclamation points for: Lindsey Andrews, Lauren Donovan, Melissa Faulner, Anna Jarzab, Rosanne Lauer, and Elyse Marshall.

Love and so much thanks to my family: Mom, Dad, Kara, Chris, Beckham, J.D., Fay, and Roger. You, too, Mr. Tumnus.

Thank you, Kiersten White. Words never seem enough when thanking you. You have listened to me talk about this novel for a long, long time. Few people would be able to do that with such genuine compassion and understanding.

Thanks to my Asheville friends: Alexandra Duncan, Alan Gratz, Beth Revis, Megan Shepherd, and Meagan Spooner. Everyone at Malaprop's Bookstore and Café. And, especially, Lauren Biehl for in-person ensuring my return to health and happiness.

Thank you to Gayle Forman and Daisy Whitney for the impeccable, honest feedback. Thanks to Jim Di Bartolo for my ongoing education in comics, Manning Krull and Marjorie Mesnis for making it look like I can speak French, Hope Larson and Delia Sherman for answering very specific questions, Brian Sulkis for being great company and an inspiration, and Jon Skovron for guiding me through the most intimidating subject matter. And thank you, Natalie Whipple, for spending so much time teaching me about something that no longer exists inside this novel. You are a fantastic ally.

Thank you to all of the kind readers, authors, booksellers, librarians, educators, and Nerdfighters that I meet on my travels. Giant bear hugs to Robin Benway, Amy Spalding, Margaret Stohl,

Laini Taylor, Jade Timms, and everyone on the retreat in San Miguel de Allende for listening and for laughing in the right places.

Finally, thank you to Jarrod Perkins. I'm crying now just because I typed your name. I love you more than *anyone. Ever. Times a hundred million billion.* Étienne, Cricket, and Josh—they were all you, but none of them came even close to you. You are my best friend. You are my true love. You are my happily ever after.

questions for discussion

- Why is Isla so embarrassed after her meeting with Josh at Kismet? Does she really have anything to be embarrassed for?

- In what ways might Isla's friendship with Kurt impede other relationships for her at SOAP?

- Does the start of Isla and Josh's relationship seem realistic? It all happens very quickly—do couples really pair off this way?

- Who is to blame for the catastrophe that happens in Barcelona? Why?

- Why does Isla react the way that she does after reading Josh's autobiographical graphic novel? What might be difficult about *seeing* your romantic partner's past relationship in detail, as opposed to just *hearing* about it?

- Why does Isla have such a difficult time reconciling the different portions of Josh's personality ("public Josh" v. "private Josh")? Does everyone have different personalities in different settings?

- Is Isla justified in her reasons for breaking up with Josh? Why or why not?

- Isla repeatedly says that she is not worth loving and doesn't really have an identity—do you agree or disagree with her assessment of herself? Why does she feel this way?

- What do you think about Isla and Josh's relationship at the end of the book? Do you think it'll work out over the long term, or not? Why?

Turn the page to read an excerpt from
Stephanie Perkins's international bestseller

ANNA and the **FRENCH KISS**

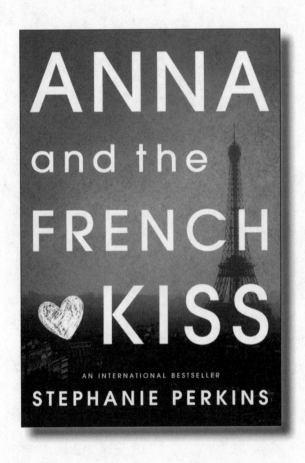

chapter one

ere is everything I know about France: *Madeline* and *Amélie* and *Moulin Rouge*. The Eiffel Tower and the Arc de Triomphe, although I have no idea what the function of either actually is. Napoleon, Marie Antoinette, and a lot of kings named Louis. I'm not sure what they did either, but I think it has something to do with the French Revolution, which has something to do with Bastille Day. The art museum is called the Louvre and it's shaped like a pyramid and the *Mona Lisa* lives there along with that statue of the woman missing her arms. And there are cafés or bistros or whatever they call them on every street corner. And mimes. The food is supposed to be good, and the people drink a lot of wine and smoke a lot of cigarettes.

I've heard they don't like Americans, and they don't like white sneakers.

A few months ago, my father enrolled me in boarding school. His air quotes practically crackled over the phone line as he declared living abroad to be a "good learning experience" and a "keepsake I'd treasure forever." Yeah. Keepsake. And I would've pointed out his misuse of the word had I not already been freaking out.

Since his announcement, I've tried yelling, begging, pleading, and crying, but nothing has convinced him otherwise. And now I have a new student visa and a passport, each declaring me: Anna Oliphant, citizen of the United States of America. And now I'm here with my parents—unpacking my belongings in a room smaller than my suitcase—the newest senior at the School of America in Paris.

It's not that I'm ungrateful. I mean, it's *Paris*. The City of Light! The most romantic city in the world! I'm not immune to that. It's just this whole international boarding school thing is a lot more about my father than it is about me. Ever since he sold out and started writing lame books that were turned into even lamer movies, he's been trying to impress his big-shot New York friends with how cultured and rich he is.

My father isn't cultured. But he is rich.

It wasn't always like this. When my parents were still married, we were strictly lower middle class. It was around the time of the divorce that all traces of decency vanished, and his dream of being the next great Southern writer was replaced by his desire to be the next *published* writer. So he started writing these novels set in Small Town Georgia about folks with Good American

Values who Fall in Love and then contract Life-Threatening Diseases and Die.

I'm serious.

And it totally depresses me, but the ladies eat it up. They love my father's books and they love his cable-knit sweaters and they love his bleachy smile and orangey tan. And they have turned him into a bestseller and a total dick.

Two of his books have been made into movies and three more are in production, which is where his real money comes from. Hollywood. And, somehow, this extra cash and pseudo-prestige have warped his brain into thinking that I should live in France. For a year. Alone. I don't understand why he couldn't send me to Australia or Ireland or anywhere else where English is the native language. The only French word I know is *oui*, which means "yes," and only recently did I learn it's spelled o-u-i and not w-e-e.

At least the people in my new school speak English. It was founded for pretentious Americans who don't like the company of their own children. I mean, really. Who sends their kid to boarding school? It's so Hogwarts. Only mine doesn't have cute boy wizards or magic candy or flying lessons.

Instead, I'm stuck with ninety-nine other students. There are twenty-five people in my *entire senior class,* as opposed to the six hundred I had back in Atlanta. And I'm studying the same things I studied at Clairemont High except now I'm registered in beginning French.

Oh, yeah. Beginning French. No doubt with the freshmen. I totally rock.

Mom says I need to lose the bitter factor, pronto, but she's not the one leaving behind her fabulous best friend, Bridgette. Or her fabulous job at the Royal Midtown 14 multiplex. Or Toph, the fabulous boy at the Royal Midtown 14 multiplex.

And I still can't believe she's separating me from my brother, Sean, who is only seven and way too young to be left home alone after school. Without me, he'll probably be kidnapped by that creepy guy down the road who has dirty Coca-Cola towels hanging in his windows. Or Seany will accidentally eat something containing Red Dye #40 and his throat will swell up and no one will be there to drive him to the hospital. He might even die. And I bet they wouldn't let me fly home for his funeral and I'd have to visit the cemetery alone next year and Dad will have picked out some god-awful granite cherub to go over his grave.

And I hope Dad doesn't expect me to fill out college applications to Russia or Romania now. My dream is to study film theory in California. I want to be our nation's greatest female film critic. Someday I'll be invited to every festival, and I'll have a major newspaper column and a cool television show and a ridiculously popular website. So far I only have the website, and it's not so popular. Yet.

I just need a little more time to work on it, that's all.

"Anna, it's time."

"What?" I glance up from folding my shirts into perfect squares.

Mom stares at me and twiddles the turtle charm on her necklace. My father, bedecked in a peach polo shirt and white

Anna and the French Kiss

boating shoes, is gazing out my dormitory window. It's late, but across the street a woman belts out something operatic.

My parents need to return to their hotel rooms. They both have early morning flights.

"Oh." I grip the shirt in my hands a little tighter.

Dad steps away from the window, and I'm alarmed to discover his eyes are wet. Something about the idea of my father—even if it is *my father*—on the brink of tears raises a lump in my throat.

"Well, kiddo. Guess you're all grown up now."

My body is frozen. He pulls my stiff limbs into a bear hug. His grip is frightening. "Take care of yourself. Study hard and make some friends. And watch out for pickpockets," he adds. "Sometimes they work in pairs."

I nod into his shoulder, and he releases me. And then he's gone.

My mother lingers behind. "You'll have a wonderful year here," she says. "I just know it." I bite my lip to keep it from quivering, and she sweeps me into her arms. I try to breathe. Inhale. Count to three. Exhale. Her skin smells like grapefruit body lotion. "I'll call you the moment I get home," she says.

Home. Atlanta isn't my home anymore.

"I love you, Anna."

I'm crying now. "I love you, too. Take care of Seany for me."

"Of course."

"And Captain Jack," I say. "Make sure Sean feeds him and changes his bedding and fills his water bottle. And make sure he doesn't give him too many treats because they make him fat and

7

then he can't get out of his igloo. But make sure he gives him at least a few every day, because he still needs the vitamin C and he won't drink the water when I use those vitamin drops—"

She pulls back and tucks my bleached stripe behind my ear. "I love you," she says again.

And then my mother does something that, even after all of the paperwork and plane tickets and presentations, I don't see coming. Something that would've happened in a year anyway, once I left for college, but that no matter how many days or months or years I've yearned for it, I am still not prepared for when it actually happens.

My mother leaves. I am alone.

chapter two

$\mathcal{I}$ feel it coming, but I can't stop it.

PANIC.

They left me. My parents actually left me! IN FRANCE!

Meanwhile, Paris is oddly silent. Even the opera singer has packed it in for the night. I *cannot* lose it. The walls here are thinner than Band-Aids, so if I break down, my neighbors—my new classmates—will hear everything. I'm going to be sick. I'm going to vomit that weird eggplant tapenade I had for dinner, and everyone will hear, and no one will invite me to watch the mimes escape from their invisible boxes, or whatever it is people do here in their spare time.

I race to my pedestal sink to splash water on my face, but it explodes out and sprays my shirt instead. And now I'm crying harder, because I haven't unpacked my towels, and wet clothing reminds me of those stupid water rides Bridgette and Matt used to drag me on at Six Flags where the water is the wrong color and it smells like paint and it has a billion trillion bacterial microbes in it. Oh God. What if there are bacterial microbes in the water? Is French water even safe to drink?

Pathetic. I'm pathetic.

How many seventeen-year-olds would kill to leave home? My neighbors aren't experiencing any meltdowns. No crying coming from behind *their* bedroom walls. I grab a shirt off the bed to blot myself dry, when the solution strikes. *My pillow.* I collapse face-first into the sound barrier and sob and sob and sob.

Someone is knocking on my door.

No. Surely that's not my door.

There it is again!

"Hello?" a girl calls from the hallway. "Hello? Are you okay?"

No, I'm not okay. GO AWAY. But she calls again, and I'm obligated to crawl off my bed and answer the door. A blonde with long, tight curls waits on the other side. She's tall and big, but not overweight-big. Volleyball player big. A diamondlike nose ring sparkles in the hall light. "Are you all right?" Her voice is gentle. "I'm Meredith; I live next door. Were those your parents who just left?"

My puffy eyes signal the affirmative.

"I cried the first night, too." She tilts her head, thinks for a moment, and then nods. "Come on. *Chocolat chaud.*"

"A chocolate show?" Why would I want to see a chocolate show? My mother has abandoned me and I'm terrified to leave my room and—

"No." She smiles. "*Chaud*. Hot. Hot chocolate, I can make some in my room."

Oh.

Despite myself, I follow. Meredith stops me with her hand like a crossing guard. She's wearing rings on all five fingers. "Don't forget your key. The doors automatically lock behind you."

"I know." And I tug the necklace out from underneath my shirt to prove it. I slipped my key onto it during this weekend's required Life Skills Seminars for new students, when they told us how easy it is to get locked out.

We enter her room. I gasp. It's the same impossible size as mine, seven by ten feet, with the same mini-desk, mini-dresser, mini-bed, mini-fridge, mini-sink, and mini-shower. (No mini-toilet, those are shared down the hall.) But . . . unlike my own sterile cage, every inch of wall and ceiling is covered with posters and pictures and shiny wrapping paper and brightly colored flyers written in French.

"How long have you *been* here?" I ask.

Meredith hands me a tissue and I blow my nose, a terrible honk like an angry goose, but she doesn't flinch or make a face. "I arrived yesterday. This is my fourth year here, so I didn't have to go to the seminars. I flew in alone, so I've just been hanging out, waiting for my friends to show up." She looks around with her hands on her hips, admiring her handiwork. I spot a pile of magazines, scissors, and tape on her floor and realize it's a work in progress. "Not bad, eh? White walls don't do it for me."

I circle her room, examining everything. I quickly discover that most of the faces are the same five people: John, Paul, George, Ringo, and some soccer guy I don't recognize.

"The Beatles are all I listen to. My friends tease me, but—"

"Who's this?" I point to Soccer Guy. He's wearing red and white, and he's all dark eyebrows and dark hair. Quite good-looking, actually.

"Cesc Fàbregas. God, he's the most incredible passer. Plays for Arsenal. The English football club? No?"

I shake my head. I don't keep up with sports, but maybe I should. "Nice legs, though."

"I know, right? You could hammer nails with those thighs."

While Meredith brews *chocolat chaud* on her hot plate, I learn she's also a senior, and that she only plays soccer during the summer because our school doesn't have a program, but that she used to rank All-State in Massachusetts. That's where she's from, Boston. And she reminds me I should call it "football" here, which—when I think about it—really does make more sense. And she doesn't seem to mind when I badger her with questions or paw through her things.

Her room is amazing. In addition to the paraphernalia taped to her walls, she has a dozen china teacups filled with plastic glitter rings, and silver rings with amber stones, and glass rings with pressed flowers. It already looks as if she's lived here for years.

I try on a ring with a rubber dinosaur attached. The T-rex flashes red and yellow and blue lights when I squeeze him. "I wish I could have a room like this." I love it, but I'm too much of a neat freak to have something like it for myself. I need clean walls and a clean desktop and everything put away in its right place at all times.

Meredith looks pleased with the compliment.

"Are these your friends?" I place the dinosaur back into its teacup and point to a picture tucked in her mirror. It's gray and shadowy and printed on thick, glossy paper. Clearly the product of a school photography class. Four people stand before a giant hollow cube, and the abundance of stylish black clothing and deliberately mussed hair reveals Meredith belongs to the resident art clique. For some reason, I'm surprised. I know her room is artsy, and she has all of those rings on her fingers and in her nose, but the rest is clean-cut—lilac sweater, pressed jeans, soft voice. Then there's the soccer thing, but she's not a tomboy either.

She breaks into a wide smile, and her nose ring winks. "Yeah. Ellie took that at La Défense. That's Josh and St. Clair and me and Rashmi. You'll meet them tomorrow at breakfast. Well, everyone but Ellie. She graduated last year."

The pit of my stomach begins to unclench. Was that an invitation to sit with her?

"But I'm sure you'll meet her soon enough, because she's dating St. Clair. She's at Parsons Paris now for photography."

I've never heard of it, but I nod as if I've considered going there myself someday.

"She's *really* talented." The edge in her voice suggests otherwise, but I don't push it. "Josh and Rashmi are dating, too," she adds.

Ah. Meredith must be single.

Unfortunately, I can relate. Back home I'd dated my friend Matt for five months. He was tall-ish and funny-ish and had decent-ish hair. It was one of those "since no one better is around, do you wanna make out?" situations. All we'd ever done was kiss, and it wasn't even that great. Too much spit. I always had to wipe off my chin.

We broke up when I learned about France, but it wasn't a big deal. I didn't cry or send him weepy emails or key his mom's station wagon. Now he's going out with Cherrie Milliken, who is in chorus and has shiny shampoo-commercial hair. It doesn't even bother me.

Not really.

Besides, the breakup freed me to lust after Toph, multiplex coworker babe extraordinaire. Not that I didn't lust after him when I was with Matt, but still. It did make me feel guilty. And things were starting to happen with Toph—they really were—when summer ended. But Matt's the only guy I've ever gone out with, and he barely counts. I once told him I'd dated this guy named Stuart Thistleback at summer camp. Stuart Thistleback had auburn hair and played the stand-up bass, and we were totally in love, but he lived in Chattanooga and we didn't have our driver's licenses yet.

Matt knew I made it up, but he was too nice to say so.

I'm about to ask Meredith what classes she's taking, when her

phone chirps the first few bars of "Strawberry Fields Forever."
She rolls her eyes and answers. "Mom, it's midnight here. Six-
hour time difference, remember?"

I glance at her alarm clock, shaped like a yellow submarine,
and I'm surprised to find she's right. I set my long-empty mug
of *chocolat chaud* on her dresser. "I should get going," I whisper.
"Sorry I stayed so long."

"Hold on a sec." Meredith covers the mouthpiece. "It was
nice meeting you. See you at breakfast?"

"Yeah. See ya." I try to say this casually, but I'm so thrilled
that I skip from her room and promptly slam into a wall.

Whoops. Not a wall. A boy.

"Oof." He staggers backward.

"Sorry! I'm so sorry, I didn't know you were there."

He shakes his head, a little dazed. The first thing I notice is his
hair—it's the first thing I notice about everyone. It's dark brown
and messy and somehow both long and short at the same time.
I think of the Beatles, since I've just seen them in Meredith's
room. It's artist hair. Musician hair. I-pretend-I-don't-care-but-
I-really-do hair.

Beautiful hair.

"It's okay, I didn't see you either. Are you all right, then?"

Oh my. He's English.

Look for STEPHANIE PERKINS's fresh take on the classic teen slasher story.

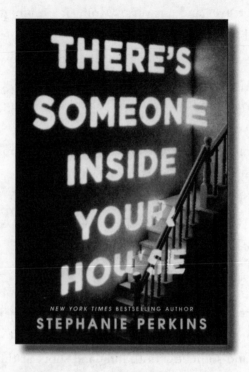

It's been almost a year since Makani Young came to live with her grandmother in landlocked Nebraska, and she's still adjusting to her new life. And still haunted by her past in Hawaii. Then, one by one, the students of Osborne High begin to die in a series of gruesome murders, each with increasing and grotesque flair. As the terror grows closer and the hunt intensifies for the killer, Makani will be forced to confront her own dark secrets.

"Perkins lulls readers into a false sense of security before twisting the knife."   —*Publishers Weekly*

"A heart-pounding page-turner with an outstanding cast of characters, a deliciously creepy setting, and an absolutely merciless body count."
        —Courtney Summers, author of *All the Rage* and *Cracked Up to Be*